Cald's mother was interrupted by a scream from the rear of the caravan. She brought the horses to a halt and looked back as someone shouted. They heard the clash of steel on steel.

"Gnolls!" The shouted alarm traveled up the length of twenty wagons, accompanied by screams from women and children.

Cald stood up to see over the piles of goods on the wagon. To the left of the caravan, from the concealment of the bushes at the side of a gully, bestial forms with bodies like men but hyenalike faces hurled spears at the settlers. Some of the monsters had used all their throwing weapons and were running toward the wagons with axes, clubs, and swords.

"Gnolls!"

Greatheart

Dixie Lee McKeone

TSR, Inc.   TSR Ltd.
201 Sheridan Springs Road   120 Church End, Cherry Hinton
Lake Geneva, WI 53147   Cambridge CB1 3LB
United States of America   United Kingdom

**To Mikey Pendleton
who is learning through
role-playing games
that heroism is a matter of heart.**

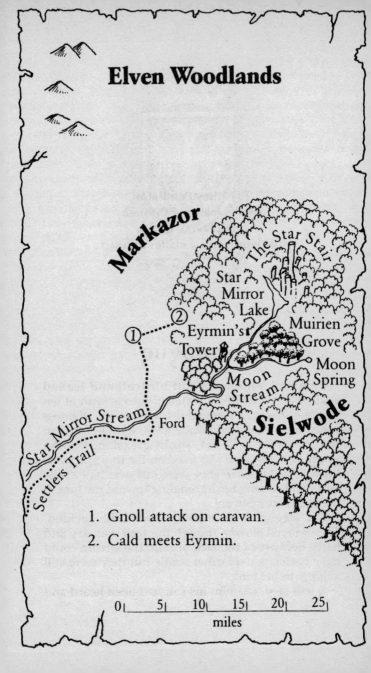

Elven Woodlands

Markazor

The Star Stair

Star Mirror Lake

Muirien Grove

Eyrmin's Tower

Moon Spring

Moon Stream

Star Mirror Stream

Ford

Settlers Trail

Sielwode

1. Gnoll attack on caravan.
2. Cald meets Eyrmin.

0	5	10	15	20	25

miles

ANUIRE

prologue

Lienwiel whistled a soft birdcall and leaned against a tree while he watched the caravan of ten wagons. His eyes were accustomed to the dimness beneath the trees of Sielwode, so he squinted against the glare on the bright, sunlit grasslands to the south. Still, his gaze was fixed on the tiny specks he knew to be humans. They were just over half a mile away and coming nearer, angling toward the ford in the Star Mirror Stream.

The wagons were heavily loaded, he decided. They moved slowly, though the trail was dry and hard. Because of the lack of rain, the stream could have been crossed farther south, but they were still aiming for the ford.

A soft step told him his call had been heard and

answered. Mielinel, a young female warrior, came in sight between the trees and joined his watch.

"Trouble, do you think?" she asked as her eyes followed his gaze, her hand fingering her bow.

"Not likely," Lienwiel replied. "They appear to be staying with the road, but we'll watch them."

The elves of Sielwode laid no claim to the ford. The elves considered the borders of their land to cease with the shadows at the eaves of the forest. Beyond lay the land of Markazor. Humans and humanoids sometimes fought for possession of it, but that was no business of the forest dwellers. As long as the humans kept to the rutted track on the plain, they had nothing to fear from the elves.

If they tried to enter the wood, they would die. Humans had no respect for the forest; they cut trees for firewood and building. Since their arrival on the continent of Cerilia a millennium before, they had ravaged entire forests. King Tieslin Krienelsira, ruler of Sielwode, had sworn to protect his forest against intrusion.

"They're traveling north," Lienwiel said, pointing out the obvious.

"Trying to settle northern Markazor again?" Mielinel asked.

They both knew the result of the first human effort to lay claim to the northern hill country beyond Sielwode. For five years, the elves had fought off the northbound settlers, who brought their axes to the edge of the forest for firewood. The goblin, gnoll, and orog population that had spread south from the Stone Crown Mountains, most under the control of the powerful awnshegh called the Gorgon, had driven the humans back. The survivors had straggled south again, dispirited and less a threat.

While the two elves watched, the wagons crossed the ford and halted for the day. The humans watered their animals, staked them out to graze, and then spread out on the plain, cutting the long dry grass. Half an hour after they returned to the wagons, thin tendrils of smoke rose from their campfires.

The elves exchanged glances, knowing they were seeing the result of a legend come to life. Neither had been in the western arm of Sielwode during the turbulent times, but both had heard the tales of Prince Eyrmin and his foster son, Cald Dasheft. It was said the young human, who had been raised in the forest, had taught a human family the elven art of cutting the dry grass, braiding it into logs, and using it for cookfires.

"We won't need to fight these for firewood," Lienwiel said softly.

"Still, if they continue north, they'll bring more trouble with the Gorgon," Mielinel remarked, her eyes filled with anger. Many of the inhabitants of Sielwode blamed the humans for the awnshegh's attacks on the forest, which had occurred while the humans were trying to conquer Markazor.

"Not to us, unless he seeks the portal again," Lienwiel replied. "Still, Relcan and the king should know the humans are traveling north. Take the message back to Reilmirid."

With a nod, she turned away. Knowing she was new to the eaves of the forest, Lienwiel whistled a note of caution, but his warning seemed unnecessary. Her head turned, and her path through the thornbushes hid her from all but elven eyes. She looked up and sidestepped a tendril of a strangle vine that looped down from a tree; then she was lost to sight beyond the thick boles of the ancient trees.

Twenty paces from Lienwiel hung the half-clothed skeleton of a hapless gnoll. It had slipped into the forest and had been caught by a strangle vine. The elves valued the natural traps of their forest and regarded them as additional barriers to incursion.

The eaves of the wood were filled with dangers, and Lienwiel had heard the other races thought all of Sielwode was dark and dangerous. Better they did not know of the beauties of the deep wood, he thought. In that belief, he was like all his kind.

The next morning he watched the wagons leave. By midday they were out of elven sight. He relaxed, giving an occasional glance toward the grasslands of Markazor, but most of his mind was tuned to the forest, communing with the trees. Joining minds with the forest was an elven pastime that delighted his race, even those who had lived through millennia.

Every hour or so he turned his eyes on the plain; toward evening he saw movement. A solitary figure crossed the plain, traveling toward Sielwode. Elf or human? The traveler was still too far away to tell, but he was definitely planning to enter the forest. Lienwiel slipped through the shadows, and when he had divined the path of the stranger, he concealed himself behind a thorny bush.

The hair on the back of the elf's neck prickled as the stranger approached. A male, a human, and large, even for one of his race. He was a warrior, heavily armed with a broadsword in a tooled leather sheath, a longbow, and a full quiver of arrows. He wore a pair of loose trousers and a tunic of thin fabric that kept the rays of the sun from heating the armor beneath it; Lienwiel recognized the faint glimmer of metal beneath the cloth. The human's dark head was bare, a concession to the heat, which would have made a metal helm an oven for his head in the sunlight of the plain.

And he walked with an *elven* step.

Humans usually led with their heels, their every step a demand that the land submit to their will; elves gave the world the respect that was its due. With each step they touched the ground lightly, asking the soil beneath their feet for permission to pass. They were taught this reverence for the land when they first learned to walk, and the first gentle touch of an elf's footstep was so automatic and so natural it was only barely audible to even another elf—possibly this human.

The man's ability to walk like an elf was puzzling, and the elf disliked the look in the man's eyes. This warrior had come prepared to die—yet he would not go like a rabbit or a deer that recognizes death at last and closes its eyes, submitting to fate. This man would go to the netherworld still fighting and goring like the wild boar, and would likely take his adversary with him.

The human was a warrior; every inch of his six foot frame proclaimed it. His dark hair was nutbrown, worn short in a warrior's cut. It waved lightly around an angular, strong-boned face. His sky-blue eyes snapped with intelligence and automatically recorded everything around him. They suddenly focused on the thornbush as if he could see Lienwiel on the other side.

It seemed impossible. The human was still in the bright sunlight of the plain and Lienwiel was concealed not only behind the bush, but in the black shadows of Sielwode. Nevertheless, the stranger stared straight at him as if looking into his eyes.

Lienwiel, a victor of many battles, knew he did not want to fight this intruder, but his task was to guard the eaves of the forest, and he would do his duty. As the stranger drew closer, he stepped from his concealment and threw out a challenge.

" 'Ware, stranger. Death awaits any human who enters Sielwode! If you seek water, a stream lies half an hour to the south. If you need fuel for your fire, I will show you how to use the grass of the plain." A few elven warriors who had just reasons for hating humans would refuse to instruct travelers in twisting and plaiting the dry grass for fuel, but Lienwiel obeyed his instructions, thinking it was not honorable to kill any being who only fought out of need to survive.

The stranger kept coming, so the elf drew his sword.

"Stay your blade," the man called back. "I have leave from your king to pass and no quarrel with you. I seek the Muirien Grove."

Though he had never seen him, Lienwiel knew the stranger he faced, and his spine seemed to freeze within his flesh. He had long ago proven his courage, but he had known on first seeing the man that it would not be wise to test his blade against him. Now he understood what he had sensed.

"You are Cald Dasheft," he said, fear and awe leaking from his pronouncement. Only three and a half years had passed since the death of the prince, but the human child whom Prince Eyrmin had raised to manhood and who fought at his side had already become a legend among the elves of Sielwode.

"I am Cald Dasheft," the human replied. To the elf it seemed less an agreement than a pronouncement of his fate.

* * * * *

Cald in turn, gazed at the elf, who pursed his mouth and gave a series of shrill whistles that would have seemed like birdcalls to the untrained ear. The first announced that the traveler was no enemy. The second called for another warrior to take his place on patrol. Cald understood the reason, and it angered him. He wanted his last walk in the Sielwode to be a solitary journey, a time when he could relive his memories undisturbed.

"I need no guard," Cald snapped.

His objection seemed to weigh on the elf, but the slender warrior stood his ground. His eyes, as he gazed at the human, held the elven sadness of impending death. The elves made a great show of grief, claiming the end of any life, particularly that of a creature born to immortality, was a terrible loss, but Cald doubted they could mourn more deeply than he.

"I am the warrior Lienwiel. My people will honor a bond of friendship and let you pass," the elf guard said. "But you must be escorted. Many have arrived in Reilmirid since you left. They will challenge you. If you seek death, Cald Dasheft, you will not find it at the hands of my people."

Cald curbed his rising anger and disappointment. If Eyrmin could see beyond the portal, he would disapprove of Cald's fighting with this new company of elves, which had taken over the protection of the westernmost tip of Sielwode. Cald nodded and accepted the escort, but the elf would be puzzled by the path he planned to take. His course would meander through the forest, approaching the grove from a different angle. His trail would be a historical walk, pausing at each of the most important points of his life—at least the points he had valued most.

For the past three years, Cald had been traveling in the human lands. He had watched the petty kings fight each other and listened to their intrigues. Except for the time he hired out his sword to escort a family of farmers from Lofton in Alamie north to the fertile hill country near Sorentier, he considered his time wasted. His human kindred, with their lust for power and wealth, had disgusted him.

Lienwiel had been right when he read Cald's readiness to die. Cald had returned to open the portal to the Shadow World. He would free the elven prince from his imprisonment in the Shadow World or join him. He had no wish to die, but if he had to give his life to enter the portal, he would still join Eyrmin, the elven prince who had been father, teacher, friend, and companion in battle—the bravest and truest being he had ever known.

Cald left the plain of bright sunlight and walked into the dense undergrowth. The elf song that softened the thorns of the barrier bushes was so soft Cald only barely heard it, but he resented the guard's assumption that he could not make his own passage. His voice was louder, rougher, less soothing on the ear, but he took a slightly different tack, making his own way.

His escort threw him a surprised look and ceased to sing. Instead he followed in Cald's wake. The dimness acted like a balm to his eyes and his heart. To other humans, this dark, seemingly impenetrable forest was a place of menace. To the human who had been raised in it, the faint signs on the ground and on the tangled bushes and vines gave evidence of paths. They were walked by people who felt the life in every plant and tree in the forest, people who broke no twigs, disturbed no leaves. In turn, the growth of the forest gave way to their passing.

A walk of just over half a mile brought Cald to the foot of an ancient oak. Its thick branches and large dead leaves provided shelter for shadows that fled only in the early spring, when the sprouting of new leaves forced the old ones to fall.

There had been new leaves on the tree when Cald had first seen it, and the tree had seemed larger. But Cald had been much smaller then.

He had lacked three months of being four years old.

It had been nearly twenty years since he had crouched at the foot of that tree, at the age where he was trying to understand the grown-up world around him. He had relived that fateful day many times, both in thought and nightmare.

ANUIRE

one

"We're going to fight goblins," announced Cald with the insouciance of a child who had not yet reached the fourth anniversary of his birth.

His mother, Sima Dasheft, who drove the second wain in the twenty-wagon caravan, glanced down at him in surprise as she shifted on the high seat. Her hair, a glossy black that usually swirled around her head like a storm cloud, had been tightly braided to keep it from tangling and blowing in her eyes while she drove the wagon. Cald thought the hairstyle made her head look small.

"Where did you hear that?" she demanded of him.

"Arthy Worsin," Cald replied, though he knew they would not be fighting goblins. Arthy's father had clouted his son lightly on the ear and told him not to be stupid. Cald had repeated the remark in hopes of enticing his mother to tell the tale of their adventure. He was bored with riding and staring out at the grassy plain of southern Markazor.

"We won't be fighting goblins or gnolls or orogs," Sima Dasheft told her son. "Fighting is for the army. We will be the first settlers in what will later be a new part of Mhoried. Benjin Mhoried has decreed growth for his nation."

"Can land grow?" Cald asked. He stared out over the fields, wondering if hills would rise up out of the rolling plain.

"Not the ground itself, but a nation can grow," his mother said, her eyes shining with the idea. "And there are times when it must. We must stay stronger than our enemies, because they are evil."

"We have evil enemies," Cald said, trying to prompt her.

"Oh, yes, and Arthy is right; there are goblins and gnolls living in northern Markazor. Before they become too strong, we must form a bulwark to protect the homeland."

"Is a bull-wark like a cow-bull?"

His mother laughed.

"No, it is like a wall, but not a real one as in a house. Ours will be a string of small forts at first, with settlers and artisans living near them to supply the needs of the soldiers. They will keep away the goblins and the other monsters."

"Uncle Mersel will fight, and we will grow potatoes, and father will make swords and arrowheads and shoes for the horses," Cald said with a sigh. "When I grow up, I'm going to go in the army and help Uncle Mersel." He was very proud of his mother's brother.

Captain Mersel Umelsen commanded the forces that had traveled north a fortnight before the caravan had started. He had promised Cald's father a great holding. The captain had also promised that the family would be protected. He was leading a caravan of settlers into the low hills of northern Markazor where the first fort should be even then under construction.

Cald had been excited about the journey. To him it seemed a great adventure to ride on the high seat of the wain and travel to a new place. After three days of riding he had become bored. The journey took far longer than he had anticipated.

It was also slower than his parents had thought it would be. They had left Shieldhaven—Bevaldruor in the old tongue—well before the spring rains were due. They wanted to reach their destination in time for the spring planting.

The army had traveled north, planning to ford the Maesil a few miles south of the border between Mhoried and Cariele. The heavy settler wagons had gone south to use the ferry that crossed the river between Mhoried and Elinie.

Their journey would be lengthened by more than a hundred and fifty miles, but the wagons could not ford the river. The plan had been for the army to arrive first and clear the area of humanoids so the settlers could plant their crops in safety.

For Cald, the journey was also marred by having to travel in the wain, wrapped in furs in the chill mornings while the other children walked with their parents or ran about, exploring the grasslands. Cald had been born with breath-rasp, struggling to breathe when he played too hard, when the weather was cold, or when pollen filled the air. Since his parents had lost three children before he was born, they were determined that he should live, and his life was a constant irritation of overprotection.

The rain had ceased three days before, and that morning the ground was drier, so everyone in the caravan was riding, and Cald was enjoying his mother's company. He had discovered a terrible disadvantage to the "Great Adventure." He missed Sermer, the playmate he had left behind in Shieldhaven.

"I don't see why we have to move," he said. As he thought about his friend, he forgot he had been excited and anxious for the journey.

"Sometimes I think it's in our nature," his mother said thoughtfully. "Our ancestors traveled to this land from far in the south, from another place, far across the southern sea."

"Did they have to leave their friends behind?" Cald asked, thinking of Sermer.

"I don't think they left their friends, but they left almost everything they owned, or so the story goes. They were running away from a terrible evil that turned creatures into monsters, and no one was safe."

"Like goblins?"

"Worse than goblins."

Cald looked out at the plain, then to his right, at the dark wood that his father and mother did not seem to like. "Can that evil come here too?" he asked.

"It came many years ago," his mother said. "All the people gathered together and there was a terrible battle. The evil was destroyed, so you don't have to be afraid of it."

"Tell me about the battle," Cald said, shivering at the thought.

"One day, when you are older, your Uncle Mersel can tell you. He is a soldier and will make a better story of it."

"Can't you tell me some of it?" Cald teased, wanting a new tale to ease the boredom of travel.

"Not until you're older," his mother said, her voice firm.

He would have teased for more, but up ahead his father slowed the first wagon and climbed down from the high seat. His mother tied off the reins and gathered her skirts in preparation for climbing down.

"Rough ground ahead," his father called back.

"You sit still and hold on," his mother said. "We'll lead the teams."

"I want to walk, too," Cald complained, but his mother was guiding the left horse around a washout that had nearly caused the lead wagon to overturn.

"Stay where you are for now," she ordered, "Or you'll be hacking and gasping before midday stop. And keep that fur around your shoulders. The wind's still chilly and . . ."

Cald's mother was interrupted by a scream from the rear of the caravan. She brought the horses to a halt and looked back as someone shouted. They heard the clash of steel on steel.

"Gnolls!" The alarm traveled up the length of twenty wagons, accompanied by screams from women and children.

Cald stood up to see over the piles of goods on the wagon. To the left of the caravan, from the concealment of the bushes at the side of a gully, bestial forms with bodies like men but hyenalike faces hurled spears at the settlers. Some of the monsters had used all their throwing weapons and were running toward the wagons with axes, clubs, and swords.

Elder Worsin, Arthy's feeble grandsire, fell when a spear struck him in the chest. The gnoll that threw it rushed forward to hack at Arthy, who was just a year older than Cald. While the boy ran away screaming, his father appeared around the end of the wagon and, lifting his axe, chopped the arm off the dog-faced monster.

"Cald, get down! Hide!" his mother shouted at him before pulling a hoe from the back of the wagon. Too frightened to object, he climbed over the seat and crouched down among the sacks of clothing and bedding.

A gnoll leapt from the bushes and thrust his spear at Sima, but she jumped aside. She brought the work-sharpened blade of the hoe down on its shoulder. Cald looked in the other direction as blood spurted from the creature's neck.

A spear sailed over Lido, the left wheeler dray horse, and struck Drens, slicing open the right wheeler's rump. The horse screamed with pain and panicked the rest of the team. They bolted, fear giving them the strength to pull the wagon at a dead run. The heavy wheels bounced over the uneven ground, throwing out baskets of seedlings, bundles of bedding, and food.

Cald gripped the side of the wagon and wiggled farther down among the cooking pots and leather sacks of clothing. In the distance, he heard his father shout his name over the screams of others in the caravan. The clamor of battle drowned out his father's words. Was he telling Cald to stay in the wagon or jump out before the horses carried him far away? Since both alternatives were unpleasant, Cald decided his father wanted him to stop the wagon.

"Stop! Whoa!" he shouted to the horses, but he had no reins to stop them, and even if he had, he would not have dared turn loose his grip on the side of the cart.

The ride seemed to last forever. The horses, terrified by the screams from behind them, raced east, into the forest. Cald had held his grip on the side of the wagon and stayed down, just as his mother had ordered. The horses slowed as they forced their way through the thorny undergrowth, but they were still moving at a fast trot when the right rear wheel of the wagon hit a root. The cart slid sideways, slammed into a tree, and broke its rear axle. The sudden jolt started the frightened beasts into rearing, and they slammed the wagon into a second tree. The collision splintered the shaft and freed the singletrees. The horses raced off into the woods, pulling the broken shaft with them.

The wagon overturned, and Cald tumbled onto the ground, protected from injury by the fur wrapped around him and the thick leaves of the forest.

At first he huddled where he lay, too frightened to move. Then, the worst of his panic drained away, and he climbed from the wreckage and looked around. Still fearing the gnolls, he moved away from the wagon and dug down within the bed of leaves, covering himself and the fur. He had no idea of time, but he waited a long while, hoping to hear his father's or mother's voice.

They would beat off the creatures and come searching for him; at first he was sure of it; later he grew irritated that they had not yet found him; when the sun sank low on the western horizon and the shadows of the trees began to stretch away as if retreating into the forest, he crept out of his hiding place and trudged toward the only safety he knew, the wrecked wagon that had overturned a hundred feet away. Behind him he dragged the fur that had been wrapped around him. He crouched under the wagon until nearly dark. Then he crawled in among his family's spilled belongings and slept fitfully.

The next morning, he dug through the pile and found a raw tuber that would probably have been his dinner the night before if the wagon train had not been attacked. He ate enough of it to take the edge off his hunger and put it aside.

Where were his parents? Why hadn't they come

for him? Were they angry because he could not stop
the horses?

Many of his family's household goods were
spilled on the ground, strung out in a line from the
broken wheel to where the wagon had finally
stopped. Perhaps if he gathered everything together
by the wagon, they wouldn't be mad at him any-
more.

He picked up the basket his mother had used to
hold tubers for peeling. The memory of her sitting
by the table and recently by the campfire, reaching
into the basket for beans to break or for turnips or
tubers to peel while she told him stories, brought
tears to his eyes. He was sniffling when he saw
movement, and he whirled around and crouched in
fear.

His tears in the morning light gave a sparkle to the
woods and the stranger standing a few feet away,
staring down at him. At first he thought it might be
one of the creatures that attacked the caravan, but
the face—what he could see of it through his tears—
had a shape similar to his own and that of his parents. The stranger's forehead was wider and his chin
narrower, though. The skin of the creature was pale
brown, like that of the people in the caravan. To the
child, that made him human.

He stood tall and straight, more slender than the
men of the caravan. He wore armor that gleamed
metallically, though it was no metal the child knew.
The breastplate, tall pointed helm, tasses, greaves,
and gauntlets seemed to change color as the elf
moved, blending with the background, and were
trimmed in tiny designs; Cald knew nothing of
magic runes.

Large pointed ears framed the stranger's black
hair, cropped short over his wide forehead. His narrowed eyes above the small straight nose were dark,

with the depth of a lifetime that stretched back through millennia. To a child of not quite four years, those eyes were filled with the kindness he sought.

He gave no credence to the elf's mouth, which was set in a cruel, implacable line. The stranger looked away, searching the forest with a quick, practiced gaze, but his mouth softened as he looked back at the child.

Cald knew he had been found at last. He dropped the basket and dashed forward, grasping the slender man around the knees.

"My mama, my papa," he sobbed. "I want my mama."

In later years he would understand the meaning of the actions and conversations that followed, but though he had never forgotten a moment of that first meeting, the meaning had passed over the head of the small child that day. He had been unable to understand the language of the elves, but some of the words had stayed with him, imprinted on his mind because of his fear. The elves, with their love of stories, had made a pleasing tale of so strange an incident. Like all children, he loved to listen to stories about himself and the constant retelling had kept every incident fresh in his mind.

A second elf had walked up behind the first and also stared at him. Cald had shrunk from the newcomer. He lacked the height and the casual assurance of the first. His eyes, as dark and large in his face as the eyes of the first elf, radiated hostility. The new arrival threw darting glances into the forest and jerked his gaze back to stare at the boy. His right hand moved restlessly from his sheathed knife to his sword and back, as if he dared not let his fingers stray far from either one.

"It's a human," the second said, his voice filled with disgust.

Cald could not understand the words, but the tone was obvious; this second stranger did not like him, or thought he had done something wrong. He took a tighter hold on the first stranger's leg and hid his face.

"A very small one, and it's dirty," replied the first. He placed his hands on Cald's shoulders, pushed the child back a step, and knelt to get a better look at the tear- and soil-smudged face.

"It's a human!" the second elf repeated.

The first looked up at his companion. "Relcan, I recognize the racial features. I agree it's a human, probably from that wagon, and likely brought into the forest by the harnessed beasts we found this morning. We can assume they were pulling the wrecked wagon, and that the child was in it."

Carefully watched over because of his breath-rasp, Cald had been more shocked at being alone for most of a day and a night than a healthy, adventurous youngster would have been. When the kneeling elf looked up at his companion, Cald pressed closer to the slender knees, seeking a reassuring touch.

"By the order of King Tieslin and your own instructions, Prince Eyrmin, we are to kill all humans invading Sielwode—" Relcan said, taking one quick step forward as if he were ready to deal the death blow.

The expression on the face of the prince sent him back a rapid pace.

Several other elves appeared and joined the first two. Eyrmin rose, and Cald, not willing to let the elf get far away, hugged his leg with one small arm. He looked from one elf to the other as the newcomers reported. Most had been searching along the eaves of the forest for other intruders. They had found none.

A final elf appeared, taller than the rest. While the others had walked, trotted, or run with the grace inherent in the elven race, this late arrival stumbled twice as he ducked under low-hanging bows. When he stopped, he seemed to have trouble deciding where to put his feet and hands. His breathing was heavier than the rest, as if he had made a long run. His haste seemed to worry the prince.

"Danger, Saelvam?" Eyrmin asked.

The tall, awkward elf shook his head.

"The beasts were doubtless a part of a caravan of human settlers," the tall warrior said, his eyes moving from the prince's face to the child and back again. His face was filled with sympathy for the youngster. "Human and gnoll bodies litter the ground just this side of a group of nerseberry bushes where a hundred or more gnolls waited in ambush. The tracks show the surviving humanoids took the wagons, all but this one." He pointed to the wreck.

"Any living humans?" the prince asked, glancing down at Cald, who still clung to him.

"None."

"Then you'll have to kill it," Relcan insisted, his eyes darting toward the tall elf as if looking for confirmation. The other warrior averted his eyes and shifted his attention to some distant point, disassociating himself from the prince's second-in-command.

The others shifted and frowned, and some sidled away. None wanted to be thought squeamish. They were warriors and used to killing. Prince Eyrmin noticed them, and his eyes sparkled with the humor of the situation. He called to two who were slipping away around a tree.

"Hialmair, Ursrien, would one of you accept the honor or ridding Sielwode of this human menace? The lights of Tallamai may lighten the path of a warrior who dares to fight such a dangerous foe."

Ursrien looked away, but Hialmair, whose bearing showed him a brave and successful fighter, turned an unwavering gaze on his prince.

"May no song ever tell of a time when I shirked my duty to my prince, but I must forego this honor. My sword is too long and my bow too large for the foe."

When he saw Eyrmin's lips twitch in a half-hidden smile, Hialmair followed Ursrien into the wood and out of sight.

The other warriors were quickly disappearing, but the prince called to Saelvam. Because his height drew attention and he had been closer to Eyrmin and Relcan, he had been more cautious in his effort to escape.

"Saelvam," the prince called. "I have a task for you."

Saelvam paused, sighed, and returned, his chin on his chest, his slow place showing his reluctance. He tried to keep his hands from their accustomed resting places on the hilt of his sword and the string of his bow, but did not seem to find a place for them.

When the tall warrior stood at the prince's side, Eyrmin disengaged Cald's arm from around his leg, took the child's hand, and put it in the palm of the other elf.

Cald, thinking he was being placed in the care of this person, looked up at him hopefully. He wondered how he could talk to these people, with their strange language, and how he could tell them he was hungry and cold.

"Can you kill this child for me?" the prince asked with a smile.

Saelvam gazed down at the child and back at his prince. He frowned.

"If you order me, I must," the elven warrior replied after a slight hesitation. "But it looks so trusting."

"You have looked into the heart of honor," the prince replied. "How do you kill a creature that doesn't know it's your enemy?" Eyrmin sighed. "Doubtless it will grow to be no better than the rest of its race, but it's too young to know or do evil."

"But it will live to become evil, and no one asked for its trust," Relcan objected.

"No, one does not ask for trust or hold it out as if it were a piece of fruit," Eyrmin said, his voice sharp. "If faith in one's honor is complete, it comes unasked and lays a burden on the receiver." His gaze, fixed on his second-in-command was sharp and speculating. "We would be nothing as a people without that knowledge."

"It can't survive alone," Relcan said, still pressing for Cald's death. He had missed or completely ignored the philosophy of the prince's explanation. "Kill it now if you want to show it mercy. It will starve in the forest if some beast doesn't get it before nightfall."

"No, to leave it is to kill it as surely as if we used a sword," the prince sighed. "Either way we destroy trust, and that is not the path an honorable warrior chooses."

"Do you mean to shelter it?" Relcan demanded, staring at the prince as if he had lost his mind.

"We will care for it until we can return it to its own kind," Eyrmin said. "I doubt it will eat much."

As Cald grew older, learned the language and the meaning of the conversations that took place that day, he never forgot the prince's signal omission when he offered the elves the honor of taking the child's life. He had not suggested Relcan do the deed. Even then, Eyrmin had known of the uncompromising attitudes of his royal cousin.

ANUIRE

TWO

". . . And each creature on the field, whether elf, human, dwarf, gnoll, goblin or the nameless deformed beings twisted by Azrai, knew the fate of Aebrynis would be decided that day."

Cald waited breathlessly for the rest of the tale. He never tired of hearing Prince Eyrmin talk about the battle on Mount Deismaar.

"When dawn lit the sky, the warriors faced each other at the foot of the mountain. Their lines stretched as far as the eye could see. They waited in silence. The stamp of a hoof or the jingle of a horse's harness caused some to jump, so keyed up were they for the great battle." Eyrmin stared out into the distance as if he could see the two armies facing each other at the foot of Mount Deismaar.

"Many of our cousin elves stood against us, allied with the evil Azrai, but not the warriors of Sielwode. Though we hated the human encroachers as much as Azrai did, we would not ally with evil to defend our homeland."

"And the morning breeze blew," eleven-year-old Cald prompted, his eyes wide. He had heard the story many times before, but the awe of it still raised gooseflesh on his arms. He was accompanying Eyrmin and several elven warriors on a slow walk through the woods. Behind the prince and child, the younger elves, who had not been at the great battle, were listening intently.

Saelvam, who was still young enough to have grown another inch in the last seven years, stumbled over a root. The other elves occasionally teased him, saying his legs and arms were too long. It did sometimes seem as if his hands and feet did not understand how far they were from his body.

"And the morning breeze awoke with the dawn," Eyrmin continued. "The standards snapped in the clear air, the great flags whipping about as if they were trying to free themselves from their poles and ride the wind, leading the attack. The great flag of the Anuireans waved from a pole that had been set on the ground, and yet three men were hard pressed to hold it. Roele's personal standard was carried by a man who rode at his side; the red dragon with his golden blade writhed in the wind. The Khinasi with their standard of the sun on the sea were to his left, and facing them were the Vos, with their snarling snow tiger on a field of white.

"Between us and Roele's army were the few dwarves who had joined the fight. They stood under a banner of crossed axes, while over us flew the Star Stair of Sielwode on a background of sky-blue." Seeing the child was growing tired of hearing about the banners, Eyrmin moved on.

"The rising sun reflected off the armor of the great warriors, but the metal would gleam no more that day . . ."

"Because Roele ordered the horns to blow," Cald said breathlessly.

"The signal for the horns was the dipping of his standard, an obeisance to his gods and a request that they aid him on the field of battle. To the left and to the right of Roele, every standard dipped in an ever widening wave as if each were part of a ripple on a still pool when a stone is thrown in. Though it was not our custom, we dipped our banner to Tallamai and asked the fortunes to guide our arrows."

"And then the horns blew."

"And then the horns blew. The challenge echoed down the line, growing stronger and stronger as each company or clan added to the sound. From across the half mile of open space, Azrai's forces accepted the challenge with horns, drums, and shouts.

"With the blowing of the horns, the two armies started forward. The warhorses screamed their challenges. They rose rearing and cantered in place, held back by their riders so they did not outdistance those who traveled on foot."

"And you couldn't see much after that," Cald said.

"Beneath the feet of the restless horses, the dust rose in roiling clouds that hid part of the field from us. But we had no time to look about, because we were then upon the enemy. The first clash of weapons as the two armies met rang a deafening roar across the slopes of the mountain. We thought no sound could be more terrible, but we would learn otherwise by the end of the day.

"Facing us was a company of man-beasts of

Aduria, twisted and given power by the evil god Azrai. We were hard pressed. They stood eight feet tall and carried spears that were longer than ours. Fortunately they seemed to know nothing of bows.

"Our shield bearers went first, and between them the spearmen. Last came the bowmen, shooting over the heads of their companions. We felled so many with our arrows that our ranks shifted and left vulnerable spots as we climbed over mounds of slain bodies. There seemed no end to the beast-men.

"We fought throughout the morning with the sun to our left, into the afternoon as it moved over us, and to our right with the closing of the day."

"With nothing to eat or drink," Cald shook his head at the idea of thirst, but his mind was on the battle. Though he wore a practice sword, he left it in its sheath as he hopped about and swung his arm in imaginary slashes and thrusts at the enemies of the tale.

Eyrmin continued as if he were not aware of Cald's movements.

"Within the first hour of battle, the line had disappeared. Small groups fought up and down the side of the mountain. At times, it seemed we were pushing the forces of Azrai back toward the land bridge. Then their troops would rally, and we would retreat up the mountain. The streams ran red with the blood of the dead and dying, both theirs and ours. The water was unfit to drink.

"Fields of grass and small forests were set afire by the mages of both sides. Many individual battles were abandoned as both friend and foe sprinted away to avoid the flames. Often, as if by some unspoken arrangement, foes met again to fight in safer territory."

"And then the gods came down," Cald whispered. He ceased his imaginary battle and stayed close to the prince's side as Eyrmin picked up with the thread of the child's thinking.

"First, there was the glow on the mountainside, for the concentration of such power cannot be hidden. The gods of the humans numbered seven, and to honor their courage and sacrifice that day, we took the trouble to learn their names. Anduiras, the noble god of war; Reynir, of the woods and streams; Brenna, of commerce and fortune; Vorynn, of the moon, who favored magic; Masela, of the great seas; and Basaïa, who humans say ruled the sun. These six stood against the evil of Azrai, the seventh."

"Six against one," Cald murmured, as he did each time the tale was told. He wanted to hear again the reason; it was not the most exciting part of the story, but to him the lesson, as Eyrmin had explained it, was the most impressive. In Eyrmin's explanation he had found a life lesson, and he liked to have it reinforced.

"The numbers counted for nothing. It was the power that mattered, much like six elves standing against one dragon. The six gods of the humans drew much of their strength from the faith of their followers. As the battle waged and the humans began to fear, the powers of their gods waned. But Azrai, the evil one, had learned to draw not from faith but from fear, and fed on his own host as well as on the weak of heart and purpose among his foes.

"So it is that if a human fears, he weakens those immortals on whom he depends, and elves who fear aid the side of evil and weaken themselves, for we have never looked to gods, though we seek the aid of good fortune from Tallamai."

Cald knew all about Tallamai. The stars in the night sky were the spirits of elves that had died honorably in battle. They looked down on their people, and often aided them in small ways. The elves of Sielwode revered them and attributed good fortune to their assistance. Still, their influence was not considered to make them gods, like those of the humans. Eyrmin went on with the tale.

Behind the prince, Saelvam, caught up in the tale, had not given due attention to the path and tripped over a fallen tree limb. Eyrmin's eyes danced with laughter, though he bit his lips to keep from smiling at the awkward elf's misstep. When Saelvam was back in line, he went on with his tale.

"Power and dread purpose lit the faces of the six gods as they moved forward to meet Azrai, who loomed before them. He alone was enough to fill every heart with terror and weaken our purpose, but his own minions feared him as much, and the beast-men we fought fled his presence. Had they not, we would not be here today. In their loss of heart, we found the courage to follow them. We chased them down the mountainside and across the plain to the east. The man-beasts had stolen many elven lives that day, and we could not let our people go unavenged.

"Our bowmen had used all their arrows, and stopped as they ran to retrieve spent missiles, pulling some from the wounded and the dead. How long the battle would have lasted, we have no idea, but the ground beneath our feet trembled and shook. Even the most surefooted stumbled and fell. One of the beast-men, looking behind him, shouted to the others, and they cowered, huddling on the ground. They ignored us as if we no longer mattered. Indeed, we soon learned we were a puny danger compared to the peril that followed.

"Their fear caused us to turn and look. From the slopes of the mountain a great blackness had begun to spread, as if night sought to hide the destruction from the sight of the sun. From that blackness came bolts of fire and lighting that showered down. So hot was the fire of the gods that trees blazed up and were gone in an instant. Rocks and soil melted and boiled.

"The ground shifted around us and sank to a depth of nearly twice our height. The surviving elves of Sielwode tumbled with the sinking earth and cried out to Tallamai. In our fear we were like children. It is our way to look to ourselves and thank those that have gone before when they send us good fortune, but that day we called to them as the humans and beasts called to their own gods. Strong arms and great skills could avail us nothing against the force of the world turning against itself. Many of us believe the power of the departed had seen our plight and had already provided for us."

The prince paused before crossing the stepping-stones in the Star Mirror Stream. He guided Cald, whose shorter legs still made his leaps from stone to stone less secure than those of the elves.

"Because you had a place to shelter when the mountain exploded," Cald said breathlessly when they reached the northern side of the stream and entered the Muirien Grove.

"Because we had a place to shelter when the mountain exploded," Eyrmin agreed. "It seemed as if the land had risen up to fall on us for daring to shed so much blood. Earth, stones, giant trees, weapons, armor and the dead rained down on the surrounding countryside. We sheltered beneath the cliff that had been created by the sinking of the earth, and so we survived. Beyond us, the beast-men were buried under a great fall of earth and rock. The dust had not settled when tumbling from the sky came the richly jeweled crown of some evil king. It glittered dimly from the top of the heap of stones and earth."

"And you would not touch it, because you thought it was evil," Cald said, his face alight with the enjoyment of the tale, but it soon became a frown. Most of his questions were rote, asking for the parts of the tale he enjoyed most or hurrying the prince along when he bogged down in the description. This day he had a new thought, a new question.

"But Eyrmin, if the humans came to this land because they feared the evil Azrai and he was destroyed, why didn't they go home again? Didn't they love their land like we love Sielwode?"

Most of the elves accompanying their prince smiled in approval, but Relcan gave a snort of disgust. His head jerked. He shot a glare at the human child, and then walked quickly away. The prince had taught Cald to love the forest with elven intensity, and any mention of the boy's feelings seemed to anger Relcan.

Eyrmin's hand dropped to the boy's shoulder. "Humans do not put their hearts into their lands the way elves do. The lives of your race are fleeting, and what seems a short tale to an elf is a long history to humans. Many had come to Cerilia generations before the battle at Mount Deismaar and had no memory of their homeland. Even had they remembered it, the land bridge was destroyed, and it is said that evil creatures now swim in the depths of the Straits of Aerele."

"They could not have loved their land like I love Sielwode," Cald said. To him Sielwode was a wonderful place, and he loved it with a fierce devotion most of the elves found surprising in one of his race. To him it was safety after the terror of the gnoll attack, which still haunted his dreams occasionally and kept his fear fresh. Part of his love for Sielwode came from his devotion to his royal foster-father. In his mind, Sielwode and Eyrmin were inseparable.

In the seven years he had lived with the elves, Cald had been well cared for and had been taught the elvish tongue, Sidhelien. He had advanced in his own language and could speak some goblin, gnoll, and orog. He was knowledgeable in wood lore.

Eyrmin had always insisted that Cald would have to return to his own people when the first surrogate human parents came within elven sight of Sielwode. Relcan had been assiduous in spotting human travelers on the Markaz plain, and at first Cald clung to the hope that the elves might find his parents.

By the time Cald knew his own people would not return, Eyrmin had become the focus of his life. Then news of humans on the plain caused him to tremble in fear of being sent away, but the prince always found fault with the travelers. He kept Cald in the wood. Finally even Relcan gave up trying to rid the elven realm of this young human, though he wasted no opportunity to show his contempt.

The elven healers had given Cald magical draughts that cured his breath-rasp, and he had grown strong as well as tall for his age. Over Relcan's objections, Eyrmin had made him a bow, and under the elves' instruction, Cald had become what they considered a fair shot. Few adult humans had as keen an eye as Cald, though he was not yet large enough or strong enough for a proper elven longbow. The prince had provided him with a sword and spears, though he was less adept with them.

On that crisp autumn morning he wore his sword and carried his bow, hoping the prince would tire of walking and he would be able to practice his skills. He thought he had perfected the moves of an intricate parry and cross-block that he had seen the prince use in practice. He refrained from asking for a bout, knowing Eyrmin and the half dozen warriors who walked with him would be communing with the ancient trees of the Muirien Grove.

Eyrmin had told him most humans believed that all elven magic was intrinsic to their race and could be used only by elves. Cald was perhaps the only human who knew that particular belief was untrue. Some of their arts were learned; he had cause to know because Eyrmin had been teaching him what he could absorb.

Only one other elf knew the human boy was learning to use elven magic. Glisinda, a warrior and the village Speaker of Lore, knew of the lessons. She also knew that the prince believed Cald would one day return to his people, and the knowledge he took with him might help to bring more understanding between the races of Cerilia.

Glisinda had kept the secret, entirely in sympathy with the beliefs of the prince. She was dedicated to learning and remembering, and used elven magic to draw to the forefront of her mind knowledge that spanned thousands of years. To her, teaching was as sacred as learning.

Cald had one failing in developing elven skills. He was unable to emotionally blend with the trees, unable to understand their thought. When he touched the trees and concentrated, he could sense life, but to know a thing lived was not the same as communicating with it. His only success had been in the Muirien Grove, but the experience had not been pleasant; he had sensed hostility and knew at least this portion of Sielwode did not accept him.

When the tale and the conversation ended, he fell back to walk behind Eyrmin and took care to tread silently. They entered the grove. Like the elves, Cald was both repelled and fascinated by the ancient gnarled trees. They were thick boled and twisted, but of no great height; some had huge rents in their trunks as if the tough wood had not been able to withstand the forces it faced. Limbs as thick as Cald's body lay on the ground. Few rotted away in the strange atmosphere of the grove. They made walking treacherous. High in the trees, the jagged boughs they had broken away from still looked raw, and jutted to the sky with accusing splinter points.

The elves collected fallen limbs in other parts of the forest. They carefully preserved every usable scrap for building, calling them the gifts of Sielwode. But they never touched a fallen branch from the grove.

The monarchs of the grove were somehow out of time with the rest of the forest. Other trees in Sielwode dropped their leaves in the fall and sprouted new ones in the spring. In contrast, the monarchs of Muirien Grove made no concession to the annual change of seasons. They had their own timing, different from each other and the world in general. Once every eighteen to twenty-five years, they shed their musty old leaves in preparation for sprouting new ones, as a few were doing now.

The elves stopped by a gnarled and twisted monarch that had dropped most of its foliage. Since the trees of the grove recognized no season but their own and dropped their leaves only to sprout new ones, the elves raised their voices in the traditional song of spring:

"Awake, feel life in all your limbs.
Your sap rises in your bole.
Greet Sidhelien. The new year begins,
And with it, life.
Greet Sidhelien. . . ."

The song continued through many verses. Cald repeated the words with his mind and delighted in the lilt of elven voices. Since he felt the grove resented his presence, he did not defile the purity of the elven song with his own voice, which, in comparison to theirs, was loud and rasping.

The elves sang for every tree that showed signs of renewing itself. Later they would sing to the others, hoping to wake them to renewal. No saplings sprouted among these ancient monarchs, and the elves were afraid the grove was dying.

At midday, they paused to sit beneath an ancient tree that had not yet begun to shed its leaves. They had brought flasks of elven wine—Cald's, in deference to his age, had been watered down considerably—and waybread, their customary traveling rations. They ate their meal, and over their wine they talked, speculating on the grove and its place in the history of Sielwode.

It had always surprised Cald that the elves were ignorant of the reason the trees of the grove behaved as they did. They could recite the history of nearly every inch of land within their domain. They knew when each patch of ground had been an orchard, and later a meadow, and in which century it was taken over by saplings to become a forest again. Even so, mystery surrounded the Muirien Grove.

Elves all over Cerilia believed that tales of ancient honor and bravery strengthened the hearts of living warriors, and the elves of western Sielwode used the same principle on the trees. When they visited the grove, they told stories of their own making, of great deeds and heroes who had inhabited Muirien, hoping to raise the consciousness of the trees and bring them back to good health. Saelvam was just ending such a tale of the grove, one made entirely from his own head.

". . . So, Time, the giver and taker of life, looked down on Ciesandra Starshine. He knew her heart was true, and she would keep her vow to wait for her lover's return.

"He wept, knowing her wait was long, and shortened it for her, placing her in the grove, where a score of years in the rest of the world would seem only one."

Cald, still too young to understand the poignancy of unrequited love, had been more interested in the imaginary lover who had traveled to a distant land to fight a great but undisclosed evil. The elven warriors were touched and sat quietly for a few moments. Then young Dralansen blinked away a tear.

Eyrmin smiled at the story, and then glanced down at Cald.

"You are developing a good voice for tales. Have you none of the grove?"

Since he felt Muirien resented his presence, Cald did not want to presume, but he knew it would break the mood of the afternoon to say so.

"No, I make up stories about the Star Stair," Cald replied, pointing north to where a series of natural stone spires rose hundreds of feet into the sky. Their uneven heights gave them the appearance of being a stair to the sky. Since the elves had never told a tale of them, they were a curiosity to the young human boy.

The words were hardly out of Cald's mouth when he noticed the discomfort around the circle of listeners. Relcan, who usually looked away when Cald spoke, snorted his contempt. He jerked his head around to glare at the boy and turned a mocking gaze on the others as if to say, "See? I was right when I said he did not belong."

Eyrmin, with a sober gaze, shook his head. "No tales of the mind's imagining can be told of the Star Stair."

"Then you know its history?" Cald sensed he should not ask, but curiosity overran his discretion.

"It is lore better not spoken of," Eyrmin said gently. "Instead we will . . ." His eyes flickered as he looked beyond Cald. Quicker than the eye could follow, he was on his feet, sword in hand.

" 'Ware goblins!" he shouted.

Cald grabbed his bow and was scrambling to his feet when he saw the humanoids. Two large goblins walked ahead of a clutch of others. They wore badly tanned, sleeveless leather coats with rusty metal disks sewn on as a type of armor. They carried large axes with crooked, badly shaped handles, mere tree limbs that had been skinned of bark. Behind the first two, four others marched, shouldering long poles from which dangled the carcasses of two slain deer.

The first two goblins stopped suddenly and threw the four carrying the deer into confusion. They all stared at the elves. Their small beady eyes glared from under low foreheads and heavy brows. Their wide noses flared, and their heavy cheeks and jowls shook as they growled a challenge. The first and largest had a single fang rising from his bottom jaw. The others all showed two fangs that were not as long.

Behind the first six, Cald could see several others, and more had slipped around the trees. The human boy had no time to make a count, but the number seemed more than twenty. Eyrmin had grabbed his arm and shoved him into a large crack in one of the trees.

"Stay there," the prince hissed.

"Knew it," a harsh voice muttered. "Can't take a step in these woods without finding elf vermin underfoot."

None of the elves spoke. They were outnumbered at least four to one, but they did not attempt retreat. This was their forest, and intruders were not allowed. Cald watched from the rent in the tree, his heart swelling with pride in his friends. He understood the odds, but never having seen any but the battle with the gnolls on the plain, and little of that, he was too ignorant of fighting to fully grasp the danger.

He knew how the goblins had gained access to the forest; they had entered some underground passage miles away and had returned to the surface through some natural fissure that opened inside the forest. If they had tried to cross the plain, they would have been seen long before they reached Sielwode. The elves were constantly on the search for entrances to the deep passages, and blocked them when they were discovered, but at least one had eluded their sharp eyes.

The elves in the western arm of Sielwode had fought under the command of the prince for centuries and had no need for orders at the opening of an attack. Three slipped behind the trees, nocked arrows to their bowstrings, and let fly their missiles.

Prince Eyrmin, to whom the responsibilities of command meant taking the burden of the greatest danger on his own shoulders, moved out into the center of the clearing, his sword, Starfire, in his hand. The ancient, dweomered blade glittered in the sunlight. As ever, he made himself a target to draw out the goblins. Without armor, because the elves had intended only to commune with the trees, he stood in great peril.

Relcan, with a frown and hasty, nervous motions, reluctantly followed the prince, taking up a stance just behind him and to the left.

The goblins, knowing the legendary accuracy of elven bows, took shelter. Three threw their spears at Eyrmin and Relcan, but the agile elves skipped away from the bad casts.

Cald quickly strung his bow and loosed an arrow in the direction of the last to throw his spear. The boy was not as quick to sight down the shaft of the arrow as the battle-wise elves, and his target had seen the tip of his arrow protruding beyond the bark of the tree. The humanoid ducked back just in time to escape death. Cald's arrow rang off a metal disk attached to the creature's boiled leather helmet. Cald delighted in hitting his first living target. Though it wasn't a kill, hitting was always better than missing.

The large goblin leader roared and charged, its axe in its hand. Cald thought it very stupid or very brave to risk the elven arrows. Then he saw Dralansen step out from behind a tree. His bow was drawn, but he held his shot. As the goblin shifted about, Cald realized it was careful to keep the two elves in the clearing between himself and the archers.

At any other time, Cald would have left the defense of so important a person as Prince Eyrmin to the elven warriors, but fearing the others were as hampered as Dralansen, he took careful aim and planted an arrow in the goblin's left forearm. He had been aiming for the goblin's heart.

Just as well, Cald thought. He had the accuracy for a potentially fatal shot, but it would have taken a stronger bow than his to send an arrowhead through the hardened leather coat with the metal disks. He had at least limited the huge goblin to a one-handed stroke with his axe. But had he helped the prince?

Three more goblins dashed into the clearing. Relcan and Eyrmin were each suddenly trying to hold off two opponents. Other goblins were surrounding the five elves. Saelvam rushed into the clearing, holding back three invaders with quick jabs from one of their own long spears. The tall, lanky elf that so often embarrassed himself with his awkwardness, was a graceful fighter. His long legs moved him quickly and deftly toward the enemy and back. Hands that often dropped goblets in Reilmirid were quick with a bow and adept with a spear and sword. While Cald watched, Saelvam thrust the point of the goblin weapon into the heart of his nearest opponent and was fending off the others again before the surprised goblin fell to the ground.

Fiedhmil was backed against a tree, fending off two others with his blade.

Malala came into sight, her light feet moving in what Cald had termed her battle dance. Spinning, dipping, weaving back and forth, she never seemed to be in one place long enough to strike at her foe, but one goblin dropped to the ground, its head severed from its shoulders. She circled the body with lightning speed and moved on to another opponent.

Cald shivered and realized his fear was not wholly because of the goblin attack. It seemed as if the grove itself had suddenly turned malevolent. It emitted a brooding evil. Even the elves and goblins seemed affected by it. The humanoids looked about with their small eyes stretched wide, as if they expected some hidden enemy to strike out of thin air.

The elves, who could have used the fear and confusion of the goblins against the creatures, were similarly affected. They glanced about quickly, seeking the source of the strange atmosphere.

In the center of the small clearing, Eyrmin and Relcan were standing back-to-back, their slender elven blades flashing as between them they parried the swings of four axes.

Since the arrows had stopped, other goblins were entering the clearing. Cald fitted another arrow to his bow and sent the point deep into the leg of the creature just taking a swing at Relcan's head.

One of the newly arrived goblins saw the shot and turned toward the tree. Cald nocked another arrow, and the point cut the cheek of the goblin, who did not pause as it stalked toward the human boy.

Suddenly the light faded to early twilight, not

dark enough to drain the red from the blood streaking down the goblin's cheek, or to wash out the faded green of his ragged pants, yet suddenly the color fled from everything else around the clearing. The world faded to shades of gray.

The forest had developed shadows, not lying on the ground like those thrown by the sun, but standing upright, side by side with the trees of the Muirien Grove.

In the darkness, the five elven blades glowed with a magical light of their own.

The battle between the elves and goblins abruptly stopped as both sides looked around, wondering what was happening. The large, single-fanged goblin spun completely around and back to face Eyrmin.

"Elf! Say what it is that happens," it snarled as if the dwellers of Sielwode were taking unfair advantage.

"It is some filthy magic of the Sidhelien," growled its companion, though he had taken a step back and eyed the prince warily.

Eyrmin, still clutching his sword, also stared at the change in the clearing. He held his sword slackly, as if he had forgotten it was in his hand.

"It's no magic wrought by my people," he said, his voice hollow with wonder. "I don't know what it is . . . unless it's a portal to the Shadow World."

The indrawn breaths of the elves were loud in the still air. The goblins hissed and snarled and grouped together for protection.

Cald trembled, his mind suddenly filled with the little he knew about the Shadow World. Eyrmin had told him that in many of the human lands, mention of it was forbidden by law. Even the elves seldom spoke of the dark and dreadful plane of existence that paralleled the world of Aebrynis. They knew little of it; it was a dark and forbidding place ruled by undead—ghouls, liches, ghosts. Eyrmin had told

him it had once been a beautiful land before the evil
taint, but even the prince claimed to know little
about it.

By the expression on the goblin leader's face, it
did not quite believe Eyrmin but had decided not to
argue. With a growl that sounded more animal than
humanoid, it backed away from the elves. The rest of
the band followed. They reached the far side of the
clearing and seemed undecided whether to retreat
or regroup and attack.

The goblins eyed the strange wood as they faced
the five elves in the clearing. One at the back of the
group snarled in surprise as someone ran past.

Into this strangeness came an eruption of more
than a score small figures with demihuman faces,
round cheeks, curly hair, and wide, frightened eyes.
They carried swords and axes made to fit their
diminutive hands. Some had bows, and others
spears. Several were armed with rakes and hoes.
They swirled around the goblins as if the humanoids
presented no danger. Several glanced up at Eyrmin
as they passed the elves and took up stations behind
the trees on the far side of the clearing.

Then Cald understood. The demihumans were
halflings from the Shadow World. They were fleeing,
but from what?

Cald soon found out. Behind the halflings came a
host of creatures that surpassed any nightmare Cald
had experienced.

ANUIRE

three

Cald stared at the gray creatures that rushed through the wood after the halflings. They charged after the demihumans in a hodge-podge of races—orogs, goblins, gnolls, elves, humans, and even a few dwarves—yet they fitted no description he had ever heard. No color showed on their flesh, but then, even his elven friends had been robbed of their natural hues.

When a large orog raced into the clearing and attacked the first goblin it reached, Cald saw a huge gash in the orog's head. Even Cald knew the creature could not have lived with that wound. He'd heard of such monsters in elven lore—*the undead!*

Their tattered, half-rotten clothing and decaying skin and flesh gave off a stink that caused his stomach to roil. Eyrmin had said that warriors of both sides at Mount Deismaar had become sick with fear, but Cald's terror had the opposite effect. The cold knot of fear seemed to freeze his stomach as well as his arms and legs.

The pursuers of the demihumans represented every race on Cerilia, but they were twisted and strange, with red-glowing eyes filled with madness. The goblins among them were misshapen, their faces more animal than humanoid, and grotesque in their undead state. The gnolls stood taller than those that had attacked the settler's caravan. On some, the doglike snouts were oversized. Others ran on twisted legs and staggered as they raced after the halflings. There were even elves, their beautiful faces twisted like their backs and arms. An aura of evil permeated the forest as the vile creatures came on.

More fearsome than all the rest was the creature who led them. He rode a giant black parody of a horse, whose legs were longer in front than behind. Steam issued from the mount's wide nostrils, set in an overlarge head, and its red eyes seemed to reflect some fire from deep within. But it was not the horse that kept Cald biting his knuckles to keep from voicing his fears. The rider was no more than a skeleton covered with skin. As he held up one hand, urging his followers forward, every joint in his emaciated fingers stood out in perfect clarity. The skin on his face was so fleshless and tight that the outline of his teeth cast shadows on his hollow cheeks. On his head sat a crown that absorbed the light around him, so that he rode in a shadow deeper than night, but still was clearly visible.

The horse needed no guidance. It charged through the grouped goblins. The king held aloft his left hand, urging his followers forward. With the sword in his right hand, he swung at the largest goblin, beheading the single-fanged humanoid with an almost absentminded motion.

Beneath that fearsome crown, deep within each eye socket, gleamed a terrible light, as if the creature concentrated all the evil and madness of his followers. Then Cald realized why the eyes were so bright. The king from the Shadow World had paused, his attention no longer on the escaping halflings. He stared straight at Cald.

The air seemed to freeze around the human boy. He felt himself being dragged from his hiding place by a will much greater than his own. Dimly he heard a voice urging him back into the split in the tree.

Eyrmin leapt forward, taking a swing at the crowned figure. The two dweomered blades clashed. A blinding blue glow, startling in the grayness, flashed out from the collision of the two swords.

In elven battle practice, Cald had often seen fire flash when two dweomered blades met. When the prince's blade, Starfire, struck another weapon, it flashed even brighter, but never with such blinding light. The sparks hung in the air as if they had a life of their own.

When the king turned to face Eyrmin, Cald felt the release of the pull that had forced him out of his hiding place. The voice he had heard had been Eyrmin's. The prince had ordered him back.

Even so, another, larger group of halflings appeared between the trees. A female, carrying an infant and followed by several young demihumans who clung to her skirt, took refuge within the tree, leaving no room for Cald. He joined a group of halfling archers that gathered behind one of the trees. While they conferred on the best place to make their stand, he watched the battle in the clearing.

The goblins, so recently at odds with the elves, had stood directly in the path of the exodus from the

Shadow World. Six already lay dead, and others were fighting off the twisted minions of the mounted king. Several of the more intelligent fled across the clearing to take up a safer fighting position.

Relcan was trading rapid, jerky blows with a huge, undead orog from the world beyond. The creature had an enlarged head that in life had suffered a terrible blow. The flesh from the right side had been slashed away and flopped down the side of its neck, leaving a glaring eye staring out from the naked bone. The wound had not slowed the monster. It howled with glee as it forced the elf back until Relcan tripped on a tree root and fell. The orog raised its blade for a fatal blow.

A goblin axe split the monster's backbone.

Relcan jumped to his feet, picked up his sword, and was poised to attack the goblin until he saw the creature pulling its axe out of its victim's back. Frustration darkened the elf's already angry face. He could not kill even so hated an enemy as a goblin when it had just saved his life.

The goblin had just freed its axe when three ghouls with large, crooked snouts crossed the clearing, howling with battle fever. Their voices, as they attacked the elf and the goblin, seemed to come from a great distance. Two fleshless humans joined the fight, and several halflings charged in with their spears.

The first halfling dashed forward, putting his weight behind his weapon as he jabbed at the smallest of the ghouls. The humanoid brought down its rusty blade with a force that cut the spear shaft cleanly in half. The halfling, suddenly disarmed, kept on running. He passed the larger creature and rounded the nearest tree. When the ghoul turned to follow him, it caught another halfling spear in the back.

All around the clearing, the battle continued. Dralansen, who found himself in his first battle, was as pale as the creatures from the Shadow World. He used a long, crooked goblin spear to hold off two orogs. The goblins from Single-Fang's band were fighting side by side with the elves and the halflings.

By some tacit agreement on both sides, the center of the clearing belonged to the fiercest battle. Eyrmin and the king from the Shadow World were trading blows with their swords. The vile, misshapen horse had fallen in the fray, brought down by a goblin spear. The king fought on foot, weaving and thrusting. The darkness that seemed to flow from his crown moved with him, an evil shadow that emanated fear. In contrast, Starfire, the ancient blade of Eyrmin's royal ancestors, blazed like a torch.

The dimness of the clearing was lightened as their clashing blades sent searing blue-white light shimmering into the air. The crown of the skeletal king seemed to absorb the light as soon as it flashed, though not quickly enough to prevent those who looked toward the fighters from being momentarily blinded.

Suddenly another light flashed across the clearing. A red lighting bolt rushed out from the desiccated hand of a magic-user and struck at the base of a tree. There, two of Single-Fang's goblins were attempting to hold off six undead members of their own scaly race. All eight died in a flash of fire.

Another goblin, smaller than the others, climbed into one of the trees, hoping for safety. Cald spared it a quick glance. In its fear, the humanoid had confused the trees; it had sheltered in one of the trees from the Shadow World.

A halfling, trying to escape the destruction, dashed out into the center of the clearing and ran blindly into Eyrmin, tripping the elf prince. Eyrmin fell over backward. The blow dislodged his grip on his sword. The king from the Shadow World leapt forward, his blade raised, but Eyrmin rolled quickly to the side and kept on rolling as his foe slashed at the empty spaces where the prince had been only moments before.

When the skeletal warrior attempted to anticipate the elf's movements, Eyrmin reversed his roll and whipped to his feet. He grabbed the sword arm of the king and wrenched the evil blade from him in a surprise move. The prince held the blade in his left hand, but with a lightning backhand stroke, he cut through the impossibly thin neck of the king from the Shadow World. The lich-lord's head fell to the ground, and the terrifying crown rolled across the soil.

Across the clearing, the magic-user drew back his hand to cast another lighting bolt, and Cald, realizing the mage was directing his spell toward Eyrmin, sent an arrow into the twisted man's arm. He was too late to stop the spell, though, and the lightning bolt flew up to strike a massive tree. An enormous limb broke away. Cald shouted, but not in time to warn Eyrmin. A heavy branch struck the elf prince, and he fell to the ground.

An armored skeletal warrior from the Shadow World had been trading blows with Dralansen, but when the lich-lord fell, it broke off the fight and dashed forward. It grabbed the crown and put it on its own head. Then, drawing back, it raised its head and shouted. The words were uncouth and unknown to the elves, but the tone was triumphant. It waded into the heavy foliage of broken limb as if searching for something.

Two warriors from the Shadow World followed it, but chasing them were two of Single-Fang's goblins. One of the undead raised its sword to strike the unconscious prince, but the first goblin rammed its spear through the fighter he had been chasing.

Suddenly a fierce wind blew across the clearing. Dead black leaves flew up into the air. The limbs of the shadowy trees tossed in the wind, but the trees rooted in the Muirien Grove were untouched by the strange gale.

On the opposite side of the battlefield, the fight faltered. The clothing of the twisted creatures of the Shadow World whipped around them in the gale. The elves, Cald, and the two remaining goblins felt no breeze at all. The halflings shouted warnings to each other and fled in all directions. They soon disappeared into the forest on the eastern side of the grove.

The undead warrior who had picked up the crown and was searching desperately beneath the thick leaves of the fallen limb, gave a scream of frustration before it was sucked back into its own plane.

As quickly as they had appeared, the shadow trees were gone and the ancient monarchs of the Muirien Grove stood alone. Moments before, the clearing had been littered with bodies of the dead, but these were swept away with the closing of the portal. The small goblin who had climbed into the tree from the Shadow World had also disappeared.

The elves blinked and looked around uneasily. All their faces seemed to reflect the same thought. Had they imagined what had occurred? They had begun a fight with a score of goblins. Now only two remained. One lay sprawled on the ground, stunned or dead. The other stood by the thick, broken limb of the tree and looked as confused as the elves.

Malala came out of her puzzled, trancelike state first and hurried to kneel by Eyrmin, who had not moved since he had been struck down by the tree limb. Dralansen grabbed the bow he had dropped, fitted an arrow to the string, and drew a bead on the goblin that stood close to the unconscious Eyrmin.

Cald dashed out of his hiding place. "No, you can't kill him. He saved the prince's life."

"It's true," Malala raised her head to agree with the human boy. "Our prince lives; he is only stunned. He would have died at the point of a sword save for this goblin. This places a grave obligation on us."

The humanoid had tentatively raised his spear but lowered it when he realized the elves were not planning to kill him. He walked over to the base of a tree where the only remaining member of his band lay sprawled on the ground.

"Bersmog! You dead?" he shouted, loudly enough to be heard across half the Sielwode.

Bersmog groaned and rolled over, looking up at his companion and Saelvam, who stood nearby, still holding his sword. The goblin seemed to see the elf first.

"I think maybe."

"I'll not kill you, goblin," Saelvam said, sheathing his weapon. "I saw you save the life of Relcan, who is of the royal kindred." he gazed at Relcan, who had crossed the clearing to help his prince to his feet. "If we are under obligation to one of the creatures for saving the prince's life, is it not the same for you? You are also of the royal kindred."

Relcan, who considered every other race an enemy of the elves, glared at the tall elf. Eyrmin stood, dazed and staggering. He nodded, though the motion seemed to cause him pain.

"Yes," he said and grimaced. As if his first speech had been painfully loud, he continued almost in a whisper. "They aided us in battle and they are free to go. We will not take the lives of those who protected ours."

Eyrmin rubbed his head as he walked across the

clearing. His eyes were directed downward, and he searched the trampled grass. Kneeling, he picked up his sword, Starfire, and turned slowly. He gazed at each of the elves and at Cald, as if assuring himself they were all present and unhurt.

He was preparing to slide his sword back into its scabbard when he gave a start of surprise and stared across the clearing. He moved into a fighting stance. The others drew their swords or fitted arrows to bowstrings, but they saw only an empty clearing.

"Wh-Who are you?" the prince asked. To his companions, he seemed to be speaking to thin air.

Even the goblins held their weapons ready, the recently stunned Bersmog leaning against the tree. His friend stood in front of him. Like the elves and Cald, they saw nothing, but they were less patient than the elves.

"Him have big bang on head?" Bersmog asked his goblin friend when no enemy appeared.

"*B-i-g* bang," the second goblin agreed.

Eyrmin relaxed and sheathed his blade, but he kept staring across the clearing. He wiped his hand across his eyes and looked again.

"What do you see?" Cald, who had come out of his hiding place, asked, fearing the Shadow World portal had opened again. None of the rest could see any danger.

"Probably nothing," Eyrmin said slowly. "A waking dream caused by the blow, mayhap." He put his hand to the back of his head and winced slightly. "I think we have disturbed the grove enough for one day."

He led the way west-southwest, toward the fork of the Moon Stream and the Star Mirror Stream, where the elven village called Reilmirid, or Watcher's Home, was located close to the western tip of Muirien Grove.

The elves traded glances, their eyes full of questions. Even Cald felt the prince had shied away from a full explanation of his experience. His excuse for their sudden exit from the grove was unconvincing and left everyone wondering.

They had not gone far when they heard a strange birdsong among the trees, and light footsteps following. Half a score of demihumans appeared from between the trees. More joined them, and soon fifty trudged along in the wake of the five elves and the human boy.

When the first halflings had begun to arrive, Eyrmin had looked back, his eyes flickering with thought. Then he turned to continue the trek to the village.

"Send them on their way. They shouldn't be here," Relcan demanded.

Eyrmin shook his head. "I will speak with them first."

"They're too weary to be sent on their way today," Malala said. She walked with a slight limp, and her shoulders slumped, a sign of her own fatigue.

Relcan nearly stumbled over a tree root as he glared at her. He hitched his sword belt higher with a series of short jerks and slapped the scabbard repeatedly in his irritation.

"Will you fill Sielwode with every race that would enter it until there's no longer room for your own people?" he asked the female elf. He was using his criticism of her to voice his objections to the prince's tolerance of the halflings.

"We will not fault these halflings for entering Sielwode. They were only trying to flee the evils of the Shadow World," Eyrmin said, biting off each word until it stood out with crisp clarity. "You fought the creatures that followed them; would you send them back rather than allow them to cross our land? Are we that poor, that we cannot give temporary shelter to those who mean us no harm?"

"How do we know they mean us no harm?" Relcan asked, glancing back over his shoulder as if he expected a diminutive spear in the back at any moment.

"I've had enough battle for one day," Eyrmin said. "Leave it for now."

The elves led the way to the Star Mirror Stream and crossed by the stepping-stones that rose just inches out of the swirling water. Behind them, several of the following halflings slipped from the widely spaced stones and fell in. They were in no danger, because the fast-moving stream was only a foot deep. The others, nearly hysterical with the relief of having escaped the Shadow World and happy to leave behind the oppressive atmosphere of the Muirien Grove, laughed with delight.

Cald turned to watch the small people and frowned. He had heard tales of the ones who lived in Sielwode. They were always described as stout and dressed in bright clothing. These halflings were nearly as thin as elves and were clothed in wellworn garments. The bottoms of the males' trousers and the hems of the females' skirts were black with the soil of travel. Dirt spotted the rest of their clothing, too, but they were not filthy. Red, yellow, blue, and green showed through the soil of travel and time, but the shades were dull, as if the dyes had been impure.

While he watched, a female plucked a leaf from a plant on the edge of the stream and held it against her dull green skirt. In seconds, she was surrounded by other female halflings, who exclaimed over the brightness of the leaf.

"They seem happy enough," Eyrmin remarked.

"So have many humans while they were cutting

trees at the edge of the forest," Relcan retorted. Though he seemed ready to make another remark, Eyrmin frowned at him, and he closed his mouth with a snap.

They were entering the trees again when from behind them they heard a large splash and a growl.

"Need more stones, Bersmog," a goblin said shortly.

"Make bigger jump, Stognad," his companion replied.

"Now you say."

The elves stopped and looked back. The goblins had given up on the ford and were wading through the water. They had brought along the carcasses of the slain deer.

When the elves halted, the halflings who followed bunched up behind them. The goblins waded through the little people and stopped in front of Eyrmin.

"Bersmog say is shame to let good food rot," Stognad said, willing to let his friend carry the blame was well as his share of the load.

"Are they going to smell up the village cooking flesh?" Malala demanded. She had been the first to admit an obligation to the goblins, but their habit of eating flesh disgusted her.

"If they cook it, they'll do it in the forest," Eyrmin said. He gazed at the demihumans, who were eyeing the carcasses hopefully. "And they can share with the halflings." He looked back at the goblins.

"Later I'll have questions for you, so you are to remain in the forest tonight. You will not be harmed."

"Then can cook meat," Stognad grinned.

Since the elves allowed no wood to be burned, they reluctantly supplied woven grass logs for fuel, and the goblins took the venison into the forest. Eyrmin ordered two of the elves to lead some of the halfling men to the plain of Markazor to cut more grass for weaving into logs. Meanwhile, the halfling women butchered the meat and set it to cooking.

That night, the woods around the elven village rang with happy, lilting voices. As was the way with their resilient race, the halflings put aside their experience of the afternoon and enjoyed their new freedom from fear.

Cald, not sure what he thought about these little people, slipped from tree to tree and watched them. He also watched the two goblins, who sat together under a tree and oversaw the preparation of their kill. From the stories Cald had heard of goblins, the silence and meek attitude of these two seemed totally out of character.

The battle at the portal had begun just after midday, and so much had happened it seemed strange to Cald that the sun was still high in the sky. The day darkened, and as he looked up, he saw gray clouds rolling in, obscuring the sun.

Watching the goblins and the halflings was more interesting than remaining in the elven village. Word of the portal and the battle with the people from the Shadow World had flashed through the village. Like those who had been in the grove, the other villagers needed to absorb this new happening. Every elf mind was turned in on itself.

Usually, important elven councils were held at night, under the lights of Tallamai. But when the visitors to Sielwode had filled their stomachs, Eyrmin called for a council to meet. The folk gathered in a pleasant, flower-dotted meadow, open to the sky and as bright as the gathering clouds would allow.

To the halflings, after the darkness of the Shadow World, even an overcast day on Aebrynis was glorious. They ran about picking the bright wildflowers until their leader shouted for them to cease lest the elves drive them out of the forest. They were so excited over the color and the light, he was unable to subdue their enthusiasm. In the end, it was not the halfling leader, but the arrival of Prince Eyrmin and Glisinda that brought the demi-humans to order.

To Cald, the prince was a constant delight of changing moods, with a full-blown personality to fit every occasion. Eyrmin could be as lively and merry as a young elf, then suddenly serious and wise, and then ruthlessly fierce. But he was most impressive of all when he acted as direct descendent of his line of kings, which stretched into historical obscurity.

The importance of the council had brought out Eyrmin's royal heritage. He stood no taller and still wore the battle-stained clothing in which he had fought. Still, the set of his face, his regal bearing, and the look of authority in his eyes brought silence to everyone in the clearing. A sense of honor, justice, and clarity of thinking robbed his expression of all petty concerns. His eyes held unfathomable depths of wisdom, and his brow was smooth and unlined.

Cald swelled with pride to think this glorious person was his foster father.

Still it was Glisinda who awed the halflings. An elf of surpassing beauty, her love of finery was legend among the elves. When she was in the village, she wore bright clothing, lavishly trimmed. She was a gleam of brightness among the greens and browns of the forest elves, like a bright bird flitting through the dark forest.

On this occasion, over a pale yellow gown, she wore the added finery of her official status. As a Speaker of Lore, she wore a deep green cloak trimmed in the pale green of new leaves. Both the colors and the decoration had meaning. The deep green of mature leaves signified the ages of elven history. The light green of the trim was made up of thousands of tiny magic runes that helped her draw on knowledge new to her.

With Glisinda to his right and Relcan, his second-in-command, to his left, Eyrmin indicated the circle for the council.

The speakers numbered ten. Eyrmin, Relcan, and Glisinda represented the elves. Five halflings—three of whom were so alike they had to be triplets, a fourth that was elderly and gray haired on head and toes, and the fifth a young woman with short, shining golden curls—represented the refugees. The two goblins made up the rest of the circle.

Relcan glared at the goblins and objected to their presence, but the prince wanted them there because he had questions for the humanoids.

Every elf, save those patrolling the eaves of the wood, was present, as were all the halflings. Many sat on the ground. Those on the outside of the circle stood to see over the heads of the others.

As prince, Eyrmin had the right to speak first, and he opened the council.

"It is said that to speak of evil in the night is to draw it to the speaker, so we will ask our questions in the light of day." He waited, giving everyone a chance to absorb his first words. Then he turned his attention to the halflings.

"It is also said that many on Aebrynis refuse to speak of the Shadow World, that by not giving voice to their thoughts, they can deny its existence. Would that we could do the same, but only the foolish deny what their own eyes have seen. We need to know of this world you left and why it is intruding on our world."

Eyrmin looked to the elder halfling, expecting him to answer. He stood and bowed.

"I am Oles Digdown, elder of our clan. My valued

companions"—he pointed first to the triplets—"are Bigtoe, Littletoe, and Fleetfoot Rootfinder, the sons of our hereditary leader, though they are not yet old enough to take on the burden of leading their people. Beyond them is Tala Hedgeneath. Tala will speak of our history," he said and sat down again.

Tala rose and took one pace out into the circle. Like the triplets, she seemed young, and her face was childlike as she composed herself and clasped hands behind her back. The hem of her soil-stained skirt swayed as she rocked slightly. Then she began the history of the halflings in a lilting, singsong voice of recitation.

"Remember the golden time of long ago when light sprang bright with the day and flowers grew. Remember laughter and dance and know you will find them again.

"The darkness came, and with it, creatures that are dead and yet walk and destroy all nature. The crops turned rank. . . ." Tala looked around desperately as if she had lost her concentration.

"Everything tasted like straw," corroborated Bigtoe, filling the gap.

"Terrible," added Littletoe.

"Made you belch," volunteered Fleetfoot.

Tala recaptured her memory and went on with her tale as if her chorus did not exist.

"The crops turned rank," she repeated with more confidence.

"Remember the flight for safety from the hordes, and slavery. Remember the hiding, the hunger, and death. Remember the good, and know the fear. Freedom is at hand."

Tala stepped back and took her seat with a sigh as if glad her part of the council was over.

Oles Digdown rose again. "The evil came to our world centuries ago, and this is all the history of our land and our trouble that we know. Tala was learning from our loremasters, but they fell in the last battle. This knowledge is all we can offer in gratitude that you opened the portal for us."

"But we didn't open it," Relcan objected. As if he needed reassurance, he snapped his head around to look over his shoulder at Saelvam and Malala.

The elves and halflings stared at each other. Eyrmin glanced at the goblins, who shrugged their shoulders in unison.

"Didn't do it," Bersmog said.

A complete stillness descended as the assembled group pondered the mystery. Even the children, sensing the importance of the council, were quiet and still. Minutes dragged by. A rabbit, knowing he had nothing to fear from the elves, hopped into the center of the circle and came to a stop two feet from Bersmog before it sensed a being that was not Sidhelien.

The forest creature panicked and dashed away, jumping first onto Relcan and rebounding off the elf and onto one of the triplet halflings before it found a way through the crowds and out of the circle. A young halfling shrieked in delight and five others followed him as he ran after the rabbit.

The contemplative spell had been broken.

Eyrmin turned his head to look inquiringly at Glisinda. As a Speaker of Lore, she would give them the answer to their questions, if any elf knew the answer.

As if obeying an unspoken command, she stood, slowly raising her arms and placing her fingers on the runes that trimmed the shoulders of her cloak. Her face was serene, her eyes staring into unmeasured distance as she lightly ran her fingers across the magic symbols that trimmed the shoulders, neck, and front of her cloak of office. Around her, the air sparkled with magic, and many of the halflings drew back. Some were fearful, but most seemed to realize there was no evil in the magic. They laughed and clapped, highly entertained.

For more than two minutes Glisinda stood enveloped in a sparkling glow. Then it faded, and she took her seat again.

"The Sidhelien have no magic to open the portals," she said quietly. "It is believed that some human wizards have the magic to do so, but we know nothing of their skills."

"Then what happened?" Elder Oles Digdown shook his gray head. "King Mmaadag Cemfrid would not provide us with an escape. If it was not you, or us, or the goblins, then was it only an accidental happening?"

"No, it was not accidental," Eyrmin said softly. Every eye turned toward him, the halflings with interest and the elves in surprise. Obviously he knew something they did not.

"During the last century, we have had several reports of halflings seen leaving the eaves of Sielwode. We know they could not have entered from the plain without being seen."

A gust of chill wind blew across the meadow. Even the elves looked up as leaves fluttered and sailed on the freshening breeze. When the gust died, the halfling elder shivered as he offered his opinion.

"The halflings you speak of must have escaped through the portal. Perhaps some can open it at will, but we do not know the secret."

Many of the elves appeared doubtful, and Oles Digdown saw their lowered brows.

"You avenged many of my people when you slew the dread king Mmaadag Cemfrid," he said to Eyrmin. "Among the avenged were our mages and loremasters. Those of us who still live are only farmers and workers of wood. We are ignorant of magic."

"There was fear and rage on both sides of the portal," Glisinda said. Anger attracts anger, and fear draws evil to it. Similar emotions on both planes might have opened the portal."

"This is true," Bigtoe agreed.

"Very true," Littletoe concurred.

"I'm thirsty," announced Fleetfoot.

No one paid any attention to the triplets, whose only contribution to the council seemed to be the chorus of agreement on points they found of interest.

The council had made no decisions, it had discovered no useful information, but even Cald knew they were not finished with the Shadow World.

ANUIRE

fOUſ

When the council in the meadow ended, the sky was growing darker, though the air had the healthy, natural feel of an approaching storm. Malala suggested the elves invite the halflings into the shelter of the village; Eyrmin, with a natural sensitivity for others, had a different suggestion. He had remembered a place where the burrow dwellers would feel far more at home.

Just a mile from the village, a low row of hills abutted the Moon Stream on the east. The year Cald had turned six, a heavy rain, a mud slide, and two dislodged trees had combined to block the stream. The churning flood waters had dug several large, shallow caves in the hillsides. When the stream had dug itself a new path, the caves had been left dry and comfortable. The mouths of the caverns were wide. Thick, flowering vines draped the entrances, giving a sense of shelter without reducing the fresh air. Cald had often played there, and occasionally the elves used the caverns for storage.

Saelvam escorted the halflings back to their temporary camp to pick up their few belongings before leading them across the Moon Stream. Most of the elves returned to Reilmirid.

Eyrmin, Relcan, and Glisinda, with Cald stalking in the shadows, waited until the others had disbursed before the prince faced the goblins. Glisinda, as Speaker of Lore, addressed them. It was her right, as she was responsible for knowing all elven law and rules of honor.

"You saved the lives of Prince Eyrmin and Relcan, who is also of royal blood. For this you have our gratitude. We owe you an obligation. You are free to return to your people."

The goblins traded long looks and shook their heads. Bersmog made a great show of scratching, first his stomach and then his neck.

"You say about obligate," he said. "This plenty strange but maybe is good?"

"An obligation is a debt owed," Eyrmin said. "We are indebted to you for saving our lives."

"You pay debt by letting us live?" the goblin pressed.

"We have said so," Relcan snapped. "You're free to go." And under his breath he muttered, "The sooner the better."

"Making us leave not paying debt," Bersmog said.

"We go, we die," Stognad added.

Eyrmin frowned. "I don't understand."

"We with hunting party. Our job to look after young Gotwart on his first hunt," Stognad explained. "Him last son of Chief Splitear. Last son.

All the others dead."

"Now Gotwart dead. Chief be plenty mad," Bersmog continued the explanation. "We go back before tribe has new chief, Splitear take skin off bodies while we still alive and feeling it plenty. We stay here. Elves no hunt for meat, so plenty food in woods." They both nodded with wide, fang-toothed grins as if, with their needs taken care of, nothing else mattered.

"Goblins, living in Sielwode?" Relcan looked ready to explode, and Eyrmin shook his head as if the idea was too much for even him.

"We'll discuss it later," the prince said. He led the way back to the village. Relcan walked beside Eyrmin, throwing angry looks at the prince. Twice he spun to walk away, thought better of it, and returned to pace the prince again. His tense movements manifested his anger and frustration, made worse by indecision.

Glisinda trailed them, and Cald brought up the rear, wondering what was wrong with the prince. Eyrmin had something on his mind. Not even the suggestion of repeated openings of the portal to the Shadow World had really intruded into that shell of thought. Not even the thought of goblins living and hunting in Sielwode mattered.

Cald was determined to learn the source of the prince's distraction, but still a youngster and also a human, he was often excluded from the more important discussions. Relcan and Glisinda also noticed the prince's preoccupation, and Cald had no doubt Eyrmin would take them into his confidence. Cald was determined to share those secrets.

Reilmirid was more a grove than a village, a grove of sielwodes for which the forest was named. In the exact center of the village stood an ancient monarch. The base of its trunk measured three hundred fifty feet in circumference, and it soared thousands of feet into the sky.

The elves called it Grove Father. Surrounding it were thirty-two of its children. They, too, were huge when compared with the more common trees of Aebrynis. The smaller ones had trunks forty feet in circumference; some would measure sixty feet, but they were still dwarfed by the parent tree. They grew close together with intertwining limbs connected by small bridges and short stairs.

Three pathways at three different levels circled the Grove Father and connected the dwellings of the village. Other, thicker limbs provided the foundations for the elven dwellings. Reilmirid, which in Sidhelien meant Watcher's Home, was to Cald the epitome of perfect adventure.

Humans scoffed at the idea that the elves could really feel a bond of friendship with their forests. With the exception of Cald, no human believed in the exchange of communication the elves claimed to have with the individual trees. Cald had often seen the elves silently communing as well as singing to the denizens of Sielwode. Eyrmin had told him the elves sang to the sielwode saplings for three centuries, asking them for a certain plan of growth.

In later years, Cald would understand that the bond between the elves and the forest was an innate magic peculiar to elves alone, one buried so deep in elven psyches that they themselves did not recognize it as such.

The result was a village barely noticeable from the ground. Bole bridges partially encircled the trees and provided access from one limb to another. Spiral stairs led to limbs on which dwellings had been built, close to the trunks of the trees.

Two lemdair, stair-gates in the elvish tongue, gave entry to Reilmirid. Not gates like those of ground-built cities, they were long stairways designed to be raised in the event of siege.

Cald hung back, then followed the elves up the eastern stair. When he reached the first and lowest of the village "paths," he turned left while the others went right. The elf songs had caused the limbs of the sielwodes to grow level and straight, with many branches paralleling the arms of their neighbors. The boy trotted along these high paths on limbs six to ten feet thick. He sprinted up and down the stairs and around the bole bridges.

Darkness had come early that evening, and torches were being lit. The elves never burned wood. In autumn, they harvested dry grass from the plain of Markazor and braided it into loglike shapes for fires, and tight ovals that fitted into the metal guards at the tops of the torch poles.

Cald raced by the light standards, where the growing wind whipped the flames horizontally until they looked like glowing war banners before a battle.

Between the three main tree trails, numerous limbs provided shorter paths to the elven dwellings. They created dead ends among the trees, and Cald turned back on one. He retraced his path and climbed down a vine to perch on a support of the dwelling he shared with Prince Eyrmin.

Through a chink in the wall, he could see into the main room of the house. There he waited, wondering if he had been wrong. Perhaps the three leaders of Reilmirid were not planning a private discussion.

From his position, he looked out over what he could see of the tree village. Even though he was anxious to learn what had so disturbed the prince, he could not look out across Reilmirid without being filled with joy.

The limbs and trunks of the sielwodes grew

straight as arrows, but everything else was angled or curved. The elves never cut into a living tree, and depended on the attrition of nature to provide their building materials. They used trees struck down by lightning or limbs broken off during storms. Every scrap of wood was carefully preserved and put to the best possible use. Sometimes they spent years considering how to use a piece to best advantage.

No dwelling in Reilmirid had straight walls or ridge poles, or square windows. They curved and bowed with individual grace and form that was an art exclusive to the elves. The shingles of the roofs and sides were overlaid with tinier shingles like fish scales. With more than fifty varieties of wood to chose from, the elves carefully worked the different types into patterns. As the shingles weathered, the changing hues brought out scenes of the forest in ever-sharpening detail.

The evening was too far advanced for Cald to see the patterns. He usually enjoyed this time, watching the flickering lights from the oddly shaped windows throw out patterns of half-ovals, triangles, and diamonds. The windows took on life from the flickering torches inside the buildings and provided opportunities to spot the prince.

Then he saw the three elves walking slowly around a bole bridge, talking with Asteriela, one of the warriors who had been on perimeter patrol that day. Cald hunched his shoulders against the cold rising wind and curbed his impatience. They had somehow been delayed, so Cald would be in time to hear what had happened to distract Eyrmin. They would not speak of it until they were alone.

Five minutes later, the three elves had entered the prince's house. Below Cald's perch, Eyrmin paced back and forth across a floor mat woven of dyed grass.

"I'll worry about the goblins later," he was saying to Relcan. He sounded cross.

"Something else happened in Muirien Grove," Glisinda said, raising the issue that had brought her to the prince's quarters. "A song you are not ready to sing?" She gazed calmly at Eyrmin, who dipped his head, acknowledging her ability to see beyond the obvious.

"One I have not yet set to a tune," Eyrmin said. "Until I have thought on its measure, I will share it with none but the two of you."

He took a flask from a hook on the wall and filled three goblets with wine. The other elves sat patiently, knowing he was gathering his thoughts.

After he had handed around the goblets, he took a seat on one of the floor cushions and gazed at Glisinda.

"It was you, I think, who suggested that anger drew anger, and fear drew fear. Could it be true also that the spirits of the dead attract other spirits, be they ghouls and skeletons or bodiless souls?"

Relcan choked on his wine and set the goblet aside with an awkward clatter unusual for an elf. Glisinda sat stone still, as if moving would destroy tenuous thoughts. When she spoke, her voice was tinged with caution.

"It is possible, but what spirits could be in the Muirien Grove?"

"Elven spirits," Eyrmin said. "Nameless warriors with faces full of longing and deep regret. Faces unknown to me, and a style of dress unlike any I know. I saw them after the closing of the portal."

"Spirits from the Shadow World," Relcan said with unaccustomed slowness, as if he were having to tug new thoughts from a mind only accustomed to age-old tradition. "Our tune will be one of woe if those creatures invade our world. . . ." He paused, his ideas dwindling to nothing as Eyrmin shook his head.

"I saw elves among the warriors of the Shadow World," Eyrmin said. "They were pathetic, twisted creatures, only a mockery of what they had once been. The ones I saw after the closing of the portal were different. They stood upright and had fair faces that could come only from pure thoughts. They held weapons, and I thought they meant to attack, but the two I confronted backed away from me. I spoke, but they gave no sign they heard me."

"You think these are the spirits of dead warriors?" Glisinda murmured. "And they are possibly the reason the portal opened, the pull of the dead on the undead?"

"Something created that opening between the two worlds," Eyrmin replied. "I'd gladly have it proved otherwise. It would be a relief."

"Why a relief?" Relcan asked. By his expression, he was exerting patience in listening to the tale of the prince, but the last statement seemed to worry him.

"At the council we discussed the sightings of half-lings leaving Sielwode, halflings who were never seen entering. Suppose they came through the portal in the Muirien Grove?"

"I see. It would mean the portal has opened before," Glisinda said, her face paling with the implications. She took another sip of her wine. Her eyes lost focus as she searched her memories.

"The portals between worlds aren't doors, framed and stationary," Relcan objected, his darting looks seeking confirmation from Glisinda. As a Speaker, she should know all about the portals. "No tale we've heard speaks of the danger occurring time after time in the same spot."

Glisinda spoke with the same patience Relcan had used earlier, though hers sounded genuine.

"The prince is suggesting these spirits not only create but anchor that door you mentioned. If the ghost warriors remain in the grove, a place no one would chose, then they must be somehow trapped. What a terrible condition."

"Judging by the sadness in their faces, it is terrible," Eyrmin said. "And for us as well if we're right about the permanence of that entry into the Shadow World."

"And none of the others saw them?" Glisinda asked.

"I saw nothing, save the prince raising his blade when there was nothing within ten or more paces," Relcan snapped. His expression suggested he did not believe there had been anything to see. "The others seemed as confused by his actions as I was. They saw no spirit warriors either."

"I saw them," Eyrmin snapped, but his irritation gave way to worry. "Why could I see them and no one else?" He ran his hand through his hair, touched the lump on the back of his head, and paused, his expression wondering. The room was still as death.

"A pain dream? Could it have been no more than that?" He shook his head in denial. "It seemed so real."

"You were wise not to speak of it in the presence of others," Relcan said. "A sennight from now, when the wound to your head is healed, you can walk in the grove again in peace. You will see nothing."

"Be sure I will," Eyrmin said. "I will rejoice in knowing I was wrong."

Certain the conversation was over, Relcan rose, jerked at his sword belt, bid the others a fair night, and left. Glisinda allowed his light footsteps to fade with distance before draining her goblet.

"You don't believe it was a pain image," Glisinda said quietly. "I'd advise you to wait the sennight.

Walk in the grove again. If you see them a second time, I will seek the answer to the puzzle."

Cald understood. Glisinda could not call on the magic twice in one day. Even once was a drain on her strength and spirit.

She rose, went to the door, and turned. "The halflings are staying yet another night?"

Eyrmin sighed. "They are too fatigued to go on. We will let them stay two more days."

She nodded, sadly it seemed to the boy watching.

Cald was glad when Glisinda left and he could climb down from his hiding place. To protect his secret spy hole, he would have to climb up to the next large limb, cross to another tree, and go down and around by three sets of limb stairs. He was hurrying on his way when Feilin and Kilrinis, two merry young warriors, caught up with him, gave a laugh, and tweaked his hair.

Kilrinis was a great jokester and talker, and Feilin loved to be the first with any news. Suddenly Cald had a brilliant idea.

"Hurry along, or you'll be wet through," Kilrinis said.

"So will the halflings and the spirit elves in the Muirien Grove," Cald said. "I wouldn't want to stay out all night in a—"

"What spirit elves?" Kilrinis asked, just as Cald had hoped.

"The ones in the Muirien Grove, the ones you can't always see," Cald said. Understanding the subtlety of the Sidhelien, he pretended to have more interest in the refugees from the Shadow World. "Are the halflings used to rain? Maybe there was no rain in their world, and they might be afraid when water starts dropping out of the sky. . . ."

The two elves ignored the human boy's chatter about the halflings; judging by their traded looks, they had latched onto what Cald wanted them to hear.

"They say Prince Eyrmin saw something in the grove," Kilrinis whispered to Feilin while Cald chattered about the halflings.

A strong gust of wind blew through the trees, and Cald grabbed for the railing, glad to have a use for his shaking hands. He had never before told a lie, and he was afraid.

"Cald." Feilin leaned close as if they were sharing a secret. "Have you ever seen the ghost elves in the grove?"

"Only a couple of times. I think they mostly hide," he said. "Maybe they have homes that we can't see up in the trees. I wish I knew if the halflings understood about the rain. . . ."

"Why would you and the prince see them and no one else?" Kilrinis asked. His eyes were searching Cald's face, and the boy was afraid to lie again.

"Because I'm human?" Cald asked. That suggestion often saved him trouble, since the elves thought humans incomprehensible at best, but he realized that in this instance, relying on his humanity would not help the prince.

"Mayhap Itrelian and Wilbien saw them." That statement could have been the truth. A few days before, while at play, the two elf children had been frightened by something on the other side of the Star Mirror Stream where it bordered the Muirien Grove.

"They're just little," Cald went on. "Maybe they only saw a rabbit or a deer—that's what the prince thought had frightened them. Still, they are old enough to know a deer when they see one. Do you think the halflings will be safe in the storm?"

Feilin and Kilrinis were trading long, thoughtful looks when the rain suddenly poured down through the trees. Cald insisted he had to get to the prince's quarters. He told nothing but the truth when he said Eyrmin forbade him to run on the tree paths when they were wet. As a human, he would never be as surefooted as the elves. On his way home, he congratulated himself, not at all ashamed.

At the next limb-stair he paused and looked back. When he had met Feilin and Kilrinis, they had been descending, but they had turned back now and were climbing up to the bierieum. In fair weather, the elves preferred sitting under the stars to tell their tales, but on chilly or rainy nights, they gathered in the bierieum—the chamber of music—which was the largest and highest structure in the elven village.

Unlike humans, elves slept little, seldom more than an hour a night. They could go for days taking short trance-rests, with their eyes open and aware while their bodies gathered strength from their stillness.

For most of the village, this would not be a night to sleep. They would discuss the news Feilin and Kilrinis brought to the bierieum, and give the incident of the frightened elf children a new meaning.

Cald had lied when he said *he* had seen the elf spirits, but he told himself he was only helping the rest of the warriors of Reilmirid believe the truth. Prince Eyrmin was the bravest, truest warrior of them all, and if he said the elves were in the grove, then they *were* in the grove.

The two elf children would be closely questioned again. They had no idea what they had seen and would say so. Possibly they had been frightened by nothing more than the shadow from a tree limb moved by the wind. Maybe they really did see a spirit elf. By the time he reached the prince's quarters and the small room where his bed waited, Cald had convinced himself the elf children had really been the first to see the mysterious people of the grove, and many elves would believe it, too.

During the night, the storm grew in force. The giant sielwodes swayed and trembled. The elves peered from their doors when they heard the scream of tearing wood and a tremendous crashing. In an instant, every elf in Reilmirid was outside, searching for the damage. Fortunately for two families, they had left their homes with the rest and were not inside when two giant limbs of the ancient sielwode fell and crushed their dwellings.

At dawn the residents of the tree village picked their way over the debris-littered ground, inspecting the damage and shaking their heads. Most hardly noticed when a number of the halflings and the two goblins joined them.

The destruction was a sign, they decided.

"The elves of Tallamai are angry," Relcan said, glaring at the goblins and the halflings.

The other elves were equally divided on whether the visitors were the cause, but they all agreed that the giant limbs had fallen by design.

Elder Oles Digdown and the halfling triplets— Bigtoe, Littletoe, and Fleetfoot—were among the most interested of the spectators, and the triplets suddenly announced their agreement.

"It is a sign," Bigtoe spoke up, as if he had weighed the matter and come to the only logical conclusion.

"It surely is a sign," Littletoe agreed, nodding his head in time with his brother.

"It's a mess," Fleetfoot said.

"Even you see it as a portent?" asked Glisinda, who had been standing nearby. Despite the destruction, she smiled at the antics of the three halflings.

"A portent."

"Surely a portent."

"A terrible mess."

Elder Oles gave a deep sigh; his shoulders

drooped. "I had hoped to reach the land you spoke of, the Burrows, where my people are gathering," he said. "But the wise ones have given their decree, and they will be angry with us if we do not do our part in fulfilling their wishes."

"And what is their decree?" Glisinda asked, no longer smiling. More than a score of elves had gathered to listen to the halfling.

"The building of the watchtower," Oles Digdown replied. "If I understand rightly, it is the decree of your wise ones that you do not injure living trees, so they have provided the timber for the building, and if I do not mistake, they have also provided the location."

Eyrmin had joined the gathering in time to hear the last statements.

"The two giant limbs are from high in the Grove Father," he said. "And large as they may be, they would not suffice to build a tower—" He paused and looked up.

"But then they need not," said the halfling elder, finishing the prince's thought for him. "The tower exists; only the stair and the platforms for the watchers need be constructed."

"And the trunk where they broke away will give the view," Saelvam suggested, so caught up in the idea that he had spoken out, though Eyrmin had opened his mouth to answer the halfling himself.

The tall elf, always more humble than the rest, perhaps because of his height and awkwardness, stepped back. His face was red with embarrassment. He trod on Ursrien's toes.

"From high in the Grove Father, we could watch the plain of Markazor for many miles around," Glisinda said, pointing out the advantages while taking attention away from Saelvam. "It is a plan we have long cherished, to have such a lookout." She gazed down at Oles Digdown again. "But why did you think the sign was for you?"

"In the ancient days, when our world was green and fair, our village was renowned for its wood-working skill," he said. "We still retain that art. Why else would the limbs fall just now, while we are in this land, if we are not to do the work?"

"Why should you?" demanded Relcan. His darting gaze lit on several warriors, as if demanding they agree with him. Several, seeing no recourse but to support the royal kinsman, nodded sagely as if he had exhibited superior wisdom. Oles Digdown, however, was equal to the query.

"Because if we assist you, you would in honor be obligated to us. In payment we would have the right to ask you to aid those of our people who follow us."

The listening elves who had supported Relcan's apparent wisdom, nodded again, seeing the sense in the halfling leader's answer.

Cald had joined Itrelian and Wilbien, the two elf children, on the lowest limb of a tree, where they had an unobstructed view of the wreckage and could hear the adults below. He had expected the elves to object to the suggestion that the halflings remain and build the tower, but to his surprise, most seemed to favor the idea.

Because of their long lives, elves were never in a hurry to do anything, even what was needed. Constructing a stairway up the Grove Father and putting a series of watch stations on it would remove the need for constant patrols along the borders. When the watchers spotted travelers, they could send a contingent of warriors to ward off any invasion.

Relcan was not happy with the thought of the halflings remaining in the forest, but not even he raised any further objections. Ever watchful to keep out the humans, he wanted the tower, and they all wanted warning of the opening of the portal.

The need to watch for invaders and help halflings were two reasons for a tower, but a third had not as yet been openly discussed. Glisinda judged the time to be right for it to be mentioned. She tilted her head to look up at Cald.

"Human boy," she called out, though she usually used his name. The subtlety of her address drew the attention of the elves gathered around the wreckage. "A tale is passing through the village that you too saw spirit elves in the grove. Is this true?"

Every eye in Reilmirid seemed to stare at him. Fearing they might hear a lie in his voice, Cald shrugged.

"For those of us not blessed with your vision," Relcan called, his voice scornful, "Describe them for us."

Cald searched his memory for what he had heard of the private conversation between Eyrmin, Relcan, and Glisinda, and then shrugged again.

"They looked like elves, but they seemed sad and they wore funny clothes."

Relcan's jaw dropped, and he stared at Cald with a new respect. The prince's face was a study in surprise. Glisinda, who was standing a little apart, turned to speak to Eyrmin, but her voice was louder than necessary; every elf in the village heard her clearly.

"He describes what you saw. If you did not speak to him of your sighting, then we must believe the spirits exist. You can cease thinking you were affected by a pain dream. Cald could not have shared it."

The prince drew a deep breath, all indecision wiped away. He stepped up on a fallen limb so all the village could see him.

"I told only Glisinda and Relcan. As she said, I could not have shared a pain dream with the human child. There *are* spirit elven warriors in Muirien

Grove," he called. "No song tells their tale, yet they are there. In their faces, I saw honor and great courage entrapped. I have thought on this, and I ask this question: Is it possible that the undead of the Shadow World are seeking the strength of the elven dead to use it for their own foul purpose?"

He paused, allowing the villagers time to express their indignation that elven honor and courage would be devoured by the creatures of the other world.

"We will not build this tower to watch for human trespass into Sielwode," he shouted. The elves stared at him, unbelieving.

"We will not build it to watch for the portal and assist the halflings." Below him, Oles Digdown's shoulders slumped.

"And yet we *will* do these things. The tower will be built to protect those helpless elves who look to us for protection." He glanced down at the puzzled halflings. "Build the tower for us, and in return we will assist your people who escape the Shadow World. In this, your need and ours coincide."

There were many heads nodding in agreement to that. No one doubted that the portal would open again.

ANUiRE

five

Czrak twisted in the cool mud of the swamp, sighing as the movement eased his discomfort. In his sleep, he had rolled onto the stump of a tree that he had broken in one of his rages. He raised his head, glared at it, and with a withering look, seared it to nothing, leaving the mud around it boiling.

A sound, an exclamation of surprise and terror, came from his left. He turned to see an elf staring at him, stunned by the horror of the creature that had risen from the bog. In one hand the elf held a knife, in the other a sheaf of talltails he had been cutting. The soft, spicy flesh of the plant was a favorite food of the elves, but more than a century had passed since any had come to collect it. Too many of their people had disappeared.

Czrak liked elves. They were his favorite race. Their innate magic and their immortal life span made their blood an excellent source of strength, bettered only by the bloodlines of kings and other awnshegh.

Czrak liked elves too well to let this one get away, so he glided forward, his thick, nearly boneless slug-like body moving across the mud of the swamp, propelled by eight insectile legs that resembled those of a giant water spider. He fixed his hypnotic eyes on those of his prey, but after a short struggle, the elf's will broke Czrak's hold, and the creature tried to bolt.

Czrak had not been able to hold it, but he had twisted the logic of its mind. When the elf tried to spring away, using its magic to increase the length of its leap, it chose soft ground that gave it no leverage. Not even the awnshegh's abilities could stop it from covering ten feet, though the elf landed flat on its back, losing the knife and the talltails at the same time. They fell in a shower around the supine figure as it pulled a sharp sword and tried to scramble to its feet.

Czrak had spent three centuries in the swamps, and he could move quickly when he chose. He glided across the soft mud, oozing the upper portion of his soft body across the elf's slender legs, preventing it from rising.

The elf's sword hacked at him, narrowly missing his head and left arm, which was still a human appendage. The blade cut deep into the shell of Czrak's left front arachnid leg, and he jerked with pain. The pain submerged beneath intense pleasure as he sunk his hollow, fanged teeth into the elf's chest. One long fang reached directly into the heart, and he felt the strength and power of the elven blood flow into him. The elf struck again with the blade before the life went out of him, but Czrak did not feel the blow. He writhed in delight as the new power filled him.

When he had drained the carcass, he dragged it back into the deep mud and buried it in the cool dampness below him. He would eat it at his leisure. He healed his wounds with a concentration of thought, and for at least half an hour he wallowed in a sense of well-being.

The successful use of his power always gave Czrak a momentary satisfaction, but his complacency lasted only a few minutes. His movements had pressed down the mud, and he caught sight of his reflection in the thin sheet of murky water. The sight of his bloated, twisted face reminded him of his condition.

He had once been human. His name then had been Czrak Revemirov-tsan, leader of the Revemirov clan. He had walked with pride; his warrior skills drew looks of admiration from men, and not just those of his clan alone. His good looks brought sighs from women, and under his leadership the Revemirovs had held the lush grasslands above Cwmb Bheinn. Their herds of horses were reputed to be the best in Cerilia.

Then *he* had come. He . . . who in retrospect had been a nameless, formless blank among the sharp edges of clearer thoughts. Czrak now knew *he* had been the god Azrai the Shadow, but the deity had disguised himself when he influenced the Vos. Azrai had planted the seeds of discontent and nurtured them until the people of northeastern Cerilia were filled with lust for the lives of those that had supposedly wronged them. Azrai had led the Vos, along with armies of gnolls, goblins, people from the southern continent, and many creatures that defied description, into the battle at Mount Deismaar.

The Revemirov clan had fought valiantly that day.

Czrak, bathed in blood and the glory of battle, had envisioned himself ruler of the great city-states of the south in reward for his valor. He and his people had been hard on the heels of a retreating contingent of the army of the Khinasi when Mount Deismaar exploded.

Death rained from the sky in boulders and tons of earth, giant trees, and corpses. For leagues around, everything living was destroyed. Czrak was one of the closest to the mountain to survive, but not *the* closest.

That was his major problem, and the source of his discontent. The power of the dying gods was absorbed by the closest survivors in varying degrees according to their proximity. Others, like the Gorgon and the Raven and the Hydra, had been closer and absorbed more of Azrai's power. Czrak and others got only the leavings: enough to grant lengthened lives, perhaps even immortality, and the ability to use some of the god's powers. This dubious blessing also twisted them into grotesque parodies of mortal beings.

No mortal frame could hold the power of a god. It was ironic that the followers of Azrai, who received the power, found themselves transformed into grotesque shapes. Some, like Czrak, had even chosen their miserable states. In their need physically to accommodate their new abilities, they had changed themselves.

At first Czrak had reveled in his powers, and his appetite for more was insatiable. He had discovered bloodtheft, the absorption of the abilities of people he destroyed. Several of the other Revemirovs had been close, and they were the first to enhance his strength. Only a few escaped him, and they were saved because he suddenly discovered he was also in danger of being destroyed. Those who had been closer to the mountain and absorbed more power than he were also in search of added strength. Like himself, they had discovered that minute amounts of power could be had from the common people, but the real power was in those who had absorbed it directly from the gods.

The power gained from bloodtheft could be acquired in a number of ways. For the awnshegh, inhaling the departing spirit was enough. Czrak had a taste for blood and flesh, as did many of his kind, but that was a personal preference. When two mortal members of the ruling bloodlines fought to the death, the winner absorbed part of the loser's power. Anyone, ruler or commoner, and a being from any race could take a larger portion of his victim's strength if he used a weapon made of tighmaevril. Luckily there were only a dozen such weapons in existence and the secret of their making had been lost.

Even with a blade of tighmaevril, or bloodsilver, few humans desired to go up against an awnshegh. Instead, they hunted and killed each other to increase their own strength.

Czrak spent many years running, hiding, sneaking out to ravage where he could, and slinking away again. Then he came to the swamps in northeast Elinie. More years passed as he concealed himself under the primeval ooze. When he could stand it no longer, he emerged with a raging appetite and ravaged the surrounding countryside.

As time passed and his body felt as if it would burst with the power he held, he allowed his shape to expand. He took to himself the additional long legs and wide, splayed feet of the small water spiders that could travel easily over the surface of the mud and water. He noticed the soft bodies of the ooze slugs that bonelessly slid over any obstacle in their way and took that ability also. By the time he discovered the mockery he had made of himself, not even his power could change him back again.

After a century in the swamps of Elinie, his appetite had worked to his disadvantage. No human who saw him lived to spread the tale of the awnshegh in the bog, but since none returned from their expeditions, fewer and fewer braved the damp region in search of swamp-cat pelts or the meat of the large amphibians that were considered a delicacy in Elinie.

For more than four hundred years, Czrak had not allowed any intelligent creature to see him and live. His main fear was that the knowledge of his existence and his whereabouts would reach the Gorgon, the Hydra, or the Raven.

Czrak divided his time between feeding and the satisfaction it brought him, and his usual mood of malice and discontent. For two days after eating the elf, he wallowed in contentment. Then he felt that strange pull again.

Something tugged at him; he had experienced it before, but never so strongly. An undefined yearning, stronger than mere physical appetite, made him restless. He knew its origin but not what caused it.

It came from that other plane, the Shadow World. His power gave him the sense of its presence. It was all around him, but not reachable except in those special places where the divisional fabric was weak and occasionally gave way. He always knew when one of the portals had opened, but by the time he had sensed the source, it always closed again. Such portals were rare, and seldom appeared in the same place twice. Still, several times he had felt the pull from the western arm of Sielwode, each time from the same place.

He writhed in the mud of the swamp, his whole being drawn to that portal. The pull became stronger, and he slithered to the west, compelled almost against his will.

After a few minutes, the compulsion ceased. He gave a sigh, a combination of relief and frustration. The portal had closed.

The portal had closed, but a power from the Shadow World remained in Sielwode! He could sense it: a sharp, turbulent potential just waiting to be possessed and used; the mighty weapon of some powerful being from that other world.

He slowly heightened his senses, searching for the minds of other awnshegh. It was a risk he seldom took, knowing if he sought them out, they might also sense him. But he found no other god-strengthened minds turned in his direction or toward the artifact that had been left in Sielwode.

He alone knew of it!

He must have it! The force he sensed would not quite put him on an equal footing with the Gorgon or the Hydra. But with it he could overcome some lesser awnshegh, and with their added strength, he might take on the Raven. Then he could become the most powerful awnshegh on Aebrynis!

He would be a *god!*

But how could he get it?

A distance of only forty miles separated him from godhood, but it might as well have been ten thousand. If he were a true slug, he could glide over the ground, or as a true spider he could have walked, but he was neither.

The journey would be slow and painful. If he were seen by the elves of Sielwode or the humans of Elinie, word would spread. He might be destroyed by a more powerful awnshegh before he reached his destination.

Minions.

Gods had minions—he should have servants.

He twitched in dissatisfaction. He should not have killed the elf. The creature would have served him better as a slave, drawing others to his service.

Never mind; he would find others. Humans would do—or goblins, gnolls. Even orogs would serve if any came up into the daylight near the swamp. Yes, he would take any and all servants that came his way. A god should not limit himself to a single race.

When he was a god . . .

What was he saying? His power was from Azrai, so he was already a god. All he had to do was take advantage of it.

He raised his misshapen head and roared, "I am a god!"

His voice was disappointingly weak and shallow. He would work on his voice—a god should have good volume. In the meantime, he would search the edges of the swamp. It had been half a century since he had traveled the borders of his domain.

Perhaps the humans had started again to hunt the fringes of the wetlands for swamp-cat pelts.

ANUIRE

SIX

Gerbid, the leader of a band of four gnolls, paused
and wrinkled his hyenalike snout, testing the air;
perhaps the humans had given up the chase. If he
had known there were so many of them and they
were so bad tempered, he would have looked for a
quieter place to raid.

He had thought the freestead was deserted. No
one seemed to be around. The four gnolls had been
so anxious to raid the house, they neglected to check
the outbuildings.

The two axes they had found made good weapons
for Ruflik and Fadaarg, maybe better than Gerbid's
old, rusting sword. He had been delighted with the
small cooking pot. It fitted loosely on his head, but
with a bit of fur tucked inside and a thong tied to the

handles and under his chin he would have a helmet as good as any human or elven warrior.

They had found some cooked meat and stuffed it in the pot, tied some sleeping furs around their shoulders, and left the house when a small gaggle of geese came around the corner of the building.

"Be getting more food," Ruflik announced. He swung his new axe, cleanly taking the head off the first of the birds. Gerbid killed a second, and Fadaarg was chasing a third when a female human, so old she tottered, came out of the nearest shed. When she saw the gnolls she started to scream.

Orsht loped across the farmyard and clubbed her down, also smashing the head of a youngling that came toddling out after the old one, but coming across the field was a third female. She set up an ear-piercing howl and ran off, shouting what sounded like names.

"Be getting gone muchly quick," Gerbid had ordered. They grabbed the dead geese, tied their feet together, and slung them over their shoulders. They were trotting across the plain when they topped a rise and Orsht shouted a warning. On the horizon they could see six humans on horseback, coming after them.

They had been running for miles, and the humans were still on their trail. Gerbid could understand anger and the desire for revenge, but why would so many humans leave the work they seemed to think so important to chase after a couple of axes, a pair of dead geese, and a pot? Surely it could not be because of the two females Orsht had killed. Neither was of any use, being too old and too young to matter.

The gnoll lifted his nose to sniff for danger ahead. The only thing Gerbid could smell was Orsht, who had stumbled into the freestead midden.

"Be getting your stinking self downwind," he

snarled at his companion and waited until Orsht trotted a few steps ahead. When the air cleared, Gerbid sniffed again. Yes, on the westerly wind he could just catch the scents of sweat and anger from the men following, and they were getting closer.

"Is still time to get moving your feets," he growled at the others, the short, stiff mane rising on the back of his neck. He could feel it pulling at the hide weskit he wore. He had smelled something else from the humans—wariness, as if they were afraid to follow much farther.

Then why didn't they stop?

While their leader had been testing the air, Ruflik and Fadaarg led the way forward. They were a good sixty paces ahead when they slowed, and none of Gerbid's commands spurred them to more speed.

"Why start stopping?" he shouted as he closed the gap between them. Up ahead, the range grass and clumps of vegetation were thicker, lusher than the shorter ground cover they had been crossing. Some of the plants looked tall enough to give them adequate cover for an ambush.

"Ground all mushing and wetly," Ruflik said, stepping carefully.

"Could be being a stream ahead," Fadaarg suggested, wrinkling his snout. His dark nose twitched as he sniffed for water. Gnolls were not good swimmers. The hair on their bodies lacked the oil to keep it from absorbing water. Their narrow feet, short toes, and long claws were good for traction on firm ground, but did not make good paddles. They also sank deeply in the mud, as Gerbid, Ruflik, and Fadaarg were discovering.

"Not liking this place muchly," Fadaarg muttered as he shifted his stolen axe from his right hand to his left and grabbed the limbs of a bush to pull himself onto firmer ground.

"Liking losing head to man muchly better?" Gerbid demanded as he waded farther into the swamp.

Privately, he agreed with Fadaarg. The clinging mud had soaked into the hair on his legs. The trousers he had stolen two weeks before were soaked and caked with slime. Between his own wet fur and his clothing, he seemed to be pulling twice his weight. He reached for a handful of tall, thick grass to his left and pulled himself onto slightly firmer ground. He waded through the grass to the end of the tussock, then leapt across a watery area to another.

"Jumping being better than walking in mud," he told the others.

He leapt from tussock to tussock, and the others followed. They had traveled two miles into the swamp when he paused to sniff the air again. The humans were far behind. The next time he checked, they were gone. They had not followed into the swamp.

"Slimeball men not liking swamp," Fadaarg said, stating the obvious. "Not jumping so good, maybe."

Gerbid ignored the others as he stared out at an expanse of what looked like wet sand.

"Is not jumping more," he said, only partially disgusted. After miles of running to stay ahead of the humans and more than two and a half miles of leaping from one tussock to another, he was tired. And he could not stand the stink from Orsht. He reached behind him and grabbed his malodorous companion and shoved him forward, out onto the damp sand.

"Be staying downwind," he snarled.

What had looked to be wet but reasonably solid ground, splashed in sluggish waves, and Orsht immediately began to sink. His eyes rolled, and his long tongue bunched in his mouth as he gave a howl of fear.

"Is not sand for walking," Fadaarg said.

"Be holding out your axe quick," Gerbid said, catching hold of Fadaarg with one hand and Ruflik with the other. While Ruflik planted his feet securely in the grass of the tussock, Gerbid grasped him, and Fadaarg leaned forward over the treacherous quicksand. Orsht grabbed the axe, and working together, they pulled him back to safety.

While Orsht tried to shake away the wet sand, Ruflik looked up at the sky and sniffed, as if he could smell the coming night.

"Is darking now. Not good jumping in night. We stay here?"

"No fire, no drying, ground too wet for sleeping," Fadaarg complained. "Think maybe no liking this place a lot of much."

"You speak many wise many late," Ruflik told his companion.

They could not go forward, and to go back they would have to wait for daylight so they could see the tussocks. The only thing left to do was to hunker down on the small area of solid ground and wait for daylight. Gerbid and Ruflik plucked the geese and, after a snarling tussle with Orsht and Fadaarg that nearly tumbled Gerbid into the quicksand, he decided it would be the better part of valor to divide with them. After the geese had been devoured, they ate the meat they had stuffed into the pot at the freestead. It was less tasty because it had been cooked by humans, but their bellies were full, and tomorrow would take care of itself.

They squatted on the damp ground, not wanting to sit, and tried to doze. Several times during the night, Gerbid jerked alert as he heard splashing in the swamp.

He had not forgotten the scent of fear from the humans when they neared the edge of the mire.

* * * * *

Czrak was working his way slowly along the edge of the swamp when the sun set. Less than ten miles from the southwestern limits of his domain was the human town of Ansien, the capital of Elinie, and if any intrepid hunter decided to enter the swamps, he would chose the area closest to the town.

But he would not come at night.

Czrak found a mire where the mud was deep and settled down to rest for the night. His constant movement for the last four days had been exhausting. He was nearly asleep when the light breeze brought the smell of blood. He raised his head, sniffing, avid to find it.

Not human blood, some sort of bird. He had tasted most species in his centuries of hunger, but it had been a long time since he had eaten goose. He noticed other smells—gnoll, human excrement. That seemed a strange combination. He moved cautiously toward the scent, careful to make no sound.

Then he found them, the four gnolls squatting on the tussock trying to sleep. His hunger and the desire for blood, any blood, made him twitch with anticipated pleasure, but he did not attack.

Stronger than his hunger was his desire for that weapon from the Shadow World. It had remained in the western arm of Sielwode. To reach it, he had to have minions, and he would begin with the gnolls. They would make poor servants, but they would be easy to subvert to his cause.

He waited throughout the night, knowing he would need to mesmerize them, impossible if they could not see his gaze.

The gnolls spent most of the night squatting on the damp ground, bracing themselves by sitting back to back. They slept fitfully, but finally their fatigue won out. The sun was well up before they awoke. The largest one, who wore a cooking pot on his head and had a rusty sword tucked inside a wide leather waist strap, was the first to wake. When he stood, the others tumbled to the damp ground.

"Sun shining makes time to leave this place," he said to the others, glaring at them as they sorted themselves out and reluctantly rose to their feet.

Czrak knew the area well, and had positioned himself so the gnolls' only escape from the tussock was across the quicksand. He slowly rose from the mud, bringing his huge, bloated body up so it was in full sight of the gnolls.

They stood gaping, the dark animal noses on their humanoid faces twitching with fear. Their long tongues rolled out of their mouths, and they seemed to be trying to draw their hyenalike faces down into their thick necks.

The largest was less frightened than the rest. He turned his head from side to side, seeking escape, but the tussocks had led them out onto a spit of semisolid land surrounded on three sides by quicksand. Czrak had placed himself squarely across the only exit. Realizing there was no escape, the gnoll pulled his rusty sword, preparing to fight. The others took their cue from him. Two carried woodcutter's axes, the other a stout club.

The awnshegh nodded, deciding the four had courage, even if they weren't the brightest creatures on Aebrynis. He might have done worse.

"You don't need your weapons," Czrak said, fixing the largest with a hypnotic stare. "You are honored above all the peoples of this world, because you are the first called to serve your god."

The large gnoll was harder to subvert than he had expected, but with an extra surge of power, he succeeded, and the others were easier.

Once they were under his power, he sat watching them as they whined and sidled around on the tussock, seeking his approval. Their eyes gazed on him with adoration, and they raised their heads to howl a hymn to his glory.

Their raucous noise disturbed the wildlife in the swamp, but Czrak enjoyed their worship.

Yes, he was a god, and they would bring him more converts. He gave them their instructions and led them to solid ground so they could return to Ansien.

Soon they would be bringing captured humans to him. He would have an army of slaves. He hoped there were enough for him to have his army and still assuage his appetite. He was tired of feeding off the swamp creatures.

ANUIRE

seven

Cald Dasheft grabbed the axe that the dead orog
had dropped. He raced forward, slashing at a black-
visaged human who loomed up in his path. He
caught the man across the chest, splitting his metal-
trimmed leather corselet. Bones crunched under the
heavy blade, and blood shot out in a red fountain.
The human's blue eyes lost their evil in that moment
of surprise, pain, and nearly instant death.

Despite his battle fury, Cald paused as he watched
the man die. He had already struck down an orog
and a gnoll, but killing his first human was a sickening experience, particularly since it was the first of
his race he had seen in almost fourteen years. At
least the man was human in death. In life, when he
had stepped from behind a tree, Cald had seen only

the twisted expression of evil.

Movement beside him caused Cald to jump to the side, but before he could swing, he recognized Stognad, one of his two goblin companions.

"Be-gelf be plenty mad," the goblin announced as his small, restless eyes watched the wood. Unable to get their awkward tongues around the musical elven names, the goblins had labeled the elves with names they could say. Their name for Prince Eyrmin came out "Be-gelf."

"You've said that ten times today," Cald replied. After the fifth time, he'd lost his temper. By the eighth time, the goblin's complaints had worn out his irritation. He knew Stognad had accurately gauged the reaction Cald could expect from Eyrmin, reason enough not to want to hear about it beforehand.

The prince usually ordered Cald to stay in the village when the elves had warning of trouble on the borders. This time, Cald had been visiting the halfling caves when the alarm came. Eyrmin had not had time to give Cald his usual orders. The youth was taking full advantage of the omission. The goblins had accompanied him, complaining all the way.

"Anyway, the prince needs all the help he can get," Cald said, glancing around. The fighting must have been heavy at the edge of the woods. The elves had to be badly outnumbered, or there would not have been invaders so deep in the forest. No other intruders were in sight. He led the way toward the sound of clashing steel and the cries of the wounded and dying.

Bersmog appeared through the trees at their right and paced Cald. The human slowed his steps to accommodate the goblins. They were good runners, but in the six years since they had first been granted the right to live in Sielwode, he had grown until he was taller than any elf but Saelvam. At seventeen, the human boy could pace the fastest of Eyrmin's messengers, though he could not match their endurance.

For years he had been developing his fighting skills. He could best a few elves with his bow, but their ability to draw their arrows, target, and shoot with a speed that blurred their movements was quintessentially elven. His ability with a sword or a spear was equal to any human and most elves, and he had just discovered he was able to use an axe effectively. To him it seemed past time for him to join the warriors who protected Sielwode.

Eyrmin always kept him away from the battles. The prince admitted he did not want Cald to fight against his human kindred. Cald also suspected that in keeping him away from the battle and giving him the goblins as guards and companions, the prince was also keeping Bersmog and Stognad away from the fight. None of the elves believed the two would stay loyal to Sielwode when they faced their own kind.

That afternoon, the three had been on their way to join Eyrmin when they found themselves on the fringes of a battle. They raced through the trees until they were closer to the sounds of the fight and Cald raised his hand, signaling the goblins to stop. Elves could run silently, Cald made slightly more noise, but the goblins sounded like a pair of wild boars on the rampage.

They walked less than thirty yards and were approaching a small, flower-dotted meadow when Bersmog grabbed Cald's arm and pulled him into the shelter of a tree. The goblin gave a wicked grin and raised one short, grubby finger to his lips. Cald heard the snapping of twigs and harsh voices grunting softly. Seven goblins came out of the forest and started across a small clearing. They all wore rusty-black hardened-leather armor with yellow circles on their shoulders.

Bersmog and Stognad hefted their axes and stepped out into the open.

"None of the elf-scum back this way," Bersmog called to them.

"Then that's the way we're going," one of the intruders announced, and turned to approach Cald's companions.

"Plenty smart, you ain't," Stognad muttered under his breath.

Both goblins stepped out farther into the small clearing and waited for the six intruders to get closer. The leader, a big fellow with a long scar down his face and an iron helmet, stood directly in front of Bersmog.

"Them tree-stinks got a village close by, think you?" He glared at the two strange goblins as if he could not quite make up his mind about them.

"Plenty trails," Stognad announced, looking at the ground, but the goblin leader was slowly working his way though the fact that he did not recognize the two who had suddenly appeared out of the wood.

"Which unit you be with?" he demanded. "How come you ain't got no yellow circle?"

Stognad rose on his toes and stretched his neck as if to look over the goblin leader's shoulder.

"One thing sure, ain't with them tree vermin back there," he announced. He jerked his head, indicating a threat behind the goblins and took a firmer grip on his axe.

The seven goblins whirled, their weapons raised. Behind them, Bersmog and Stognad swung their axes, dropping the leader and his largest companion. Unfortunately, Stognad's axe struck the iron helmet before it cut through the neck of the leader, and the clang brought the other four around in a hurry.

"Plenty smart, who ain't?" Bersmog demanded as

he dodged a spear and stepped in to take a swing at his attacker. The other goblin jumped back, and a second stepped forward, its spear deflected by the heavy buckle of Bersmog's belt.

Cald had stayed in the shadows, fretting because he was not in the fight, but understanding his two friends had something in mind. Deciding they had exhausted their abilities at trickery, he stepped out and loosed an arrow. His shaft was true, but his target, the second spearman attacking Bersmog, tripped over a clump of grass and fell. Bersmog jumped forward to take advantage of his opponent's fall and barely missed stepping into the path of the arrow.

Bersmog's axe made short work of the fallen goblin, and he whirled to swing at his first attacker, who was again agile enough to jump away.

Cald rushed to the aid of his friends, meeting one well-armored humanoid axe to axe. Both drew back, their arms and hands tingling with the shock that had traveled up the normally absorbent handles. The dry wood had been no match for the blows.

Knowing his hands were useless for a moment, Cald used an elven trick. He leapt into the air to kick his opponent in the face. His jump was not quite high enough, and one booted foot caught the goblin in the throat. The humanoid fell with a gasp. Cald had crushed his windpipe.

The human had only just landed and righted himself when another goblin, eyes filled with bloodlust, charged with his spear. Cald twisted to the side and hacked ineffectually with the axe, still gripped in his numbed fingers. He held it by strength of will; his arms still felt rubbery.

He danced back and forth, unable to take his eyes off the spearpoint to check the ground behind him. The meadow seemed to be getting wider; that meant he was being worked back toward the trees. The goblin, his spear giving him the advantage on reach, forced Cald back until he tripped over a root and fell sprawling on his back. Just before the breath was knocked out of him, he kicked out, catching the humanoid's right leg and jerking it sideways.

The goblin tumbled, and Cald tried again to use the axe, but, unable to control his arms, he had swung too fast. One edge of the blade bit into another thick tree root. The goblin fell on top of the other edge. The humanoid rolled over, and the axe, dislodged from the root by the goblin's impact, stayed buried in his chest.

Cald rose shakily to his feet to see Bersmog standing in the middle of the field, leaning on his axe handle, while at his feet lay the sixth goblin. He was watching Stognad, who faced the last of the group. The last of the goblins in black and yellow was a clever fighter. He met each of Stognad's parries with a block and delivered a thrust of his own.

Stognad was the more intelligent of the two goblins living in Sielwode, and while most of the elves' teachings seemed foolish, he had tried to learn those things he thought might be useful. Seeing he was unlikely to win with goblin battle tactics, he attempted a trans-leap, jumping about to confuse his adversary.

The goblins had never truly understood which elven battle tactics were accomplished by skill and which were aided by magic. Stognad's flat-footed leaps reminded Cald of the jumps of a spastic frog. Stognad didn't seem to know where he would bound next. Fortunately his opponent didn't either. When he tried to second guess Stognad, he missed his thrust. Stognad was on target. As the life went out of their last enemy, Cald and Bersmog approached Stognad.

"You need to wash your pants?" Bersmog asked,

stopping a good distance from his friend.

Stognad frowned at him but addressed Cald.

"Him hit on the head?"

"I don't think he recognized your strategy," Cald grinned. "It takes elven magic to do a trans-leap."

"Thought something was wrong," Stognad looked down at his feet. "Jump plenty good, but not like elf."

"Jumped like your pants full," Bersmog said.

"Worked," Stognad glared at his friend and led the way through the forest toward the major battle. "Nose keep me on the ground," he gave his explanation as they walked through the wood. "All full of awnshegh stink."

That was a new excuse for failure, Cald thought as he led the way toward the eaves of the forest. Fewer battle noises reached them through the forest now. The sounds had stopped completely by the time Cald found Malala sitting on the trunk of a fallen tree while Kilrinis bandaged a wound on her arm.

She used the other to point, and Cald followed her direction. A hundred yards farther on, he found Eyrmin facing a burly human whose clothing was torn and bloody and whose hair, molded tightly to his head, clearly showed where it had been pressed down by a helmet. His headgear lay on the ground a few steps behind him.

The prince stood straight and slender, looking like a reed defying an oak. Even so, in authority and power of will, Eyrmin drew all eyes. His slender blade appeared to be no match for his adversary's two-handed broadsword, but the prince parried the blows with surprising ease. As they circled, stepped in, exchanged blows, and stepped away again, the human seemed to realize they had an audience of elves.

"Kill me, elf," he panted, "And a thousand like me will be on my heels." He lunged for Eyrmin, who seemed to melt from the spot where he had been standing and appeared four feet away.

"There could not be a thousand like you," Eyrmin taunted. "Despicable as your race is, they could not spawn that many fools."

"Soon you'll see what fools we are," the man shouted, lunging at the elf again. He leapt forward, but hesitated after his first step. Three times before, Eyrmin had trans-leapt to the left after a decisive thrust from the human. The human swung to guard his right but found nothing. Eyrmin had not moved. He raised his blade and caught the man in the throat, severing his spinal cord in one quick strike.

The prince watched the man fall. As he turned slowly to face Cald, his wide, slanted eyes flinched from the boy's gaze. Eyrmin's ruthlessness in defending his homeland was legendary, yet he shrank from having the boy he had raised see him kill a human. Then he noticed the blood on Cald's clothing.

"Are you injured?" he came striding across the clearing. Until then, Cald had forgotten about the blood. He looked down in surprise.

"My race contains a lot of blood," Cald said, "but none of it is mine."

Before he could continue, Stognad interrupted, telling about the battles they had fought on the way to join the prince. They had accounted for twelve of the enemy, but the goblin, with his peculiar idea of truth, increased the tally by a score. Cald and Eyrmin exchanged glances that said they would discuss the matter later. The elves were gathering around, trading long, speaking looks.

Cald admired Eyrmin's patience in letting the goblin finish his boast. The others were still keyed up after the battle and were less tolerant of the bragging. When Bersmog, who had been adding to the story, stopped for breath, Saelvam interrupted.

"Why do they keep coming?" He shifted his bow from hand to hand and stared north, toward the eaves of the forest as if another attack would come at any moment.

"They want something from the Sielwode," Eyrmin said, stating the only obvious part of the mystery over the frequent attacks. He stooped to pick up a handful of leaves, using them to clean his sword. Around the small clearing, the others did the same.

Several strange elves stared suspiciously at Cald and the goblins. They were new arrivals in the western arm of the forest. For six years they had been coming—one, two, ten at a time, drawn by the spreading tale of the spirit elves in the grove. They could be depended upon for two emotions, distrust of nonelves and disappointment because they could not see the spirit elves. None seemed to doubt that ghosts of dead warriors roamed among the ancient, twisted trees.

At least *most* were disappointed; a few claimed to have seen something, a moving shadow out of the corners of their eyes, nothing they could identify, but they were certain in their own minds they had seen the spirits, and each tale added credence to the story.

"Hope has eyes of its own," Eyrmin had once told Cald. Since they were the only two who had ever claimed to get a good look at the spirit warriors, they had been joking about the elves who might have mistaken the shadows of a windblown tree limb or a fleeing deer for the spirits. Cald had never admitted his lie, and he had never added to it.

Those six years had become increasingly active ones for the elves guarding the western arm of Sielwode. The attackers from the north invaded more and more often. If the intention had been to conquer the elves in the forest, the most practical strategy would be to travel due south from Mur-Kilad, attacking Siellaghriod, the capital. Instead, the forces from the north continued to attack the western arm of the Sielwode.

"They must be seeking the spirits in the grove," Malala insisted to Saelvam. They had both been present when the portal opened and could not imagine anyone wanting to pass to the other plane.

Eyrmin's eyes darkened. "They will not pass us to reach them," he replied. "The ghost warriors cannot fight." The elves nodded. They remembered his challenge when he first saw the spirit elves.

"Some magician may have discovered a way to use them," Ursrien suggested.

"Little good it will do him," Eyrmin decreed. "Though we may join them in death, we will not let our old heroes be used for fell purposes."

The goblins made a show of sitting on the ground, their eyes rolling as the elves repeated the questions, speculations, and dedications to the ghost elves in the grove. For six years, every battle, every gathering in Reilmirid brought on a repeat of the conversation. The elves never tired of discussing a puzzle.

Glisinda had used every source of magic available to her, but no elven Speaker of Lore had any information on the spirits of the grove.

Cald was often impatient with the subject, but that day he stood quietly, hoping it would continue for hours.

A war of emotions was taking place in Eyrmin's eyes. He was clearly proud of Cald's success in his first battle. The young human had proved he had absorbed all the training the prince had given him. Battling against Eyrmin's pride was a deep anger that Cald had disobeyed his foster father's wishes. Clearly he did not count his single omission in ordering Cald to remain in the village as license for the human to join the battle.

ANUIRE

eight

The fight had not yet ended when the local carrion crawlers, smelling blood and sensing fatal injuries, emerged from underground lairs in search of a feast.

The elves removed their dead and abandoned the battlefield, leaving the predators to their grizzly pleasure. Two giant saber-toothed cats had sent their ominous roars ahead to announce their arrival. Until the bones had been stripped, that stretch of border would be defended by the scavengers.

The battle had been decisive, and for three months afterward, the western arm of Sielwode was quiet. Then, within a few days, two happenings occurred that sparked Cald's curiosity. To the first, he would get no explanation for years to come. One afternoon, the two goblins trotted out of camp with the

announced intention of hunting. They would bring
back a deer and have venison for their dinner.

An hour later, they returned faster than they had
left, and were empty-handed. Their small piglike
eyes were stretched wide, and their only explanation
was Bersmog's "Wanted some meat, not too much
meat. Some deer too big to hunt."

Cald asked them questions, but they gave him no
answer he could understand. He knew something
had frightened the goblins; they stayed close to the
village for weeks. When their dislike of elven food
and a hunger for meat forced them to hunt, they
cajoled Saelvam into going with them.

The second puzzle was the disappearance of
Ursrien. The skilled warrior had not been injured in
the last battle, but he had suddenly disappeared
from the village. Three months later he returned,
entering the prince's quarters early one morning.
His tired face split in a grin of victory, and he carried
a large, awkward looking bundle on his back. Hialmair, Malala, and Glisinda had entered the room
behind him, and they, too, seemed to be filled with
happy anticipation.

Cald watched with interest as Ursrien gave the
bundle to the prince. The elves exchanged speaking
looks as Eyrmin carried the strangely shaped load
across the room and laid it on the floor before the
young human.

"Warriors of Sielwode should be fully armed," he
said with a smile and stepped back a pace. The other
elves took a step forward as Cald grasped the meaning of Ursrien's absence and realized what the long,
slender, carefully wrapped item sticking out of the
top of the bundle could be. With trembling fingers,
he carefully removed it.

"Yes, very careful, it might break if you grip it to
hard," Malala said with a laugh as Cald gently

unwrapped the bow. The pale wood of the grenathian tree had been laminated to wafer-thin strips of silver alloy that held elven magic. The spells would assist him in hitting his targets. Wrapped with the bow was a quiver trimmed with runes that represented a spell to keep his arrows in place. They would remain in the quiver though he turned it upside down, or tumbled into a roaring stream. Only his hand could remove them.

The bundle held more surprises.

With shaking hands and a heart bursting with pride and happiness, Cald removed a full suit of elven armor. Breast- and backplates, greaves, cuisses, kneepieces, gauntlets, tasse, and helmet all gleamed softly, picking up the color of the floor as he laid them out in display. Every piece was trimmed with runes to protect him in battle—a suit fit for an elven prince, as fine as Eyrmin's. Added to it was a sword, many runed and light in his hand.

More important than the value of the gift was the knowledge that he had been accepted as a warrior among the elves. Cald's happiness was too great for him to manage donning his new gear himself. Eyrmin, Glisinda, and Malala were assisting him when Relcan entered the prince's dwelling. He stopped in momentary shock as he realized the significance of the scene. His face twisted in anger, and the glare he gave Cald was one of hatred.

A human boy being raised by the prince was a matter of contempt, but when that same boy became a man and a warrior, he would have an implacable enemy.

Cald tried to shrug away the cold feeling in the pit of his stomach. Relcan was only one enemy while hundreds of other elves were his friends. Nevertheless, the prince's second-in-command had taken part of the joy from what should have been a glorious day.

A week later, Eyrmin received a message from the king. He told no one what it said, but grew quiet and withdrawn. Sensitive to his new position, Cald had been worried, fearing Relcan's influence at the elven court might drive him away from Sielwode.

After three days of deep thought, Eyrmin decided to scout the southern border of the western arm. Cald, in his new armor, went with him, accompanied by the two goblins. They left Reilmirid in the night to reach the eaves of the wood at dawn. They stood looking out on the flat plain as the growing light fed to the eyes details that had been obscured by darkness.

Cald had waited for Eyrmin to speak of the message from the king, but the elven prince had not mentioned it. He seemed lost in thought, and the young man had left him in peace, but finally Cald could stand it no longer.

"Have you been ordered to kill me or send me away?" he asked.

Eyrmin's eyes flickered in surprise. He seemed hesitant to speak, and Cald feared the worst. Finally the elf shook his head.

"King Tieslin has never understood why I allow you to stay, but he has not ordered your banishment," Eyrmin said. "Understand, he knows humans only by their destruction of the forest."

"And likes goblins plenty not much, too," Bersmog added. A sharp look from the prince sent both their humanoid companions wandering away to the west. Eyrmin stared out over the plain for a few minutes as if trying to decide whether or not to share his concerns.

"No, the message dealt with another subject." Obviously the prince did not want to discuss it, and Cald respected his wishes.

At least I am not being deprived of my home, he

thought. He had been raised to love the forest, and the thought of leaving it filled him with sadness and a little fear—fear of loneliness away from his friends. His repeated assertions that he should be allowed to stand patrol duty and help with the fighting had always met with a refusal. He had proved himself a warrior loyal to Sielwode; he felt he had earned his place. Prince Eyrmin was hard pressed to defend the borders of the western arm of Sielwode from the armies of the north, and Cald felt it was his duty to do his part. Now that he had his armor and would be allowed in battle, he would be able to prove his loyalty to the people and the prince who had adopted him.

"You have proven yourself in battle," the prince said, as if he had heard the boy's thoughts. "Tieslin would not turn away skilled and loyal warriors. He might even use the halflings, if they return," he said in a rare show of lighthearted spirit.

The little people had been gone for nearly three years. They had stayed to build "Eyrmin's Tower," as they had called the lookout stations high in the Grove Father.

In the six and a half years since the battle in the Muirien Grove and the arrival of the first fifty halflings, the portal had opened four times, and another one hundred fifty-four halflings had escaped the Shadow World. The second group had consisted of only seven escapees, arriving a year after the first group. They had remained with the first fifty.

Half a year later a larger group, eighty-three all told, came dashing through, and the portal closed after them, again before the elves could reach the grove to protect the spirits there. The elves had been astonished and concerned with the number of refugees, but the halflings had no desire to remain in the forest. When the newcomers left, all but twenty of the original fifty went with them. True to their part of the bargain, the best of the woodworkers had stayed to finish the lookout.

The portal opened twice more after the halflings had finished their work on the Grove Father, and more than sixty escapees had followed the rest, each group staying two nights in the burrows that had been excavated in the high banks overlooking the Moon Stream. Then they had left, seeking a place where they could dig their burrows, plant their crops, and live in peace.

The halfling triplets had remained. Bigtoe, Littletoe, and Fleetfoot still lived in the caves by the Moon Stream. They were the sons of the hereditary leader of their village, and one of them, as the oldest son, would take the position of leader when he came of age. A mix-up at birth meant no one knew which baby had been born first, so they did not know who was the rightful leader.

Once they reached the age of thirty-five, the problem would have to be settled, but that birthday was years away and did not seem to bother them. They had shown a surprising sense of responsibility toward their people in their decision to remain in the forest. They kept a close eye on the Muirien Grove, ready to assist and guide any halflings who escaped through the portal.

The elves liked the halflings and found them amusing. Three was too few to upset the peace of the wood. They also admitted their obligation to the halflings. Every member of the village had climbed the thousands of steps that spiraled up the Grove Father to see the watch stations. Some made regular journeys up the tree to stand watch over the western arm of the forest.

As the elves had envisioned, the tall watch stations in the Grove Father allowed them a view from which they could alert their patrols, but it was still necessary to station the protectors of the woods near enough to the eaves to warn off intruders and defend the boundaries.

Cald, walking at Eyrmin's side, fretted, wanting to take an active part in guarding the wood. He was so caught up in his discontent, he didn't realize he had heard a scream until it sounded a second time. Eyrmin was already several paces ahead of him, stringing his bow as he ran.

They raced west, staying just within the shadows of the trees, until he saw the single wagon, stopped a hundred yards from the edge of the forest. A human woman was running toward the wood, her weapon a planting hoe. From beneath the trees, a boy of about eight and two girls, one nearly grown and the other about ten, were backing away from Stognad.

Bersmog approached from the west. Eyrmin and Cald had appeared from the east. The woman had reached the children and stood in front of them, her eyes starting with fear as she brandished her hoe. The older girl, who seemed to be about the same age as Cald, held a short, broken limb. Dead leaves clung to the side; it had been lying on the ground. At her feet lay a pile of old, dead wood. The boy was empty-handed, but the smaller girl still held an armload of short branches.

Bersmog grunted in disgust. "No men, no sport," he grunted in his own tongue. The goblins also missed being allowed to fight.

"They have no axes," Eyrmin said, lowering his bow, a sign he did not mean to exact the regular penalty for entering the Sielwode. He used elven speech; to Cald it meant he did not want the humans to know he understood their language. With a significant glance at Cald, he sent a message the young human interpreted.

"You are not welcome in this forest," Cald said. "Accept your lives as a gift and go."

The woman stared at him for a moment, glanced at the two goblins, who understood the elven tongue and had lowered their weapons. She tugged at the children, pulling them away. The girl remained where she was.

"We weren't hurting your precious trees," she snapped. "We only wanted a little wood to start a fire, and we only picked up fallen branches that would have rotted into the ground." She pointed to a small pile at her feet.

"Jelia!" The older woman's voice trembled with fear. She took a step toward the younger one, pulling at her arm, but the girl shrugged her away and glared at Cald.

"You're a selfish and greedy lot that denies hungry people the right to cook their food."

"Aebrynis provides for its people without disturbing the trees," Cald replied, stung by her remark.

"Then tell us how we make fires without wood, and we won't come near your miserable forest," she snapped.

Cald stared at her, new feelings springing up in him, as if he were a flower just discovering sunlight. This was a human female, possibly his own age. In the growing light he could tell her skin was pale, and her long hair, blown by the light breeze, was reddish brown like new bark on a conifer tree. Her snapping eyes were the dark blue of a clear, early evening.

Beside him, Eyrmin's mouth twitched. The elf stared up at the sky, making it obvious he was leaving this battle to the humans. Cald was loath to turn away, and she had offered a challenge, one that might aid the elves of Sielwode, he decided. Still, he would be giving her the knowledge of an elven craft, and he could not do so without Eyrmin's permission.

"If humans understood the resources on the plain, perhaps they would stay away from the forest," he said, explaining what he wished to do.

"It might prevent battles with the travelers, but not with those who wish to settle and build houses," Eyrmin replied. "Still, I would be interested to see how humans accept new ideas."

"If you wish to learn, I'll show you," he said to the girl, handing Bersmog his bow. He led the way out onto the plain. A chill wind blew from the north, so he walked to the leeward side of the wagon. They could use its protection for both the instruction and the fire. The two goblins followed, and Eyrmin brought up the rear, strolling along as if he were used to being ignored. Cald took note of the prince's unaccustomed humility and left him his anonymity.

Beyond the eaves of the wood, the sunlight and the rich ground allowed the range grass to grow nearly waist high in summer. In autumn it died away and lay flat. He knelt and pulled a number of large clumps away.

"Pull up the clumps in a circle. Clear a place for your fire and make a pile here," he told the two younger children.

Eyrmin took a seat on the ground and watched.

Cald took three of the clumps and handed them to Bersmog to hold for him. Working deftly—he had spent many hours braiding dry grass tightly around torch poles—he plaited the clumps of grass together until he had a tight bundle four inches in diameter. He added other clumps, weaving them in before he cut off the dirt clods at the end. Soon his "log" was nearly five feet long.

With his knife, Cald cut away the earth-covered roots at one end and divided the log into two short lengths. He showed them to the girl.

"They will burn more quickly than wood, but not like individual blades of grass," he said, handing her the two short, fabricated logs. "As I said, the world provides if you know how to take advantage of what it offers."

She stared at the tightly braided grass and inspected the ends, noting how the rough edges of the individual blades clung together and did not unwrap.

"Would you show me how you did that?" she said, her voice a little breathless. "We haven't had a fire for days. Finally we were desperate enough to risk the eaves of the forest. We can't live off raw turnips and tubers forever."

To the disgust of the goblins, Cald ordered them to get a fire started, using the two logs he had cut. Then he sent them out to find some game. The plain abounded with rabbits.

While the older woman, Jelia's mother, set a pot of water to boil, Cald sat on the ground and taught Jelia how to braid the range grass into logs. The work, the rays of the rising sun, and the fire warmed him quickly. He removed his new elven helmet.

Jelia stared at him, or more accurately, his ears. He felt himself blushing under her regard. She noticed and dropped her eyes.

"I'm sorry," she said softly. "I thought elves had pointed . . . I'm sorry."

He understood. "*Elves* have pointed ears," he said. "As you see, I'm not an elf."

"But elves hate humans!"

Cald glanced at Eyrmin, who sat watching. No flicker of his eyes indicated he had understood a word of their conversation.

"Elves don't hate their worst enemies." Cald corrected her. "Hatred is the thief of strength and purpose. Elves gain part of their strength from noble thought. They will fight to the death to protect the forest, but that's because they have an understanding of it that humans will never be able to share."

"I don't understand," she said. Her questioning eyes seemed sincere.

"I have lived with them most of my life, and even I cannot share their gifts, though I see their abilities," Cald said. "When the humans first crossed the land bridge and came north, the elves accepted, some even welcomed, them. Pull that braiding tighter or the logs will burn too fast. The wars between the races didn't start until humans began cutting down trees."

"Why did they accept you?" she asked.

Cald told her about the settler's caravan and how Eyrmin had found him.

"Then you are Sima Dasheft's son," said her mother, who had been tending the fire. "I knew her well. I remember you as a child. I'm Damasina Archolin. As a child you played with my son, Sermer."

"I think I remember Sermer," Cald replied. In truth he remembered missing his playmate more than missing the boy himself.

"We traveled in the second settlers' caravan into northern Markazor." Damasina continued. "Your parents had invited us to join them in whatever shelter they had been able to build, but of course, when we arrived, we discovered they had not survived the journey."

"My uncle . . ." Cald paused, not sure what he wanted to say. He had a vague memory of some kinship that he had valued, but no face or name remained. The woman seemed to understand.

"Captain Mersel Umelsen, your mother's brother," she said with a nod as she added peeled roots to the pot of water. "He sent out searchers, but never learned what had happened to the first caravan. He built a line of forts in the hills of Markazor, and held back the mountain monsters for years." She flicked a quick glance around the camp, looking for the two goblins, who were crossing the plain and carrying two rabbits they had caught in their snares. They were still out of hearing range.

"But more than a year ago, three of the forts were destroyed."

"By the soldiers," the boy, whose name was Remin, announced with disgust.

"Not by the real soldiers," Jelia snapped. "I've told you before, they were the Gorgon's people who had fooled the captain, making him think they were from Shieldhaven." She stopped braiding the grass logs and gazed at Cald, who had noticed the flicker in Eyrmin's eyes. "There were more than three hundred of them. They rode in from the east, wearing the uniforms of the Mhoried military and using the trail across the ford near the border of Cariele. Captain Umelsen was glad of the reinforcements and stationed them in all the forts. For weeks they seemed to be just regular reinforcements. Then one night they slipped from their beds, killed the guards, and set fire to the walls of the stockades. In five of the forts, the soldiers were able to put the fires out, but three burned, killing everyone in them." She dropped her eyes. "Captain Umelsen, my father, and Sermer died in the first fort to burn."

Cald felt the wound of having lost his last known kinsman and his old playmate. Still, he had barely remembered he had an uncle or a friend; the loss of some of his elven friends had hurt worse.

"There were a few goblins and gnolls in those forts," Jelia's mother said, her voice low so the approaching Bersmog and Stognad did not hear her. "Not many, but some humanoids fear and hate the Gorgon more than they hate humans. They decided the blue and black of Mhoried was safer than the black and yellow of the awnshegh in the mountains."

Jelia held up a long, four-inch-thick fabricated log and looked at it appraisingly. While she inspected her work, Cald and Eyrmin traded long looks.

Many of the attackers on the northern borders had worn black clothing with yellow circles that could be interpreted as a crown. The habitat of the most powerful awnshegh on Cerilia was called the Gorgon's Crown.

"I wish we could tell the others how to make these logs," Jelia said. "There will be a string of refugees leaving the hills of Markazor. They say the Gorgon is growing stronger every day, and gathering armies—" She shrugged. "Fear could make the stories more than truth, but in Markazor they fear him, and the armies that have attacked the forts are organized."

For several centuries there had been rumors of an awnshegh to the north, where the Hoarfells and the Stone Crown Mountains met. They had even heard the name Gorgon, and knew it must be Raesene, who had absorbed power from the evil dying god Azrai, destroyed at the battle of Mount Deismaar. The elves of Sielwode knew the Gorgon was enslaving some of the humanoid races, but they had not known he was raising armies.

Bersmog came trotting up, his usual, leering grin absent. He handed Jelia's mother two rabbits.

"Trouble," he said. "Plenty much and coming plenty fast."

"It's Relcan," Eyrmin said in the elven tongue after listening with his sensitive hearing. "Go and meet him. I wish to hear these humans speak when you are not here to listen."

Cald rose and walked around the wagon toward the woods, watching the prince's second-in-command as he trotted across the plain accompanied by half a dozen elven warriors. Relcan's face was contorted by a combination of pleasure and contempt, neither emotion able to gain a victory.

"So, you have taken up with the humans," he said, a fierce smile winning the battle of his expression. "You have left Sielwode, so go with them."

Cald had always known Relcan distrusted him, but he had not expected the elf to attempt to banish him. Worse, Relcan's dislike of the human could lead to a breach between the prince and one of the royal kindred. With the Gorgon's armies attacking, it was unthinkable.

"Relcan, you don't understand. . . ." He took a step toward the elf, but seven arrow points suddenly turned his way.

"Take another step, and I'll kill you," Relcan threatened.

The whir of a flying arrow preceded a missile that passed between human and elf to bury itself in the ground. The fletching on the end of the arrow carried the markings of the prince.

"Am I also banished from Sielwode?" Eyrmin called as he stepped out from behind the wagon.

Relcan stood with his mouth gaping as the prince approached. The warriors who had followed Relcan were backing away, and Cald, seeing the set expression on Eyrmin's face, hurried back toward the wagon. He decided it would be best to be out of hearing when the prince spoke to his second.

Back at the wagon, Jelia was busy braiding more grass into usable fuel, while Bersmog and Stognad skinned the rabbits.

Cald watched the small human family as they smiled in anticipation of a hot meal. He wondered what it would be like to live among humans, live with a female like Jelia. The dreams were pleasant, but a glance to the east reminded him of the forest, so dark and forbidding to the rest of the human race, but a place of constant delight and wonder to him.

When his keen hearing told him the conversation between Eyrmin and Relcan was over, he bade the little family farewell and turned back to Sielwode, firmly putting Jelia out of his mind.

Eyrmin stood in the sunlight, waiting. Beside him was Relcan, his face white with fury. Eyrmin dismissed him. Relcan's short glance at the prince warned Cald that Eyrmin had turned the smaller elf's animosity into hatred.

But Eyrmin had other things on his mind. He waited until they were again joined by the goblins and were back in the wood. A thin tendril of smoke rose over the camp by the wagon. The wind brought the aroma of cooking meat.

"Bersmog say shame to leave cooking meat when hungry," Stognad groused. He had a habit of attributing his complaints to his friend.

"What did the women say after I left?" Cald asked the prince.

"The younger female was suspicious of me, but the woman told her I would do them no harm, since I was one of *your* people. She also expressed the hope that we would not suffer if the awnshegh's forces came south. They seemed to think, if I was an average elf, we would not be physically strong enough to hold them off. I believe they told us the truth."

"Already come south in plenty numbers," Bersmog said as they started away. "Smell Gorgon stink."

Cald threw the goblin a searching look. "You said something about awnshegh stink in the battle at the northern edge of the wood," he said and flicked a glance at Eyrmin. "I didn't pay any attention then."

"Tell me about this smell," Eyrmin said to the goblins. He paused in the deep shade of a huge, low-limbed tree.

Bersmog busied himself with scratching his body, his legs, belly, chest, and ears. Cald and Eyrmin waited, knowing it was the usual occupation of the goblins when they struggled to explain anything that was in any way out of the ordinary.

"Not a nose smell," Bersmog struggled for words. "But is there."

"Then how do you know it's from an awnshegh?" Cald persisted. The goblins had not quite convinced him, but he remembered the remark from before, and the goblins had probably been correct.

"You know smell in forked fire from sky?" Stognad asked. "Not like made fire from camp."

"I know it," Eyrmin answered, staring at the goblins as if mesmerized. He gave up any pretense of traveling and sat on a small, broken limb, motioning the goblins to rest on the ground on a bed of ferns. His expression was intense, and Cald noted he placed his restless hands on his knees to keep them still.

"Gorgon, him have that smell," Bersmog said.

"You've seen the Gorgon?" Eyrmin pressed, doubt narrowing his eyes.

"Me see him little bit." Bersmog nodded. "Me plenty big warrior in clan. Go with Splitear when he see Gorgon, only have to call him Prince Raesene or him get plenty mad."

"How did you look on him without becoming one of his minions?" Eyrmin demanded, his face suddenly hard with suspicion.

"Not able to look—just see in blinks," Bersmog replied with a complacency that was close to triumphant. "Bad eye sickness, all stinging and burning.

Happened on the way to the mountains. When reach Gorgon's Crown, not able to look at anything but in a quick blink."

"Bersmog have to be led most of way out of mountains," Stognad said. "Him die if me not lead him back."

"Did you see the Gorgon, too?" Eyrmin asked the second goblin.

"Him not great warrior, not important enough to see Gorgon," Bersmog said.

"Save your life, you have plenty obligating to me," Stognad retorted, bearing his fangs at his companion.

"Never mind," Eyrmin said. "Describe the Gorgon for me," he ordered Bersmog.

"Is big, plenty big, and like is made of stone, but moves like people," Bersmog said. "Long horns on head of bull, and legs like goat. Funny little hard hooves that crack rock when he walk. Plenty hard, plenty mean, those hooves. Eyes all fire and smoke come from breathing like big blaze inside."

Cald thought the goblin was making up a tale and had started to smile, but the intensity of Eyrmin's expression changed his mind.

"Gorgon, him smell like forked sky fire," Bersmog went on. "Once smell Gorgon, feel smell on people who been near him." The goblin shifted restlessly. "Go hunt now? Eyes plenty good, all healed, but seeing is not filling belly."

"Go and hunt," Eyrmin said. While the goblins trotted away, he sat staring down at the crushed ferns.

"You believed him," Cald said, still doubtful. His remark was almost an accusation of gullibility.

"He doesn't smell anything," Eyrmin said. "He felt the power and the evil of the Gorgon, and he senses a touch of it on the awnshegh's minions. He associates his feelings with an odor."

"You don't think he's boasting?" Cald asked, still not satisfied.

Eyrmin rose, slowly, as if he were very tired. He led the way back toward Reilmirid.

"Few have ever seen the Gorgon and returned alive and untainted, but I have heard that description before, and I've heard about the smell. No, Bersmog is not boasting; he recognizes the influence of the awnshegh. Let that be a lesson to us. We are an intelligent people, and because of our knowledge we often ignore the abilities of others. In that we depart from wisdom."

Cald noted that the prince had included him with the elven race. Then he found a question on his tongue, one he hated to ask, but knew he must.

"Can we be sure Bersmog is untainted?"

"Yes. He's been with us too long; we would have seen some sign of it by now. He has the callousness of his race, but there's no true evil in him. I suspect the eye sickness he spoke of protected him. He was fortunate. He could not keep his eyes open long enough for the Gorgon to invade his mind."

"Then we can trust his statement that he smells— he *feels* the power of the Gorgon on the invaders?"

"I'm afraid we must," he said.

"What is the Gorgon?" Cald asked, wondering why he was the only one who seemed ignorant. The humans had known of the awnshegh, the elves and the goblins knew, but until that day he had never heard of the creature. "If it's such a powerful monster, why have you never told me of it?"

"Why speak of evils we are not ready to challenge? For centuries he has been far away and out of our thoughts," Eyrmin said. "It is not good to darken the day with tales of horror and wickedness."

"But if this foe endangers us, should I not know about him?" Cald asked.

"Later I will tell you all I know, but for now I must turn my mind to other things."

Cald understood. Learning about the power of the enemy attacking the northern borders had taken the prince's mind from the message of the king and the problems with Relcan, but they would have to be faced.

Relcan had always looked upon Cald as an enemy, but now the prince would also have an opponent within his own forces. Though the boy could not lay the blame on the humans, he wished he had never set eyes on them. Eyrmin did not need more trouble in the camp; he was already surrounded by it on all sides.

ANUIRE

nine

"Another twenty warriors have left the villages to the south, Sire. They're on their way to Reilmirid." Brechian Adraail announced the fact, weighting his voice until it sounded like a bell tolling the doom of the nation.

Tieslin Krienelsira, king of Sielwode, ruler of Siel-laghriod, stood on the balcony outside his quarters. Immediately below him, the faceted and polished spires of the Crystal Palace caught the light of the setting sun and glittered in a shattered rainbow of color. Arching bridges, ribbons of light, stretched between the towers, giving a continuity to the bright spires that rose against the dark forest, but the king took no joy in the sight.

He looked out over the forest of Sielwode. To the

east lay Kiergard, where fewer than fifty miles of hill country acted as a buffer between the forest and the humans who had begun to settle along the shores of that land. Baruk-Azhik, Coeranys, and Elinie lay to the south. The dwarves in the mountains were not interested in the forest, but humans lived in the other two lands and were working their way north. In addition, some unspeakable evil had moved into the swamps in Elinie, something feared by both elves and humans.

He worried over what was happening in the north. The unrest of the dwarves in Mur-Kilad, and the forays of the gnolls and goblins coming down from the mountains, were additional concerns.

To the west, the human settlers from Mhoried were being driven out of Markazor by forces from the north. Let them fight it out and kill each other, he decided.

Sielwode was surrounded by enemies, but at the moment he was more concerned over a friend turned possible foe. One that might threaten him personally—and even worse, a threat to the throne and the unity of the nation.

He mentally cursed the day, more than ten thousand years before, when Dorainaval of the Erebannien had entered Sielwode. He tried desperately to lay the blame for the troubles of his kingdom on her shoulders, but it would not rest where it did not belong. No one could fault her because her honesty had been as great as her beauty. Those who had been alive then said she was golden haired, golden eyed, full of laughter and wit, and possessed of a wild spirit. Those who had seen her said her beauty surpassed all other females, but that she made nothing of it. She had fled her own land rather than marry Prince Corristen, refusing to be tied, even to a throne. She had been heard to say she would give her life to a just cause, but her heart to no one.

Why every adult elf, even the king, made a fool of himself for her sake was a question not easily answered. It was said even human, dwarven, and humanoid males held that kinship with elves.

The throne was then held by Ealresid Veyamain, Prince Eyrmin's grandsire. Ealresid and Glaimal Krienelsira, royal kindred both, sought her attentions, and their rivalry led to a challenge that included not only the right to the lady's favor, but the throne of Sielwode as well.

Glaimal, Tieslin's grandsire, had won the battle, but after having killed his friend, he took no joy in the throne. The woman for whom he had fought scorned him. Since Ealresid had wagered the crown on the fight, the elves of Sielwode accepted Glaimal as king. But he never felt they gave him their love, nor did his grandson, Tieslin, feel it. Glaimal, along with Unismalin, Tieslin's father, had been lost at the battle of Mount Deismaar, and the crown had descended to Tieslin.

Eyrmin's father, Maerimil Veyamain, had also died in that battle. He had accepted Glaimal's reign, and Eyrmin had never shown any envy for the throne, but in the years he had been guarding the western borders, he could have changed his mind. If he had, Tieslin had no doubt many of the elves of Sielwode would support his claim to the throne of his ancestors. Others would honor the outcome of the fight between Ealresid and Glaimal and support Tieslin's claim. Therein lay the danger to Sielwode.

"Sire, something must be done about Prince Eyrmin," Brechian said, breaking into the king's thoughts. "The court is concerned."

Tieslin turned and walked back into his private audience chamber. When he had stepped out onto the balcony, the cushioned crystal seats had been bare of sitters, the room empty. Now, six of his most trusted advisors had gathered. They rose when he entered the room. Their long faces and the tension in their movements warned him they too had heard the news.

He wordlessly crossed the room and took a seat on the small throne, disliking the use of it but knowing it was necessary. The seat was uncomfortable in its own right. Worse, it bore the stigma of unwelcome decisions, times like this one when he had to take official notice of his advisors' concerns. He motioned them to sit and looked from face to face.

Listainel, who had been a close companion of his grandfather, was still famed for his warrior's skills and was a great leader in the field. Like most elves who had celebrated their tenth millennia, his face was sharp and strong, and his deep eyes showed wisdom.

With Listainel sat Adair, Cleomid, and Jainnar—all royal kindred and mages—as well as Biestiel and Romsien, two of Tieslin's ablest generals.

Tieslin sat back and gazed at their set faces. He could not prevent his smile. He spread his hands in a helpless gesture.

"I confess, I don't see the danger," he said. "Twenty warriors—and since I have heard no complaints of desertion, I take it they were not on active defensive status—have decided to go to the west, seeking adventure. What in that can worry us? No one expressed such concern when two score went adventuring in Aelvinnwode two centuries ago."

"But they did not join forces with a claimant to the throne of Sielwode," Biestiel replied.

"I tire of this," Romsien announced, impatiently slapping the arm of his chair. "Your pardon for my outburst, Sire. I think you show wisdom in believing there is nothing to these rumors of disloyalty in

Prince Eyrmin. If he desired the throne, would he not be here, seeking powerful allies? Instead, he chooses to defend the western borders."

"He could hardly raise an army here in Siellaghriod," Brechian snapped.

Listainel, the oldest and most revered of Tieslin's council, shifted in his chair, a sign he wished to speak. The others turned, waiting to hear him. When he knew he had their attention, he began slowly.

"I would discredit the tales, save for the reason the warriors give for joining Prince Eyrmin. No song tells of elven ghost warriors trapped on Aebrynis after death. Perhaps our wise mages can settle my mind on the issue."

"The plane of the dead is Tallamai," Cleomid announced. "They walk the paths of the white forests in the clouds, and though the woods of Sielwode, Aelvinnwode, and Erebannien are beautiful, none would seek to stay on Aebrynis when he or she has access to Tallamai."

"And the claims that these spirits have been seen?" asked Romsien. "How do you account for the tales?"

"Who claims to have seen them?" Brechian demanded. "Prince Eyrmin himself, the human child he has raised—an abomination, a pollution to Sielwode. The other stories are always of having seen something not quite identified." Brechian sat back, his face grim. "I believe the tale of the spirits to be a hoax, a trick to bring warriors under his banner."

"You believe it," Romsien demanded, his eyes hot, "or you wish it to be so? The lovely Vritienel is growing up. Does she still have stars in her eyes when she speaks of Prince Eyrmin? Does she still turn her face from your attentions?"

"Cease!" Tieslin snapped. "My kingdom was rent once before because of madness over a female. It will not happen again."

"Then do not doubt Prince Eyrmin, Sire," Romsien said quietly. "You have the loyalty of a brave and honorable warrior. He would give his life in your cause and for the good of Sielwode. Can you ask more of him?"

Tieslin rose, suddenly very tired. Only his predecessors knew the fatigue that came from the weight of the crown—only his and Eyrmin's ancestors.

"All I ask of anyone is loyalty, if not to me, then to the nation. We face enemies all around and a growing threat from the north. To be divided now would bring destruction on all our people. This distrust aids our enemies, and I beg it will cease. Now, I bid you a fair night."

He left the room, moving into his private quarters. After a few seconds' shuffling, the others left the audience chamber.

Tieslin thought about Romsien's assurances. He had said Eyrmin would give his life for his king, but when he had sent the prince a message, Eyrmin had refused to send a contingent of warriors accustomed to fighting gnolls. The king had not told his advisors about the message he had received from the west that day.

To be fair, Eyrmin had not refused to send warriors. The king had asked him if he could spare warriors who understood the new tactics being used by the humanoids who came out of the north. He had not specified any number nor had he made the request urgent. The prince had sent back a message saying he was hard pressed on the northern border of the western arm, but he had sent one of his experienced troop commanders to advise.

Both Romsien and Brechian would have twisted the incident to their own purposes, so the king had kept his disappointment to himself. Listainel, who had taught Tieslin strategy as a boy, would have asked the same question that bothered the king; why would the enemies of the north attack the western arm of the forest when they could conquer Sielwode only by taking Siellaghriod? Did they attack despite Eyrmin or because of him. Was there anything in the story of the spirit elves?

Tieslin spent a restless night; before daybreak he was up, pacing the terrace. When Wistilia, his personal servant, entered the chamber to bring him his morning fruit and tea, he sent the trusted minion on an errand.

Dawn was just lightening the sky when Garienel slipped into the king's private quarters by a secret stair. The young elf's eyes still glistened from his night of wine and song, but his face was sober, knowing he would not have been summoned by the secret way without just cause. He sketched a careful bow.

"You have need of me, Sire?"

"Do you believe the spirits of elven warriors walk in a grove in the western arm?"

Garienel grinned. "In truth, Sire, I think the wine of that region must be more potent than ours in Siellaghriod."

"It would suit my purposes to have you believe," Tieslin said quietly. "Your devotion to their protection would serve the throne."

"Then I believe, and I am devoted," the young elf said smoothly, his mood changing at once. "Do I take it I would be serving my king by offering my sword to their service?"

Tieslin smiled. The wine that coursed through Garienel's veins had not dulled his wit.

"You've heard the rumors," Tieslin said heavily. "I must know the truth." His decision firm, he crossed the room, raised the lid of a crystal cask, and took out two golden rings, one with a white stone and the second with a black gem.

"One of these will be my sign. Send the ring with the white stone if Prince Eyrmin is still loyal to the throne; send the one with the black jewel if he plans to challenge me." The king turned, leading the way to the balcony off his sleeping chamber. He gave a soft *coo*, and almost immediately, a dove lit on his shoulder. The bird stretched its neck as it eyed Garienel. In the growing light the iridescent green spots on the bird's neck glowed like emeralds.

"Brissel will meet you on the trail and accompany you. When you have your answer, fasten one of the rings to her foot and send her back to me. Use the command 'alandas.' "

The king stroked the bird's feathers and looked out over the forest.

Thinking he had been dismissed, Garienel had turned to leave and was halfway through the door when the king spoke again.

"Know, Garienel, that the security of the throne—possibly the nation—depends on you."

ten

Hernan Beekkoleran swept back the hood of his cloak, exposing a face that was still handsome, though the influence of Czrak had set a cruel twist to his mouth. The power of the awnshegh traveled with him in the guise of a clump of swamp mud, encased in a small leather pouch strapped to his left palm. From the damp earth pulsed an energy that heated his blood and coursed through his body with a painful awareness, an energy he desperately needed to unleash. Even so, he knew he must carry it until he used it in Czrak's service.

"It's hot down here," he complained, partly in surprise. He had expected the natural tunnels and passages beneath the surface of the world to be cool. The external heat made all the more uncomfortable the internal heat of the awnshegh's power.

"And there's not much air," Soramat, his second-in-command muttered. He had been gasping for more than an hour.

Gerbid the gnoll, who walked ahead of Hernan, glanced back over his shoulder. In the light of the torch he carried, Hernan could see the humanoid's open mouth. Gerbid's head shook with silent laughter.

Hernan had long ago decided he hated the gnolls, not because they were stupid, untrustworthy, dirty—which they were. He cared little that they stunk of their own filth and the blood of animals they had killed and eaten raw, or even that they would steal anything they could lift. He hated them because of that constant laughter. At least Gerbid was silent. In front of Gerbid, Fadaarg and Ruflik gave out with their *hee-hee*s and *ha-ha*s with irritating regularity.

"Maybe you like wind blowing through, sending muchly warnings to elveses? They hear gooder than humans, even gnolls, and smell everything."

"They could smell you without wind or noses," Hernan snapped. The close air of the natural tunnels, and the heat, aggravated by the torches, intensified the odor rising from the filthy fur and clothing of the gnolls. Hernan felt he might gag.

"Humans have their own stink, *hee-hee-hee*, smell muchly," said Orsht, who walked behind the leaders.

Soramat turned and raised his spear, planning to give the gnoll a sharp blow for his insolence, but Hernan, with quicker reflexes, grabbed his shoulder and hurled him into the wall.

"Leave him alone," Hernan snarled.

Soramat righted himself and sucked on the bruised and scraped fingers of his left hand. He stared at Hernan with a combination of hate and fear. Hernan turned away, knowing he had nothing to fear from the smaller man.

Hernan had been a mercenary, his sword for hire to the owners of small caravans traveling Cerilia. He had journeyed through Vosgaard, into the land of the Khinasi, the Heartlands, and to the western coast.

Four years before, he had served as a watchman for a small caravan traveling from Ansien, in Elinie, to Ruorven, in Coeranys. One night as he stood watch, he was surrounded by a blackness that blinded his eyes and his soul, and he fell unconscious. He had awakened to find himself securely bound, along with six others from the caravan. The prisoners bounced against each other in a rough cart that traveled across open country to the swamps of Elinie. His struggles to free himself ceased when the cart stopped at the edge of the swamp in northeastern Elinie, and Czrak rose up out of the muck.

Hernan's fear turned to worship under the baleful stare of the awnshegh. Czrak did not speak, but Hernan, a bitter man because wealth and power always seemed to be beyond his reach, suddenly knew he had found the key to his dreams. He would be the leader of armies, the one human all Cerilia would fear. All that was required of him was worship of Czrak and unquestioning loyalty.

Though he was impatient with the gnolls and generally hated their species, he hadn't forgotten that the four who led him through the tunnels had brought him to Czrak. He excused many of their faults and their insolence because they had brought him to his good fortune.

Only two of the first seven humans had survived the first two weeks: Hernan and Vilcher, the second mercenary. Of the five others, two were weak-minded cart drivers who were just bright enough to care for the animals and follow the carts in front of them. They had been driven mad under the spell of Czrak. The three others were stout, soft-bodied merchants who proved too weak to serve the awnshegh in any way except as food.

The awnshegh began strengthening Hernan, preparing him to be the Sword of Czrak. Meanwhile, Vilcher was given command of the gnolls and sent them out on raiding forays to find and bring in other converts. Within six months, they had increased their band of humanoids to twelve. Vilcher, strong in both arm and mind, had been an unimaginative sort with a lazy streak. He had made the mistake of capturing too many humans out of the Elinie capital of Ansien, the city closest to the swamp. When the nightly patrols disappeared as easily as the citizens, the locals built a strong palisade around the city. Czrak had been enraged, and Vilcher became an additional meal.

Behind Hernan, the sounds of shuffling feet and the spitting of badly made torches were overlaid with complaints. The men hated the dark and what seemed like aimless wandering through the twisting natural tunnels, and they distrusted the gnolls who guided them. Their concern over their path, the lack of good air, and the uneven walking made them edgy and tense. Too tense, too edgy, and that led to emotional fatigue.

Hernan could have made the journey easier. With the power given him by Czrak, he could have drawn fresh air into the tunnels and produced light by magic, eliminating the need for torches, but he chose not to. He might need all his powers against the elves. Soramat, who walked immediately behind him; Nissening, who brought up the end of the line; and Hernan himself were the only three Czrak had trusted with even a portion of his power. They all wore the mud-filled pouches in their left palms and could call on the powers of the awnshegh.

"We need to stop," Hernan told the gnolls. "Find us a place where fresh air blows down from an opening above."

"And be smelled by elveses?" Gerbid taunted, his yellow eyes gleaming, his head shaking with laughter.

"Just do as I say," Hernan snapped.

Hernan could not afford to risk the strength of his small party, either to fatigue, tension, or falls in the darkness. More than two hundred captives had been brought to the swamp, but most were city dwellers, caught while traveling on family business or trading. Their minds as well as their bodies were soft. Eight out of ten died and became tidbits to sate the growing appetite of the awnshegh. Only one in four of the captives survived. They resembled Hernan in experience and desire. The most useful were dissatisfied mercenaries like himself, or criminals.

With that discovery, he led a small band of good fighters into the stews of Shieldhaven, Ruorven, and Dhalaene. He searched out the strongest of the criminal element, taking only one or two at a time. Hernan had found the rest of his band on the roads: snatch-purses, robbers, and murderers escaping the cities. He captured bandits while they lay in wait for rich caravans. Still, it had taken more than three years to gather a force of fifty, and he knew better than to push them too far.

Hernan, the only one who knew Czrak's purpose, advised caution and the gathering of a larger force, but the awnshegh was too impatient to wait.

In a grove in the western arm of Sielwode, lying on the ground under a pile of leaves and a rotting tree limb, was one of the most powerful concentrations of magic on Aebrynis. It came from the Shadow World, a different plane, and had been dweomered by the great Azrai himself. A sword called Deathirst. How it had entered the other plane and then returned to this one was a mystery, but it was within the reach of Hernan; therefore, Czrak must have it.

Then, three weeks before Hernan had set off with the gnolls, Czrak had reached out, seeking to sense Deathirst and make sure it still lay safe. He discovered the Gorgon's mind had also found the sword.

In a frenzy to possess the sword, Czrak had ordered Hernan to lead a force to get it. At nearly the cost of his life, Hernan delayed, insisting an attack on the closely watched borders would lead to disaster. He persuaded Czrak to send the gnolls underground to travel the fissures and caverns beneath the surface until they were near the area where Deathirst lay hidden. When they insisted they were as near as they could get, Hernan had set them to digging their way to the surface. Now only a thin layer of dirt needed to be pulled away to open the tunnel mouth. He was ready to invade Sielwode from within.

Soon Deathirst, given power by the god Azrai, would be in his hand, a weapon to be used in the service of Czrak. With that blade, Hernan would conquer all of Cerilia.

In the service of Czrak, he reminded himself, and then wondered why he felt the need of the added reinforcement? He was totally loyal to the awnshegh, but as he got farther and farther from the swamp in Elinie, remembrance of his personal ambition had begun to wriggle back into his mind.

Up ahead, Gerbid stopped. Loose soil blocked the way, but the gnoll looked back, his canine mouth open in his perpetual laugh.

"Up above is elveses—muchly elveses," He said, pointing to a steep incline that had been newly dug.

"Lead the way," Hernan ordered, his hand gripping the sword at his side. As they climbed over the loose dirt, he heard the sounds of digging. Occasional showers of dirt sprinkled down on him and his followers. Behind him he heard complaints and a couple of panicked voices.

"Is just digging through littlest last bit of dirt," Gerbid said, and Orsht laughed at the fears of the humans.

"Seeing tree roots," Orsht explained, pointing to the jagged ends that had been cut away. "Holding dirt in place, is tree roots. No falling ins of dirt."

Hernan grudgingly admitted the gnolls had done well. They were right; the roots of some ancient tree supported the ceiling of the newly cut tunnel, and some roots served as handholds and steps. The last of the dirt came showering down, bringing fallen leaves with it.

Minutes later, Hernan led the first of his forces out of the newly dug shaft and into the dim light of Sielwode. Behind him, Soramat scrambled out of the hole and gave all his attention to shaking the soil from his clothing. Hernan grinned. Before he had been enlisted by Czrak, Soramat had been a mage, but only a user of lesser magic, and not a very competent one. He had relied on trickery and showmanship. He hated to soil his ornately trimmed robes.

"Keep the men here while I find out where we are," he said softly. Gerbid and the gnolls had promised they would emerge from the tunnels within the western arm of Sielwode, but not even the humanoids could say exactly where they would come out. Their choices had been limited to places where the natural underground caverns and passages would bring them within digging distance of the surface.

Through the trees, Hernan could see more light—

a clearing. With Gerbid and Orsht acting as escort, he led the way forward. He approached the small meadow from the north, and from the eaves of the forest he saw only more woods. Working his way through the shadows, he circled the open area until he reached the southeastern side. He could just make out the Star Stair, more than ten miles away. Left of it was a grove of huge trees, the fabled siel-wodes, and in the middle, one tree towered hundreds of feet above the others.

His destination was somewhere between the two, and closer, possibly not more than five miles. He nodded in satisfaction.

"You've done well," he told the gnolls.

Gerbid shook with his silent laugh, but Orsht gave out with a loud cackle, cut off in midlaugh by an arrow.

"Fool!" Hernan hissed and kicked the dying gnoll as he fell. The human ducked behind a tree and looked out.

Across the clearing, an elf showed himself briefly as he looked for another target. Hernan was ready for him.

He pointed a finger and, with the power given him by Czrak, he threw a bolt—silent, invisible, and deadly. The elf was cut in two by the force. Another elf, who had remained out of sight, gave a piercing whistle. It was picked up by others, and the sound rang through the forest like an echo.

The surprise Hernan had counted on had been lost.

"Forward!" roared Hernan. "To me! To me!"

Across the clearing, his men appeared and sent a shower of arrows after the fleeing elves. Hernan pointed out their direction.

"It will be a running battle to the grove," he told them. "The sooner we reach our destination, the sooner we can make a stand. Keep up or get picked off by the enemy."

Once in the grove, they would be able to move slowly from tree to tree, and when he had found the sword, he could drive the elves back with the power of the blade. Getting to the grove was everything. He led the way at a run.

ANUIRE

eleven

"It is a long climb up those stairs," Bigtoe
Rootfinder puffed as he entered the treetop dwelling
of the prince.

"A long climb indeed," Littletoe agreed.

"It will be shorter going down," Fleetfoot said as
he followed his brothers across the room to sit on
three cushions near Cald.

The halflings barely resembled the thin demihumans who had fled the portal years before. Their
hearty appetites had been sated by elven bread
made of wild grains and honey, abundant fruits and
nuts, and meat supplied by the goblins. They had
gained weight until they were stout, with rosy
cheeks. Their bright hair gleamed in the morning
light. Their original clothing had worn out years

before, and they were now dressed in trousers and tunics of soft elven fabric, but they adamantly refused any footgear.

Eyrmin had been pacing the large room while he spoke to five elves from the eastern side of Sielwode. They had arrived the night before, and he had been instructing them on their duties. Elves were normally a patient people, but these, like all the rest who had come to join the prince, were restless. They wanted to hear about the ghost warriors in the grove. The prince obliged them.

Through the years, he had seen the spirit warriors several times. His wonder over their existence had changed to sympathy and pity; recently the thought of them seemed to give him pain. His face showed it as he continued from where the halflings had interrupted.

"They finger their weapons, not with anger, not even with hope, but with a long unfulfilled desire to take part in the defense of Sielwode," he said. "They seem to be helpless. We must protect them." Eyrmin's face glowed with purpose, and the newcomers seemed to draw their determination from him.

"My prince, are we allowed to enter the grove?"

"Only in time of need," Eyrmin said. "And for my part, I hope that will be long in coming."

The young warriors tried to hide their disappointment, but the quick eyes of the prince had seen it.

"Their song has never been sung, so we have no way of knowing why they are there, or if our intrusion could be harmful to them. We will keep the evil of the Shadow World from them if we can. They do not seem to hear our speech, nor we theirs. If you are called to defend them, and if they approach you, do not fear their swords. That is all I can tell you about the spirit warriors," he said. The five newcomers shifted, but Eyrmin raised his hand.

"Stay. I have yet to speak of a second and possibly

greater problem. It came upon us a few months ago for the first time, and in the beginning we did not know what we faced. You will understand when I tell you we are being attacked by forces under the control of the Gorgon."

Cald, who had been waiting for Eyrmin to find the time to explain the awnshegh to him, saw the startled and fearful looks that passed among the five elves. They, too, knew about the creature. He sighed, thinking he was the only one on Aebrynis who knew nothing about the awnshegh.

"These three halflings who remain in our village are here to assist their people who escape from the Shadow World. They know nothing of the awnshegh, and neither does our young human friend. You can help me explain the monster, and I would hear what you know of its activity.

"But what is it?" Bigtoe demanded.

"That is the question," Littletoe agreed.

"I don't want to know," Fleetfoot said, giving his opinion.

"I do," Cald snapped at the third halfling. He had been waiting several weeks for Eyrmin to explain.

"The awnsheghlien, those with the blood of darkness, were servants and allies of the evil god, Azrai," Eyrmin said, keeping his voice low, as if to speak of evil too loudly would call it to him.

"They have great power. We believe they have the immortality of elves. Azrai's power is shared among them, so none are as powerful as the god, but they all seem to match him in evil. When Azrai was destroyed at the battle of Mount Deismaar, his power showered over his servants. Those closest to him, or most favored, received the greater share. Others received varying amounts. The Gorgon—Prince Raesene, as he was then—is thought to be the most powerful next to the gods."

"Did . . . ." Jiamial, a young warrior from one of the central villages of Sielwode, said. When he realized he was interrupting the prince, he blushed crimson with embarrassment. "Your pardon, my prince."

Eyrmin smiled at the young elf's embarrassment. "This is no formal audience, and we have time. Ask your question."

"Did you meet Prince Raesene at the battle of Mount Deismaar? I wondered what he was like when he was human."

"Even as a human, he had some height and a handsome face, though by the time I met him in council, lines of cruelty had marred his features. He was a mighty warrior, but arrogant."

"In council?" Cald was confused. Why, he wondered, would enemies be consulting together. The halflings were also shocked.

"Yes, there are some tales, tales of Sidhelien shame, that I have never told you," Eyrmin said, his gaze holding Cald's. "For a time, the elves of Cerilia were under Azrai's influence, though we were not aware of the evil with which we were aligned.

"When the first humans crossed the land bridge from Aduria, we accepted them, thinking we could all live together. It was not so. They saw our forests only as trees to cut, using the wood for building and for their fires. When we tried to stop them, we faced magic we did not understand and were driven back. The great forests that once covered Cerilia were dwindling, and the loss of each tree was a blow to our hearts.

"When Azrai sent his servants among us, feeding our frustration, our anger . . . our hatred"—Eyrmin hesitated for a moment as if the memory gave him pain—"we listened, hearing only how we could kill those who destroyed our forests."

"*You* could never align yourself with evil," Cald

insisted with the desperation of his love and admiration for the prince.

"Not knowingly," Eyrmin agreed. "But we were less wise in those days. We heard honeyed words and had not yet seen the allies promised us. Azrai's messengers were careful not to hint at whom we would follow into battle. It was not until we were at the foot of Mount Deismaar and we attended the war council that we knew."

"And you would not fight for him," Cald said, too used to their lessons to worry about interrupting the prince.

"A few elves stayed with Azrai, but most of us crossed the field in the night and took up stations with the humans." Eyrmin said. "We had no love for them, but as I once said of the goblins, callousness is not true evil. When we understood the nature of Azrai, we knew that to join with the humans was our only hope of keeping the god of malice and cruelty out of our lands.

"Malthriever," Eyrmin addressed one of the newcomers, "Deldemriod is the northernmost village in Sielwode, therefore closest to the land of the Gorgon. What tales pass among your people?"

Malthriever, who had been listening enraptured, gave a startled jerk when the prince spoke to him. He was small for an elf and compactly built. Cald had been watching him, thinking the warrior had the hands and feet of a child. When he spoke, his voice was lyrical, even through the roughness of emotion.

"The Gorgon's evil is passing through the mountains of Mur-Kilad, though we have not faced any concentrated attack," said the warrior. "It's the belief of the people in Deldemriod that the invaders of the northern forest are just raiding parties."

Cald and Eyrmin exchanged glances, and the human understood what was going through the prince's mind. The Gorgon was not attempting to conquer the elven forest. His minions were trying to reach the grove.

"Maybe the black deer will get them," Fleetfoot said, speaking first for a change. He curled one leg under him and began to pick at his thick toenails.

The six elves in the room jumped as if someone had dropped a carrion crawler in the middle of the room.

"He could drive them off," Bigtoe nodded.

"He surely could," Littletoe agreed as he watched his brother groom his feet.

"The black deer?" the prince asked. His voice sounded hollow, as if he were keeping some empty space inside himself, waiting for the knowledge they would impart to fill it.

When the halflings volunteered no answers, Eyrmin stared down at Bigtoe, who usually spoke first.

"Tell me about the black deer. You have seen the Stag of Sielwode?"

"I don't know about the Stag of Sielwode," Bigtoe said, and when he paused, for once he had no echo of agreement. "We saw a big black deer with silvery horns, drinking from the Moon Stream a few weeks ago."

"It was indeed large," Littletoe said.

"Thought it would drink the stream dry," Fleetfoot said.

"A black deer?" Cald had never heard of the creature.

"It is not for the halflings, the goblins, or you to seek it," Eyrmin said when he saw Cald's interest. He had read the youth's curiosity in his face. He knew Cald might hunt the creature, not for the sport of killing or for meat, but only to get a sight of it.

"The Stag of Sielwode is also an awnshegh, though it may have gained its power from the other gods and not Azrai. Elves do not fear it, though all creatures of the power are capricious, and one never knows what they might do, so we leave it alone. It could consider any non-Sidhelien its enemy, so avoid it if you can."

"I've never heard of it," Cald groused, wondering just how ignorant he was.

"It usually roams the eastern and southern borders of the forest. We have never known it to come to this area," the prince said.

Eyrmin paused; his head jerked slightly, and he stood listening. As if with one mind, the five newcomers were on their feet. The prince turned to the wall and hastily armed himself. Cald rose and hurried for his own weapons. He had not heard the alarm, but he did not have elven ears. The prince grabbed him by the arm.

"Remain here," Eyrmin ordered.

Cald was about to object when he heard the message being relayed through the forest. Dimly, in the distance, Cald heard the whistle of alarm that had sent the elves into action. The birdlike sounds formed a limited language understood by the elves and Cald.

Invaders!

Humans! They were deep within Sielwode.

Others, closer by, echoed the call. It passed throughout the tree town of Reilmirid, alerting those who might be resting or meditating. When the call had echoed around the tree town, it rang back out across the forest again, passing from mouth to mouth, alerting the elves to the location of the enemy.

Cald understood the reason for Eyrmin's order. The prince cared for him as a son and had raised him in the elven tradition, but he never forgot Cald was human and did not want him to fight against his own race. The prince's consideration for the human boy and Cald's determination to take his part in the defense of Sielwode and the grove had been the cause of several arguments between the human and the elf. Each was determined to have his way, so Cald said nothing.

He stood by while the prince armed himself and left. As soon as Eyrmin was out of sight, he rushed for his own armor, strapped on his sword belt, grabbed his quiver and bow, and looped them over his shoulder. By the time he reached the limb path, Eyrmin was leading the first group of warriors through the trees. Cald followed with the next group, keeping to the rear to remain out of the sight of the prince.

Just ahead of him, Belrinien and Flamarier, two elves who had recently joined the warriors of Reilmirid, glared at him and fell back as if they planned to keep an eye on this human interloper. Cald had heard that their village, on the eastern edge of the forest, had been attacked by a large party of human hunters, so he tried to tell himself their distrust was understandable. Still, he had been raised by the elves and was ready to give his life for their cause. He could not help resenting the attitudes of these two newcomers.

With his human limitations, Cald had no idea where the alarm had originated. He watched the elves around him as they paced themselves for the run. They were loping easily. None broke into a fast sprint, so the distance would be more than a mile, yet it must be close enough for them to feel they could run and arrive with energy enough to fight. Less than fifteen miles, he decided. If the distance had been greater, they would have been walking.

The direction led through the southern end of the Muirien Grove, through the clearing where the portal had opened. Every elf, even the most recent recruits, knew about the clearing, and they glanced around furtively. Cald grinned to himself, knowing

how elven warriors hated having anyone notice
their fears.

They were well past the clearing and near the edge
of the forest when word came down the column that
when the prince had passed by the edge of the grove,
he had seen the spirit warriors massed by the Moon
Stream. The day was clear and dry, but western Sielwode was steaming after two weeks of rain, and the
creek was high. Ahead, through the trees, Cald could
see the elves massed in a group. They crossed the ford
one at a time. His group slowed to a walk.

Until the human had taken part in his first battle,
he had never understood the emotional pitch that
came with knowing he was preparing to face the
enemy. Now he understood the trembling he had
seen in many of the elves just before a battle. He felt
it himself. Fear played a small part; Eyrmin had
often said he distrusted a warrior who had no fear.
Yet it was not a lack of courage that caused hands
and voices to shake, but anticipation, an automatic
emotional construction of fell purpose. He had discovered there was nothing worse than delay when a
warrior was primed for the fight.

Impatience at the bottleneck by the ford set his
mind to working, and the resentment of his self-
appointed guards gave it direction. As his party
slowed, he walked around a tree, came to an abrupt
halt, and backed up, giving a respectful bow though
nothing visible barred his way.

"Your pardon, brave warrior, I did not see you,"
he said, changing course to walk around the other
side of the tree. As he turned away, he saw the looks
of astonishment and discomfort that passed between
Belrinien and Flamarier.

As he continued toward the stream, he paused
twice again. He begged pardon and turned sideways, as if he worked his way through an unseen

crowd. The two elves followed in his footsteps, turning as he did, taking extreme care to keep their spear points and the ends of their bows from injuring the spirit warriors.

Cald grinned at their discomfort. Still, he was taking unfair advantage of the old lie that he could see the ghost warriors. He had been careful never again to actually say he had seen the ghosts of the grove. His reticence had given him a reputation for modesty. His revenge had been shabby, but he was stuck with it.

Less than half a mile beyond the Moon Stream, the low trills of bird whistles alerted the elves to take cover. Cald worked his way forward from tree to tree and found himself sharing the shelter of a bush with the one elf he had hoped to avoid.

Eyrmin, crouched to take advantage of a thick clump of bushes while he watched for the enemy, spared Cald an angry glance.

"I must teach you to obey orders," he snapped.

"Do the rest of your lessons mean nothing?" Cald retorted. "If your purpose is just, can you deny me a right to uphold it? How can I gain manhood if I turn my back on honor?" He had worked on that speech during his run through the forest, and he saw his success as Eyrmin's eyes clouded with doubt. When the prince looked away, watching for the approaching enemy, Cald knew he had won his right to participate in this battle.

And the fight was not long in coming. The elves had carefully chosen their place of ambush. They had stopped at the western edge of a dry wash, a fifty-yard-wide strip of sturdy grass and rock that often flooded in times of heavy rains. No saplings could stand against the spates of water that occasionally flowed through it, but the recent rains had not been of sufficient force to prevent the enemy from crossing.

The guardians of the forest watched in silence as they heard a sound of breaking twigs. The canine snout of a gnoll appeared from behind a tree. The creature sniffed the air, but gnolls were not overly sensitive to smell and the wind was blowing from the east. Every elf had an arrow knocked to his bow, but they waited, knowing Eyrmin's first shot would signal the attack.

Two more gnolls peered out from the cover on the eastern side of the wash, suspicious of the open area. Behind the last appeared a human in a cloak that seemed to fade into his surroundings. Only his uncovered head was clearly visible. He stared out across the clearing, saw nothing, and roughly pushed one of the gnolls into the open.

"Get going," he snarled, and followed the humanoid, urging him on to greater speed.

Cald kept a tight grip on the arrow he held nocked to the string, but he had not drawn it. He was afraid to, afraid his excitement might cause him to loose the shaft before Eyrmin gave the order. The prince was also ready with his bow, kneeling, relaxed, waiting.

The three gnolls were two yards ahead of the first human and several paces out into the clearing when behind them appeared at first a score, and then more than twice that number of humans, all cased in strange armor. A few wore conventional metal breastplates, tasses, and cuisses; none wore greaves; most were loosely covered with the two-foot-wide, gray-green leaves of the swamp-growing atwer bush. The wide, thin leaves were loosely tied to cover the trunks of their bodies, arms, and legs with an unlikely protection. As they came closer, the prince frowned and seemed puzzled. Like the cloak of the human leader, the leaves faded into their surroundings.

"It's some sort of magic," Cald breathed, wondering if the elven arrows could penetrate the dweomered leaves.

Eyrmin gave no sign that he had heard. He held his shot until the gnolls were within ten paces of the western edge of the wash. They had relaxed and were hurrying forward with confidence when he loosed his arrow. Eyrmin's shaft was aimed at the human leader, and his aim was true, but when the arrow was within three feet of the strangely cloaked man, it veered away as if it had ricocheted.

Cald had better luck. His missile caught the first of the gnolls in the throat.

True to Eyrmin's teachings, he immediately jumped away from the place where he had been kneeling; a clump of bushes was an adequate shelter from enemy vision, but offered little protection from a retaliating spear or arrow. Unlike Eyrmin, he was unable to use elf magic to leap away faster than the eye could see. He felt the heat of a fire bolt thrown by the cloaked human but had moved quickly enough to escape being scorched.

Elven arrows showered the intruders, but only two reached vital targets. The other missiles veered away as Eyrmin's had done. One dropped a human warrior by catching him in the side, where the leaves did not cover, the other caught a man in the throat as Cald had caught the gnoll.

"Human magic," a voice behind Cald hissed, and he turned to see Belrinien. The elf glared at Cald as if it were his fault. "If you are loyal to Sielwode as you say, tell us how to fight this abomination."

Cald stared at the elf. Didn't the warrior know Cald had been raised in Sielwode? If there was any way a human could hold off human magic, he knew nothing of it. Before he could explain, Belrinien stepped out from behind the shelter of the tree and raised his bow. Cald peered around the other side and saw another cloaked and hooded figure raising his hand. The young human reached out and grabbed at the elf, jerking him back. He saw the hatred flash in Belrinien's eyes, but Cald's attention was on a bush just behind where the elven warrior had stood.

Half the bush remained. As he watched, the rest was withering into a dead and shriveled shape. Belrinien saw it and stared at Cald, his distrust lost beneath the realization that he had just had a brush with death.

"That could have been me," he muttered.

"I think you fight this magic by avoiding it until you get a clear target," Cald said slowly, still staring at the bush.

"That sounds like wisdom," the elf replied and stayed closer to the tree, peering out with more caution.

The elves kept showering the invaders with arrows that arced toward their targets and veered off like stones skimmed across a pond. They could not understand their failure, and their lack of success heartened the magically protected humans.

Eyrmin gave the call to withhold their shots, and for a moment quiet reigned in Sielwode. In the clearing, the robed leader stared into the shadows beneath the western eaves and ordered his troops forward. They were an undisciplined lot, laughing at the failure of the elves and making shying motions with their hands, mimicking the arrows that had turned away from the magic that protected them.

"Forward!" roared the robed leader, but they seemed disinclined to follow his orders until two of the warriors, too confident of their protection, had turned to speak to their companions. When Eyrmin put an arrow into the side of one, and another elf dropped a warrior farther up the line, they started backing away, toward the eastern eaves of the wide, dry wash.

Eyrmin whistled several commands. A score of elves using magic known only to their people rapidly scaled the boles of the trees, their hands and feet clinging to the bark as if invisible steps had suddenly appeared. They hid themselves in the leaf-shrouded limbs. Several others, Belrinien included, disappeared into the thick trunks as if the trees had absorbed them. The others melted back into the forest, slowly retreating in plain sight of the enemy.

As usual, Eyrmin had taken to himself the most hazardous position, climbing into the tree beneath which the robed leader would pass as he entered the forest. Cald slipped behind the cluster of partially burned bushes, and using the elf magic he had been taught, blended into the bole of the same tree.

The elves called it Accepting the Embrace of Sielwode.

Cald had practiced this spell often, and Eyrmin had pronounced him adept at it, but the young human was still unsure whether he developed an invisibility as he pressed his body against the bark, or whether he actually entered the tree itself. Around him, the forest seemed dim and foggy. His arms and legs seemed under restraint. He could move neither right nor left nor back, but at will he could step forward, out of the Embrace.

The defenders of the forest were a well-disciplined group of fighters, and in fewer than twenty seconds, the ambush was set. Half the elves had climbed the trees or disappeared into the tree boles, and the others, playing lure for the trap, had shown themselves fleetingly as they retreated.

The invaders took heart and charged beneath the eaves of the forest, their blades and spears in their hands. A few had bows and arrows, and they sent shafts into the forest ahead, aiming at every elf they saw. Flamarier, a little too slow to jump behind a tree, took a shaft in his left forearm. He would have yet another cause to dislike humans.

The invading fighters accepted the retreat at face value. All humans knew elves could not cope with human magic, and they charged forward. The robed leader was not so sure.

"Halt," he roared, but his minions ignored him. They advanced with the battle light of Czrak in their eyes, their faces bestial as they anticipated the slaughter.

Eyrmin's plan was sound, but being an elven warrior, accustomed to immediate and exact obedience to his orders, he could not have anticipated the lack of discipline in the attacking force. The human fighters charged into the wood and would soon be out of sight, leaving the warriors in the trees without targets. The number of fleeing elves who acted as lures were too few to stop them. The prince had no choice but to give the signal to attack while beneath the trees the three unarmed magic-users stood watching.

Taking the greatest danger to himself, Eyrmin fired the first arrow as he whistled the attack command. Directly below him, the robed leader looked up, raised his hand, and muttered an incantation.

"No!" Cald shouted, and he launched himself from the security of the Embrace of Sielwode. He leapt toward the magic-user. The tallest of the other two saw him and gave a foul oath that seemed to blacken the shade of the forest. He, too, raised a hand and prepared to throw a spell, but Cald was on the leader, grabbing his right arm, forcing it down. Cald had spoiled the aim of the spell, which was flung out across the clearing. A huge tree split apart in a shower of sparks and a deafening roar.

Cald jerked the man off his feet and they rolled on the ground. The boy's attention was on his adversary, but he was aware of the other magic-users moving about, muttering their spells, waiting for their companion to get clear of the young human defender of Sielwode.

Up in the tree he heard Eyrmin's shout. A spear with the silver markings of the prince came hurtling down, narrowly missing the tallest of the mages. While his companion continued to circle Cald and his opponent, the intended target of the spear looked up, trying to locate Eyrmin, who was descending the tree, snapping twigs in his rush.

"Yi-i-i-i!" came a shout from another tree, and Belrinien showed himself briefly as he shot an arrow at the mage who searched for the prince.

The arrow veered away, but the mage redirected his spell, and Belrinien screamed and collapsed. By the time the elf's body hit the ground, it was nothing but a misshapen cinder.

Cald kept a desperate grip on the magic-user leader as Eyrmin dropped from the tree. His fall was broken by the tallest of the mages. They, too, rolled on the ground, tripping the third mage. He fell on the feathered end of the last arrow Belrinien had shot. The mage screamed and jerked. The arrow, its head caked with soil, pulled free of the ground, but eight inches of the feathered shaft had penetrated the mage's chest. He gave one gurgling gasp and died. Belrinien had revenge on his killer.

Cald struggled and gasped as he felt himself touched by a powerful evil in the mage's left hand. Hatred, bloodlust, and voracious appetite surged through him. His blood felt as if it boiled in his veins. He could feel the heat as it coursed through him. He glared into the mage's eyes and seemed to see not a human but some nightmare creature that was part spider, part slug.

He snarled in a rage he had never experienced, while a part of his mind tried to shrink from the unaccustomed feelings. Nearby, he heard a second snarl, one that had the faint overtones of Eyrmin's voice, but it sounded more beast than elf. Cald heard a muffled cry and then the sickening sound of cracking bones.

The mage gave a mighty heave and rolled over Cald, pinning him to the ground. Cald was losing his hold when, just above the man's head, he saw the face of a goblin. A friend—Stognad. Only a part of Cald's raging mind recognized an ally, and out of the corner of his eye he saw Eyrmin, rising from the ground, glaring at the humanoid as if he had not recognized him. The goblin ignored the elf and swung his axe. Cald felt the weight of the blow as the blade dug into the mage's back and the heavy body pressed down on him. Stognad frowned at Cald as he rolled the dead body away.

"Plenty much danger in fighting with mages," he grumbled at Cald. "Better hunting deer and gnolls."

Cald struggled to his feet as Eyrmin pulled his sword and hacked the necks of the three mages, beheading the bodies and kicking the heads away.

"They won't be destroying more of Sielwode," he said, his voice still a snarl.

Stognad's gaze shifted from Eyrmin to Cald and back, his expression worried. He kept the rest of his opinions to himself as they hurried west, toward the dying sounds of battle.

Cald was filled with the need to kill. He leapt over fallen limbs and bushes in his desire to reach the enemy before the elves killed them all.

He had to have his share of death and blood.

Eyrmin caught up with him just before he reached a group of five intruders taking shelter behind three large trees. The invaders were watching the wood ahead and had not heard the elf and the young human approaching.

When Cald took his first swing at an unsuspecting warrior, he felt the resistance of the magic protecting the man, but it did not stand against his determination. His first blow was only partially successful. He struck the large quiver of arrows that was slung down the man's back.

His enemy turned and met him blade for blade. Cald jumped back to avoid the larger slashing sword. He parried three blows before he found an opening and stepped in with a thrust through the man's heart.

Shouts and cries indicated Eyrmin had been busy, and by the time Cald had killed his foe, two lay dead at the feet of the prince and another had fallen to Stognad's axe. The fifth had lost his will to fight and raced through the forest the way he had come.

Cald and Eyrmin stood panting and staring at each other. The savagery that had invaded the boy ebbed. He slowly regained control of his emotions. The prince was drawing deep breaths, as if trying to pull fresh, clean air into his lungs to dispel the foulness that had invaded his body.

"What happened to us?" Cald asked Eyrmin.

"We have touched the unclean," the prince replied. "We have experienced pure evil. I felt the same when I briefly held the sword of Mmaadag Cemfrid. It is some terrible human magic."

"Not human magic," Stognad said, shaking his head. "Awnshegh stink."

Eyrmin glared at the goblin. He was usually tolerant of the two humanoids who lived in Reilmirid, but a residue of his rage still gleamed in his eyes.

"You know nothing about it," he snapped.

Normally the goblins stayed well out of the way if any of the elves were out of sorts, but Stognad stood stolidly in front of the prince and shook his head.

"Elf prince plenty smart, but he not know awnshegh power when he feel it," Stognad said, but Eyrmin threw up a dismissive hand and turned away.

"It like dark that not be seen with eyes. It dark on mind and plenty evil," the goblin called after the elf.

Eyrmin stopped and turned, staring at the goblin with eyes narrowed in sudden interest.

"Does this also carry the smell of the Gorgon?" he asked.

"They came south through the deep passages," Cald said in a rush. "They missed coming out in the Muirien Grove. . . ." His skin crawled as he realized their enemies could find many other ways into Sielwode.

"And had turned back toward it," Eyrmin finished the boy's thought. "There's no mistake; they are after the spirits in the grove. We'll increase the watch."

The prince saw two elven warriors in the distance, raised his hand, signaling them to wait and hurried in their direction, seeking news of the battle. Cald and the goblins followed.

"Feeling like Gorgon's vermin, but not same," Stognad said to Cald as he shouldered his axe.

Cald, whose mind was occupied with the danger to the spirits of the elven heroes, barely heard the goblin. He had looked back over his shoulder, irritated with Stognad, but he had seen something in the distance that made him forget the spirit warriors as well as his disapproval of the goblins.

Disappearing into the trees had been the hind end of what he thought was a deer, though the animal was larger than any he had ever seen. The rump and rear legs, all he had seen of it, had been black as night.

Did they have another enemy to fight?

ANUIRE

twelve

"Well?"

Klasmonde Volkir had silently entered the chamber, but Ulcher had been aware of the lich when he reached the open doorway. The flaming torches in their wall sconces and the huge candelabrum on the long table had dimmed until the large book Ulcher had been reading was nearly lost in the darkness. He could barely see the flames that usually provided illumination in the chamber; their light was being eaten by the Crown of Darkness, worn by the new lich-lord of Castle Gough.

"Well?" Ulcher snapped back. "How do you expect me to search when I can't see?" He turned to glare at the blackness through which he could barely discern the face of his new master.

Ulcher's attitude was a departure for him. He would never have spoken to Mmaadag Cemfrid in that tone, but the old lich-lord held the true power, and Klasmonde did not. Klasmonde's time on the throne of Castle Gough would be limited, and Ulcher needed to give serious consideration to his own security. Klasmonde was strong, and Ulcher dared not try to escape, but if he wanted a continued existence, he should leave Castle Gough before its present ruler fell to a stronger lord.

Ulcher knew his timing had to be perfect if he were to save his life. Defecting even a day too early could cause Klasmonde to kill him. A day late, and the new ruler would take his life. His plans were not firm, and he put them aside, not sure how much power the Crown gave Klasmonde, or whether the new lich-lord could read his mind. Instead, he concentrated on Klasmonde's impatience and its reason.

"I still have six tomes to search," he said in a more reasonable tone of voice. It would not be wise to try Klasmonde's anger too far.

"The ones stolen from the castle of the Black Prince?" Klasmonde demanded.

"The same. He can travel into Cerilia and has been able to stay there for extended periods of time." If the Black Prince had not lived in Cerilia—it was said he was known by the name Gorgon when he was on that plane—Castle Gough would probably be a heap of broken stone in retaliation for the raid on the Black Prince's domain. "If the answer exists, it must be here."

"What do you mean, *if* it exists?" Klasmonde's voice went up an octave. He tried to make himself sound enraged, but Ulcher heard the fear behind it. Without Deathirst, the blade of Azrai, Klasmonde was a figurehead, helpless against the attacks of Gough's enemies.

Deathirst was in an elven grove in Cerilia, left behind when the portal had closed.

"Creating portals and passing through them at will may not be a feat of magic, but a result of power," Ulcher said. "I warned Mmaadag of it many times."

"It's not power!" Klasmonde shouted. "It's in here!" With two long strides he approached the table and opened the book. He peered down at it, but the Crown of Darkness prevented him from being able to see the words. In frustration, he picked up the book and threw it on the floor. The ancient binding disintegrated and pages flew all over the chamber.

"Get them!" he ordered Ulcher.

"They don't matter," the undead mage replied as he picked up the larger portions of the book. "I had just finished this one. There's nothing in it to interest us."

"Then get on with the others," Klasmonde ordered, and left the chamber. With him went the influence of the Crown of Darkness. The sudden light thrown out by the candles and the torches caused Ulcher to blink. He picked up the loose pages, took ten minutes to put them back in place, and carried the heavy tome back to the shelves that lined one wall.

The weight nearly caused him to fall, and he frowned down at his withered left leg, still remembering a time when it had been as strong as the right. That had been before the battle of Mount Deismaar, when he had stood behind Emperor Grayconel Adriss, Supreme Emperor of Justminia, most powerful of the rulers of the southern continent and the most favored of the servants of Azrai. Like most in the Shadow World, he remembered that day with perfect clarity.

Emperor Grayconel wore the Crown of Darkness,

which showered blackness and terror like a metal spear point dragging across a large rock spreads sparks. In his hand he held Deathirst, a fell weapon that had been forged and dweomered by Azrai himself, and against it no weapon could prevail.

While they waited for the battle to begin, Ulcher eased away. A young mage then, he was impatient with the delay and his inability to see beyond the blackness thrown out by the Crown. He moved down the line of warriors, trying to find a place where his magic could be most effective. Small of stature and lacking the strength and abilities of a warrior, he stayed away from the battle lines, casting his spells from afar. He escaped the explosion that destroyed the gods, Grayconel, and most of the heroes on both sides.

He regained consciousness on a different plane. The world in which he found himself was much like Aebrynis in the beginning, though the only intelligent people were a race of short demihumans known as halflings. His arrival coincided with that of thousands of others who had been in the armies of Azrai.

The most powerful of the suddenly imported leaders gathered armies and claimed vast reaches of the new lands, killing or enslaving the halflings. Through Ulcher's power as a mage, he discovered that Deathirst and the Crown of Darkness had survived the explosion. They had been flung miles away by the force of the destruction. Mmaadag Cemfrid found the sword. The Crown of Darkness was discovered by Klasmonde Volkir, but to save his life he relinquished it to Mmaadag, who became one of the most powerful rulers in the new world.

Ulcher, whose left leg had been withered by a stray spell from an opposing—and dying—mage, decided his best chance of survival would be to offer his services to Mmaadag. Klasmonde, in order to keep his life, did the same, but his hungry gaze often strayed to the Crown.

In the beginning, the new world held promise, but with the arrival of the minions of Azrai, the sky and the world changed. Dark clouds, at first thought to be part of a coming storm, hid the sun. At first they gathered and then dissipated, but each time they formed they lasted longer, until at last they became a permanent part of the sky. Forests twisted into grotesque shapes, as if the limbs and branches were contorting in an effort to find more light. The rich grasslands became rank in the dimness, and foul plants grew in the shadows. The halflings whispered that the evil newcomers tainted the land, and even Ulcher believed it.

Through the centuries, the land became known as the Shadow World.

Four hundred and fifty years later, weary of life and his deformity, Ulcher was still serving in Castle Gough, searching old records, trying to find a dependable access back into the world of Aebrynis. There were many records and books of magic. Most of the mages of the southern continent had brought their books and scrolls of magic spells with them when they accompanied the armies. During the battle of Mount Deismaar, they looted the possessions of the dead mages of Cerilia for more. When Mmaadag Cemfrid fought and killed another lichlord, he always confiscated any books of magic lore.

But Mmaadag Cemfrid was dead, killed in a battle at a portal. Every time Ulcher thought of the battle and the incident that caused it, he suppressed a giggle.

When the servants of Azrai arrived in the Shadow World, they set about enslaving the small natives. The halflings were a spirited people, kept in check only by death threats, not to themselves but to those they loved—a weakness the new arrivals used against them. Many fled to areas the lich-lords had not claimed, and some remained hidden for generations.

When Mmaadag Cemfrid learned of a small group of halflings living two days' journey away from the borders of his lands, he sent a company of soldiers to take them captive and bring them into Castle Gough. The soldiers who returned after the battle reported the halflings had fought back with rakes, hoes, and goat dung, the last of which they had thrown in the faces of his warriors. They had knocked Mmaadag's standard out of the hands of its carrier, and one spirited halfling had stomped on the banner.

As Ulcher visualized the insult to the lich-lord, he giggled again.

After centuries of accepting fear and servility as his due, Mmaadag Cemfrid was stunned speechless. His shock turned to ungovernable rage that cost the lives of the messengers, as well as those of two stable hands who had not been fast enough to saddle the lord's war-horse. Mmaadag had chased the halflings through a portal that led into Aebrynis and fell in battle with a group of Cerilian elves and goblins. The shock of his death was so great, the skies above Castle Gough had lightened for five days.

Klasmonde Volkir returned from the portal with the Crown of Darkness. Without Deathirst, though, he could never defend Castle Gough. Klasmonde lived in fear, and Ulcher was carefully considering not only the fear, but the lich's reactions. The mage's only chance for survival was in defection, but what was his wisest course? He paced the room, limping on his bad leg until a scream drew him to the high window.

It was midday in the Shadow World, but the dimness of the landscape was like deep twilight on Aebrynis. From the window, high in the tallest tower of Castle Gough, Ulcher could see only a portion of the courtyard below, and a section of the outer, defensive walls. The dimness partially hid the fields beyond. He could barely make out the wood in the distance because of the darkness.

Immediately below him, the work on the broken wall held his interest; it had always roused his curiosity. The break had been Mmaadag Cemfrid's major frustration and was even more important to Klasmonde. Why did every stone placed in that break fail and fall? The defenses of Gough were impregnable except for that one spot.

Klasmonde's first act when he took the Crown of Darkness was to order the repair again. Ulcher watched as the soldiers used whips to drive the slaves faster as they pulled huge stones up the dirt ramp that had been used five times for the same purpose.

Klasmonde needed to complete the defenses of the castle in order to hold it. He was too insecure to ignore any opportunity to strengthen his position. He was accepted as lich-lord in Gough, but only because his minions believed the power of the throne rested in the Crown of Darkness.

For four hundred fifty years, Ulcher had known Klasmonde had wanted to regain possession of the Crown again. He had tasted power and hungered for it. Through four and a half centuries he hated knowing his life was dependent on his service to Mmaadag Cemfrid. Klasmonde gave his lich-lord his loyalty in fact, if not in spirit, and secretly drew bloodpower where he could until even Mmaadag gave him a measure of respect.

Ulcher heard Klasmonde's voice raised in anger and leaned forward to peer down into the courtyard. The captain of the guard stood backed up against the barrack wall. Klasmonde was upbraiding him for the lack of progress on the wall, but to Ulcher, the rage seemed largely feigned. With a lunge, Klasmonde attacked the man. His long, clawlike nails dug into the soldier's neck. As the captain writhed and crumpled, the lich seemed to grow, absorbing the blood strength of the dying man.

Ulcher drew back from the window, his face a study of indecision. In the past three days, Klasmonde had killed four minions and drew what power he could from each. None of them had offered much, but vast oceans were made up of single drops.

The mage had told him the portals might be opened at will by a creature of great power. Ulcher had made the suggestion in order to deflect the anger of his master while he searched for the secret. The horrible irony suddenly occurred to him. If Klasmonde Volkir decided to grab power where he could get it, even from his own minions, then Ulcher had put his own life in danger.

thirteen

Czrak rolled in the thick mud near the southern edge of the swamp. His eight spider legs thrashed. His sluglike trunk moved slowly, though for him the effort was tantamount to a full tantrum.

That fool, Hernan Beekkoleran had committed the ultimate sin against the awnshegh; he had failed in his mission and had been killed in the process. Czrak regretted the death of the former mercenary. Hernan had been the strongest and most intelligent of his servants. The awnshegh had known of the mercenary's ambitions, known he would have to kill Hernan sooner or later, but that privilege he had reserved for himself. Part of his rage came from the knowledge that the elves had taken that pleasure from him.

Only two of Hernan's group had survived the battle in Sielwode, and they had attempted to escape Czrak's wrath by running away. Luckily Czrak had anticipated some deserters and had stationed a party of gnolls at the entrance to the tunnels. They captured the human warriors and brought them back to the awnshegh.

The two men stood before him on a tussock clump and shook with fear. Their clothing was caked with soil. The dank, musty odor of the deep caverns still clung to their boots. Both were bleeding from small cuts. Demloke Winsin had an arrow wound in his arm.

"Th-the elves were everywh-where, as if they expected us," the tallest, Demloke, stammered. His eyes were starting in terror. "Berdin, our group leader, charged ahead and ordered us to follow; Hernan Beekkoleran ordered us back. Some ran one way, some the other."

"Some of the elves ran away. When we chased them, others dropped from the trees behind us. . . ." Lishet Romeser babbled, but Czrak cut him off.

"I gave you protection!" he roared.

"And mighty is the power of the awnshegh," Lishet spoke up quickly. "But the elves had a deadly aim with their bows and aimed for arms, legs, and throats."

"When the battle was lost, we decided to return to you with the news, mighty Czrak," Demloke added.

Czrak knew the man was lying, and his rage boiled up again, but he controlled himself with an effort that was new to him. He rolled in the mud and considered the news. His rage had drained him. His hunger grew with every twist and turn, but he decided not to eat the humans. They were the only ones left. He would reinspire them and send them to find more followers.

Luckily a large band of gnolls, chased out of Coeranys, had tried to cross the southern end of the swamp, and he had caught them with his power. They, under the command of the humans, would help him rebuild his army.

But how large a force would he need to drive off the elves and reach the area of the portal? Even the Gorgon, with his superior strength and larger armies, had not succeeded. The mightiest awnshegh on Cerilia had not even drawn all the elven warriors to the northern borders.

Elves! The awnshegh gave in to another rage, rolling and thrashing.

Elves! Elves! Elves!

Elves!

Czrak wondered how he could have overlooked the obvious; he had concentrated on pitting an army against the elves of Sielwode. What if he pitted elves against their own kind? He needed elves to learn what force he faced, and to bring him word of the weaknesses of the defenders of the forest. He rolled to face the two humans again, his face twisted in a grimace that served him for a smile.

"Swift and deadly is the justice of Czrak," he said quietly and watched with pleasure as they trembled. "But he also rewards loyalty. You returned to me with news." Only because they were captured and brought to me, he thought, but he kept that thought to himself.

"You were wise to flee the fight when nothing could be gained." They had fled in fear; he could read it in their minds. The next work he had for them would not require as much physical courage.

"Those who were unwise enough to lose their lives will not share in the greatness of my victories, but you will. Rest while I consider."

Czrak's hatred of the elves grew with his rage

over being thwarted, but he had to admit a grudging respect for their determination and their expertise as warriors. He decided on a plan, and then spent three days turning it over in his mind. To fail again would be worse than not trying. His followers, the few he had left, would lose respect for his power.

He made his decision, gave his minions their instructions, and sat back to wait. In four days, the two humans and ten gnolls returned from Sielwode with three elves, bound and gagged.

To Czrak's astonishment, he had to work a full day to suborn each elf. Their will was stronger than he had thought any mortal's could be. But then, elves were not mortal in the true sense, he reminded himself. Their lives had no predetermined span; if they did not die in battle or of a sickness, they lived forever, and their minds were strong.

Three days later, he wallowed in exhaustion, but he had learned from them all they knew, and had sent them west with their instructions.

Demloke and Lishet left with the gnolls to bring in more captives, and Czrak took a much-needed rest. The next time he would not fail in his attempt to get the sword.

ANUIRE

fourteen

"There was a time when Eisermerien bred brave warriors," Relcan said. He stood in the doorway of Eyrmin's dwelling, looking out over the village of Reilmirid. His restless hands moved from his sword to the frame of the door and back. He was reluctantly expressing doubts about two elves from the southernmost village in Sielwode.

Eyrmin and Cald sat at their ease. The prince and his youthful human companion had just returned from the northern border, where they had been inspecting the elven defenses.

The Gorgon had made another strong attempt to invade the forest. The elves had not been able to hold the powerful awnshegh's forces out, and the battle had raged from tree to tree. The elves retreated nearly a mile before they rallied and drove out the enemy. Fifteen elves had died in the battle.

The entire western arm of Sielwode was in mourning. Fifteen deaths among a people who could live forever was a tragedy beyond the understanding of those who measured their lives in centuries or less.

Returning with Eyrmin and Cald were eight warriors who had been severely injured and would need time to heal. Two others, Iswiel and Farmain, had insisted they needed recuperative leave from the border, but their wounds had been slight.

They were newcomers to the army of the western arm, from the village of Eisermerien. Their village guarded part of the southern border of Sielwode, in an area generally safe from invasion, since it bordered the swamp of northern Elinie. In centuries past, they had spent a great deal of their time gathering wild rice and talltails from the edge of the swamp, but some evil had taken over the bogs and they no longer traveled the fens.

Iswiel and Farmain had joined Eyrmin's forces less than a month before, yet this was the second time they had returned to Reilmirid with slight injuries, claiming they were in need of rest and healing.

"It has been nearly four centuries since the people of Eisermerien fought pitched battles," Eyrmin said. "Give them time to become hardened to war."

Cald watched as the prince frowned over the attitudes of the two new elves. Though he himself would not admit it, Eyrmin, a hero of the battle of Mount Deismaar, shared Relcan's difficulty in understanding the attitudes of the newcomers.

"Perhaps there's something strange about their food," Cald said, seeking a reason. Eyrmin raised his brows as he looked at the young human. Relcan turned from the doorway and frowned at Cald.

"I mean, mayhap they feel more pain from a slight wound than we do . . . a different type of food . . . perhaps it makes them more sensitive. . . ." He shrugged. "It's the only thing I could think of." He had only wanted to lighten the prince's mind.

Relcan gave a snort and turned away, showing his contempt for the opinion of the young human. Eyrmin mirrored Cald's shrug, though his eyes were thoughtful.

"No song of lore mentions it, but then we have discovered other new things that require new tunes." He sighed, a despondent sound that wrenched Cald's spirit. "Let them have their rest."

Relcan shook his head in disapproval, but when he opened his mouth to disagree with his prince, Eyrmin's look, stiff with determination, stopped him. He turned and had just disappeared through the doorway when a shrill whistle pierced the silence. The message was plain.

The portal had opened!

Cald was tired from their all-night trek from the northern border, but he was on his feet as quickly as the prince. They grabbed their weapons and raced out of the dwelling, disdaining the stairs in favor of the ropes that allowed faster access to the ground.

Cald was ten paces behind the prince when they entered the Muirien Grove. Ahead of him ran Iswiel and Farmain. From the high platform in the Grove Father came another, longer, whistled message. The portal had closed again, but not before a score of halflings had entered Sielwode. The messages kept coming; the halflings had been the only intruders, and they were hurrying southwest, directly toward the elven village.

Thirty elves had followed Eyrmin, but he called a halt to the run and ordered all but Relcan, Glisinda, and Cald back to Reilmirid. Cald watched, feeling a familiar pride in his foster father. Eyrmin knew the halflings that came through the portal were usually terrified because of the evils that chased them. A large, armed force of strangers would just add to their fear. Often merciless in battle, Eyrmin could be sensitive and thoughtful to those who intended no harm to Sielwode.

The prince watched the other elves as they left, and was turning to meet the halflings when Cald touched his arm.

"Relcan's complaint may be justified," he murmured so only the prince and his second-in-command could hear him. He pointed to the two elves from the southern forest. Both were limping pathetically as they followed the rest of the warriors.

"Why are they here if they're too wounded to fight?" Relcan asked, but Eyrmin was quicker in understanding.

"They traveled at a quick pace to get so far so fast," he said, his eyes darkening with suspicion. "Yet now their limping makes it appear they can hardly walk."

"They've not been telling the truth?" Relcan had difficulty accepting the idea of dishonesty among his own people. His head jerked with quick little movements and his hands twitched. He put up no argument; he had been the first to suspect that their courage was not all it should be.

"They may require more consideration," Eyrmin said. Pain filled his eyes. "I confess to a lack of understanding—and trust."

"Here come the halflings," Glisinda said as she pointed toward the sound of cracking branches behind them. Bigtoe, Littletoe, and Fleetfoot Rootfinder came dashing into the grove. They wore elven helmets and carried small weapons made by their hosts to fit their smaller hands. As usual, Bigtoe led, Littletoe followed on his heels, and Fleetfoot brought up the end of the line.

"You missed the entire battle," Cald shouted. The elves laughed.

Bigtoe glared up at Cald, his arms akimbo. Littletoe eyed his brother and did the same. Fleetfoot shrugged and sat on a fallen limb.

"There was no battle," Eyrmin assured them. "Twenty or more escaped. Find them and assure them they are welcome to rest here for a few days."

"We will find them," Bigtoe said, leading the way.

"We surely will," Littletoe agreed, and then followed his brother.

Fleetfoot stood up. "And search for a battle that isn't there," he said, stomping off.

In a few minutes the triplets returned with the refugees, who eyed the elves with suspicion. When Stognad and Bersmog came up behind them, however, they opted for the company of elves rather than goblins. They gathered around the human, Eyrmin, Glisinda, and Relcan.

"What are you doing in the grove?" Relcan demanded of the two goblins who circled the frightened halflings and joined the elves.

"Was not in place of half-dead trees. Plenty nothing good there," Stognad replied with a sneer. Neither goblin liked the grove. "We on other side when heard the call."

"Came to help fight," Bersmog added. "Been tracking a deer, but it be gone now. Nothing to eat but elf slop."

"And then get hard-mouthed by elf," Stognad griped.

"Go back to your hunting, but not in the grove," Eyrmin said, his mind on the small refugees. "The halflings need food, so you can hunt for them as well."

"And likely not get to feed ourselves," groused Bersmog. "Plenty trouble, living with elves."

"You want to go back to Chief Splitear?" Stognad asked as they turned to leave.

"How come old Splitear not got himself killed by now?" Bersmog asked as he followed his friend through the wood. By the time Stognad worked out an answer, they were too far away for Cald to hear it.

The halflings stood wide-eyed throughout the conversation between the elves and the goblins, and when the humanoids trotted away, Glisinda gave the new arrivals the speech that had become customary.

"We know you flee the evils of the Shadow World. We will allow you to rest near here and then travel through our land as long as you obey our laws while you are in our forest."

"And you can repay us by giving us news of the Shadow World," Eyrmin added. With intruders attacking from the north and the south, all apparently attempting to reach the Muirien Grove, at first he had thought the elven spirits were the sole reason. A month before, he had decided the portal could be a rallying point for evil, but how and why and whether the ghost elves drew them was a puzzle he had not worked out. He had spoken of his thoughts only to Cald. Both sensed he was right, but their reasoning was still fuzzy and without form.

Eyrmin ordered the halfling triplets to lead the escapees to the caves that had been used by scores of refugees from the Shadow World. One sturdy little warrior, who was armed with a scythe and seemed to be the leader, shook his head when they called to him to follow.

"If the news we bring is to aid you, we should lose no time in the telling," he said, still panting a little from his run. He introduced himself as Furfoot Tunnelgood. "Is the name, Klasmonde Volkir known to you?"

"The Klasmonde Volkir who served Mmaadag Cemfrid?" Eyrmin asked. The elves had questioned the halfling refugees and had learned a few names. Since the halflings who had escaped the Shadow World had been in hiding for generations, most of their tales were rumors, many confused and contradictory.

"Mmaadag Cemfrid was killed at the portal," Furfoot said. "Klasmonde Volkir is now lich-lord of Castle Gough. He is seeking the blood of everyone not necessary to the defense of the castle, seeking enough power to come through the portal."

"It is said he is mad with the desire to reach Aebrynis," announced a female halfling who had come to stand by Furfoot. On her back was strapped an infant, bound to a board. She carried a hoe as if it were a weapon.

"Curlytoe speaks true; it is said that Volkir thinks of nothing but reaching this world," Furfoot said.

"How do you open the portal?" Glisinda asked. The question had been asked of most of the refugees. Like those who had come before them, the halflings glanced at each other and shrugged.

"It just appeared," Furfoot said.

"It's not there all the time," Curlytoe added. "We have passed that spot many times and never have we seen a passage into this world, but we returned to the area inside the forked streams because the lich-lord has been seeking the portal in that place."

"Then he seeks the grove," Eyrmin said, staring out into the dimness under the trees.

The group of twenty-two halflings had little other news. They had fled their village when the soldiers of Castle Gough had come in search of slaves who had been living in the forest. They had gleaned their story from an escaped slave, but he had left them before they discovered the portal.

The triplets led them toward the caves above the banks of the Moon Stream while Eyrmin returned to Reilmirid, deep in thought. Cald and Relcan followed, allied and walking together only because they were not being made privy to the prince's consideration.

In the main room of his dwelling, Eyrmin paced, indecision, consideration, and later, determination showing in his eyes. He kept his thoughts to himself, and that raised resentment in Relcan, who sat on a cushion and shifted as restlessly as the prince. His hands moved over the edge of the table at his side, filling his wineglass often until his eyes glistened with the drink.

Cald felt so keyed up he wanted to scream, just to break the tension.

Two hours later, Glisinda arrived in Eyrmin's dwelling in response to a message from the prince. She had hardly stepped into the room before the prince whirled to face her.

"I believe the Gorgon and the lords of the Shadow World hope to meet in the Muirien Grove. Whether they are allies or enemies we have yet to learn. I need your knowledge. Have you discovered any reason they've chosen our land?"

"No." Glisinda shook her head, her eyes dark with worry. "It could be as you have said; they may be seeking the portal because of the spirit warriors. Else, why not open the portal in the Stone Crown Mountains?"

"Because of spirits we cannot see?" Relcan's voice was a little slurred by the drink. His accusing glare at Eyrmin threw Cald into a rage.

"Spirits *you* cannot see," Cald snapped. He would have said more, but a chopping motion of Eyrmin's hand cut him off.

Eyrmin's eyes flashed with anger, but he kept his temper under control. He took a deep breath, marshaling his patience. "If it isn't the spirit warriors, why did the evils of the awnshegh and the lich-lord pick the Muirien Grove?" he asked his second-in-command.

Relcan struggled to his feet as if he had been weighted down by the wine, but once he stood upright, he was steady. His eyes gleamed as brightly as Eyrmin's.

"I'll answer with a question. Elves of good heart go to Tallamai when they die, so why didn't these you claim to have seen? Could it be that they are evil and drawing evil to them?"

"No! There's no evil in them," Eyrmin said.

Relcan looked pointedly at Cald, who knew he was expected to reinforce his foster-father's description, or deny the existence of the spirits. His head whirled, trying to remember everything Eyrmin had said about the elven ghost warriors. Lying did not come easy to him, but he made an effort.

"I could feel their hope. It seemed faint, but it's there. They seek aid from *us*, not from people of the Shadow World, nor the awnshegh," Cald said, first giving a general paraphrasing of Eyrmin's description and then adding what seemed logical.

"True!" Eyrmin said, his face alight with assurance. "It is to us they are looking for help—protection. They are—were—our people, and doubtless they lost their lives in our cause."

"Then it is our duty to protect them," Glisinda agreed. "But how?"

"By withdrawing our forces from the borders," Eyrmin said.

"No!" Relcan shouted. "We have a duty to Sielwode!" The prince's second-in-command stood flat-footed, his legs slightly apart, his hands formed into fists. Eyrmin stared at the smaller elf in surprise, but his warrior's reflexes automatically shifted him into a defensive stance.

"We can't guard all the eaves of the western arm and the grove as well," Eyrmin said, trying to bring logic and order back to the conversation.

Relcan brought himself under control. "If we hold the Gorgon's army at the eaves of the wood, they will not come together," Relcan said. "The halflings have told us this Klasmonde Volkir does not know how to open the portal."

"But he'll soon realize others can open it for him," Cald whispered. The thought that had suddenly entered his mind filled him with cold terror, and the words came out unbidden.

The three elves stared at him, and as usual, Eyrmin's more agile mind caught the meaning behind Cald's sudden remark.

"The halflings," he breathed, his voice shivery with awe at the simplicity of the idea, and the danger if Cald were correct. "He can reach Cerilia by driving them through the gate before him."

"The halflings claim they cannot open the portal," Relcan reminded Eyrmin.

"But they must be able to," the prince countered. "The gate has opened several times, always to let the refugees through. The lich-lords have not always been at the gate."

"They could be lying when they say they don't know how to open it." Relcan suggested. He seemed more than willing to find another target for his anger. His eyes gleamed as if he had discovered a reason to deny the halflings the shelter of the forest.

"No, they speak the truth." Glisinda said. "I believe they have an innate magic that is triggered by fear or desperation. Perhaps there is no magic involved. Fear and desperation could be all that's needed. I don't believe they realize they can do it."

"But once Klasmonde realizes it, he'll use that knowledge," Eyrmin added. "We can no longer leave the grove unguarded."

ANUIRE

ғifteen

Cald stood leaning against one of the ancient trees
in the Muirien Grove, grousing to himself, though
his conscience told him he was getting only what he
deserved. Or part of what he deserved, he amended.
The lie he had told years ago—that he had seen the
elven spirits—was still believed by the elves, and he
had recently reinforced it. Because the elves believed
he could see the ghost elves, he had been given the
command of a unit set to guard the grove.

He did not deserve the honor of commanding a
large party of elves who were much older and wiser,
and better fighters, than himself, nor did he deserve
their trust. His conscience pricked at him like a
thorny vine.

He had been given his command a month before

and had doggedly stuck to his duty, leaving his post only to bathe in the Moon Stream when he decided he had become offensive. He slept only when fatigue drove him to it. He stood at the edge of the clearing where the portal had opened several times in the past few years. In any battle, Eyrmin always took the forward and most dangerous position. Cald decided he could do no less.

In the month he had held his command, the portal had opened once. Five halflings had escaped through it. In the distance, he could see the soldiers of Klasmonde Volkir racing toward it, but the gateway between worlds had remained open for less than a minute, and not one of the pursuers had reached the opening.

Still, the news of their experience would bring the lich-lord of Castle Gough a step closer to understanding the secret of opening the portal. It would be only a matter of time before he figured it out.

The young human blinked at the bright sunlight of the early afternoon and stepped back farther into the shade. Most humans, seeing the dark eaves of Sielwode, would have a hard time believing there were places in the forest full of sunlight, flowers, and even meadows.

But no flowers grew in the sunlit clearing of Muirien Grove. Cald had long since decided there was more to Saelvam's tale of Ciesandra Starshine than just imagination. The tale of star-crossed lovers might be a figment of his imagination, but the trees lived in a different time from the rest of the forest. Even the fallen leaves that lay on the ground in the grove were untouched by time. In the rest of the forest they would have long since rotted away.

In the center of the clearing, a broken tree limb lay, still retaining its thick leaves. It had been accidentally broken by the misdirected spell of a mage from the Shadow World during the battle between Eyr-min and Mmaadag Cemfrid. Cald spent hours star-ing at the only evidence of that first fight with the denizens of the Shadow World.

He heard the blundering noise he had learned to recognize as the goblins, and turned. Glisinda was walking toward him, and following her were Stog-nad and Bersmog and another ten elves.

"Plenty better places to stand than here." Bersmog peered into the shadowy depths of the grove.

At first, the atmosphere of the ancient trees had not bothered the goblins, but to the surprise of the human and the elves, the two goblins had developed a sensitivity to the forest. They would take long detours to avoid the grove and several other areas. When questioned, Stognad had said, "Plenty angry trees some places. Plenty happy trees other places. Trees in Sielwode be thinking kind."

Neither goblin had been able to elaborate on his feelings except to say that the small copses in the hills of Markazor and the woods of Mhoried were not like those of Sielwode. Cald knew the influence of the elves gave their forest an awareness. Why the goblins were more sensitive to the trees than a human raised by the elves was a puzzle to the boy.

"I've come to give you a break," Glisinda said to Cald. He was about to object, but the elf could read his expression. "And I've brought new forces to free the others. No one, not even elves, can go indefinitely without rest."

Cald nodded, admitting to the fatigue that came from waiting. The idea of walking the two miles to Reilmirid, eating a meal at a table, and hearing the news from the border filled him with new energy.

"I will remain for two days," Glisinda advised him. She pulled her bow from her shoulder, fitted an arrow to it, and took Cald's place in full sight of the clearing. Cald shouldered his bow and replaced the arrow that he had held through many weary hours of waiting. The vanes were frayed, and the end of the slender shaft was dark from the oil of his hands.

He bade Glisinda a peaceful watch and had just turned to leave when Eyrmin arrived. The prince had been off on a tour of the new defenses set up well within the depths of the forest, and Cald had not known of his return. The prince quickened his steps, turning in Cald's direction, but suddenly he paused, stopping by two of the replacement elves, Iswiel and Farmain.

"You are healed of your injuries?" He asked pleasantly.

"Indeed, Prince, and ready to take our places to protect the spirits of the dead heroes," Farmain replied.

"We are honored to be able to do so," Iswiel added.

"I once heard the people of Eisermerien are far-sighted," Eyrmin said. "I deem your talents could be best used on the high platforms of the Grove Father. I release you from your duties here."

Cald had joined Eyrmin while he was giving his orders and saw the looks of dismay on the faces of the two elves from the southern village. They seemed ready to object, but the prince's mouth had drawn into a thin line and his eyes had darkened with determination. They knew better than to argue. Cald and Eyrmin watched as the elves reluctantly headed for the village.

"If you hurry, you'll be in time for the change of watch," Eyrmin called after them. His gaze followed the two elves as they quickened their pace and broke into a trot.

"Mayhap they will not wound themselves on guard duty," Eyrmin said when they were out of sight. Cald remembered the sham limping of the two southern elves and knew the prince did not trust their courage.

Eyrmin watched them until they disappeared through the trees, then turned to speak to Malala and Ursrien. Cald had been watching the goblins, who pointedly stayed away from Iswiel and Farmain.

Stognad and Bersmog, who had arrived with Glisinda, had apparently decided to join the prince and Cald. Though the two goblins had lived in Sielwode for years and had proved themselves good fighters, when they went into battle, they were never asked to stand watch. The new arrivals distrusted them; the others appreciated their fighting prowess but put no dependence in their discipline.

"Them elves plenty good fighters, but not good watchers," Bersmog said. "Best send them away. Them not good elves."

"Why do you dislike them?" Cald asked the goblins.

"They stink," Stognad replied.

"I wouldn't let Eyrmin hear you make remarks like that," Cald warned, irritated with the goblins.

"Not elf stin—smell," Bersmog said, his narrow forehead wrinkling in worry. "Same as mages that came from underground."

"Then, you said you felt the Gorgon's influence," Cald reminded them. "Elves don't serve him."

"You smell that wrongness, you don't forget," Stognad said.

"Elves don't serve the awnsheghlien," Cald said. "I wouldn't say that to anyone else, or you may find yourselves banished from the forest." He turned away from the goblins. Life had been quiet around Reilmirid for a month, and the warriors had been bored and restless. During those rare times, the goblins often suffered from the contempt of the idle warriors. They were probably looking for a way to increase their status with the prince. Accusing elves of serving the Gorgon was not the way to do it, but Cald decided not to report them to Eyrmin.

The prince spent more than half an hour walking among the elven warriors, speaking to each, before he was ready to return to the village. Cald followed him a few paces along the trail to Reilmirid and paused, glancing back at the clearing.

"Something frets your mind?" Eyrmin asked.

"I don't trust Klasmonde Volkir," Cald said; his concern blinded him to the absurdity of this complaint. "I've waited there for a month, barely taking time to sleep, and it would be just like him to come through the portal while I'm in the village." Cald read the laughter in Eyrmin's eyes and frowned. "I've stood by that tree for a month, a boring month with nothing to do but wait. If the portal opens, and he comes through while I'm gone . . ." He noticed more laughter in Eyrmin's eyes. "Well, it wouldn't be fair," he said, thinking he sounded like a complaining four-year-old.

"And it could be years before he comes through," Eyrmin said. "Humans lack patience."

"Don't like patience plenty much," Stognad announced. "Waiting don't be getting."

"It's not the waiting. It's missing the fight," Cald said as Eyrmin led the way south.

They had not taken thirty steps when a sense of eerie foreboding descended over the grove. They had felt it before and recognized it as the atmospheric forerunner of the opening of the portal. The elves and goblins exchanged glances and turned, cautiously retracing their steps to the Muirien Grove.

"I knew it would happen," Cald said, feeling vindicated.

"Don't need patience," Bersmog surmised as he

took a good grip on his spear.

"Not missing battle." Stognad grinned at Cald as he trotted at the human's side.

"There may not be one," Cald reminded the goblins. Through the years, the portal had opened several times, but only one group of escaping halflings had been followed.

"Didn't come to pick flowers," Stognad growled, as if Cald owed them a fight and would be held accountable if the goblins were disappointed.

The prince, Cald, and the goblins arrived at the edge of the sunlit clearing. The sky was cloudless, but the sunlight dimmed as if a dark storm-front had moved across the sky. The air lost its freshness; it became stale and fetid. As a deep twilight descended, the trees developed shadowy duplicates that first appeared like a light haze, then took on form and substance. As the number of trees around the clearing doubled, some areas, already crowded with large tress, became impassable.

The elves who had never experienced the opening of the portal cried out in astonishment and dodged the developing wood. Cald watched, so mesmerized by the duplication as the two planes met, that he nearly lost his grip on his bow.

Movement to his right caught his attention, and he saw Flamarier taking shelter behind one of the shadowy trees. Cald remembered the goblin who had disappeared when the portal closed.

"Get away from the new trees," he called to the elf, but he had no time to make sure the warrior took his advice.

Ten halflings appeared between the trees, their short legs pumping as fast as they could go. They threw terrified glances over their shoulders at more than fifty mounted warriors who chased them at a distance of fewer than ten yards.

Leading the pursuers, but flanked by two warriors on each side, was a shadowy form. Darkness rode with him and emanated from the crown he wore. His horse looked as black as his spiked armor, but inside that shadow, the defenders could not be certain of the color. They knew only that Klasmonde Volkir had chanced on the portal, or he had discovered how to use the halflings to open it.

The halflings entered the clearing and dashed about frantically, seeking escape. The doubling of the trees blocked them at almost every turn, and where they found an opening, they saw a fierce elf, standing with a bow drawn.

Cald watched their faces and realized the difference between desperation and a complete loss of hope. In desperation, they had been diligently seeking; but now, believing death to be inevitable, they made a collective decision to fight with their last breath. One raised his short sword, one of the few demihumans to carry an actual weapon, and advanced on Cald.

"Get out of my way!" the human snarled at the halfling and raised his bow. He sighted on the lich who rode beneath that blackness. As the arrow fled from his bow and disappeared without noticeable effect, Cald growled. He should have known better than to waste a perfectly good arrow, but one without magic.

Eyrmin would not fault him for it, since the prince's own arrow had suffered the same fate.

Glisinda, Flamarier, and Malala had each found targets among the four mounted warriors that flanked Klasmonde Volkir. Malala's arrow had found an opening in the armor of a huge, undead, bestial creature that looked half goblin, half human, though larger than both. Her shaft was buried deep in the creature's chest, and it fell with an oath that seemed to deepen the twilight.

Eyrmin shot another arrow at the lich-lord, but it, too, disappeared. Realizing that his arrows would not stop Klasmonde, the prince dashed out of his shelter, dodging the milling halflings and mounted invaders as he sought to reach Volkir. In his hand was the legendary Starfire, dweomered in the ancient days of elven magic. It gleamed with a power that lessened the influence of the Crown of Darkness.

A new group of mounted warriors surged into the clearing, and Cald lost sight of the prince.

"No—no," he murmured, some inner wisdom warning him not to shout, though he could not keep silent his fear for Eyrmin. He shot three more arrows into the mass of milling warriors from the Shadow World, but though he heard cries from the wounded, he did not look to see what damage his shafts had done.

More than a dozen elves had left their shelters and were fighting hand to hand with warriors of the Shadow World. Twenty of the invaders had been unhorsed. Stray arrows had struck several mounts. None suffered fatal injuries, but their shrill neighs of pain and fright had caused the rest to rear and plunge.

Glisinda, Malala, and Flamarier had closed with the warriors, and through the melee, Cald caught sight of Eyrmin, in mortal combat with Klasmonde Volkir. The lich had also been unhorsed, and against that tall figure of darkness and terror, Eyrmin's armor stood out brightly. Starfire glowed like a torch, and the power of the elven sword gave light to the prince's armor. The magic runes sparkled and glowed. Light fought darkness as the glowing elf matched blows with the ruler from the dark world.

All around the clearing, elven armor that normally blended with the natural forest of Sielwode glowed brightly in the darkness that had invaded their world. Cald, wearing his own battle gear, discovered that every detail of the ground was illuminated by his own armor, and he dared not look at his sword lest it blind him.

Behind Eyrmin, an armored humanoid was jockeying for a position to strike the prince from behind. Cald felt the fear he often felt when the prince so casually risked his life, and shot an arrow in the direction of the humanoid. It struck the bestial creature and distracted it, but the Shadow World armor was too strong for the slender shaft.

Then, whipping his bow over his shoulder, he pulled his sword and started after the monster.

Two halflings, realizing he was fighting their enemies, had taken up a stance directly in front of him. Cald impatiently pushed them aside.

He strode out into the clearing and barely dodged a cantering brute of a horse ridden by a gross parody of a huge goblin. The creature swung at Cald with a morning star—a heavy, spiked metal ball on a chain. Cald ducked, nearly falling beneath the hooves of the horse as he tried to crouch and run at the same time. He tried to swerve to the left, but the halfling with the short sword ran at his side. He tripped over the demihuman and stumbled, falling into a tangle of branches from an old, fallen tree limb.

Thin, dried branches splintered and broke under his weight. One sharp twig narrowly missed his right eye and cut his cheek. He lost his grip on his sword. Cald scrambled under the meager protection of the branches as he searched beneath the leaves for his sword. His seeking fingers slid into the basket and onto hilt, but the cold handle did not belong to his weapon.

Evil surrounded him, left him gasping for air as if

he could not breathe. The cause was his proximity to the ruler from the Shadow World, he thought. Eyrmin and Klasmonde Volkir were trading blows on the other side of the clearing.

Some small part of his brain noted the sword in his hand was not his own, but he did not heed it. Nor did he listen when his mind urgently told him he had not felt that terrible evil when the lich-lord had first appeared.

The greater portion of the human youth's mind was taken up with the bloodlust that rushed into him, and he hacked at the dead branches as he strode out of the tangle. The strange weapon cut through them as if they had been blades of grass.

The huge goblin was waiting for him. The brute had been poking into the heavy, dry foliage but had not wanted to get too close, not wanting to risk a severed limb if Cald struck suddenly from the depths of his shelter. The goblin swung the morning star in defensive sweeps before him. Its small eyes were red with battle lust, and it charged forward, confident its heavy weapon would make short work of the human.

All caution had disappeared from Cald's mind. He felt as if he were invulnerable. The small portion of his mind that retained its sanity seemed to withdraw, watching with horror as he strode forward and raised the slender blade to ward off the morning star. That same small, sane part of him watched in shock as the blade bit completely through two spikes on the ball and the heavy bar, and then the goblin's hand.

The humanoid stared in surprise as blood spurted from the stump of its hand, but the pain had not reached its small brain by the time Cald leapt into the air and, with an impossible thrust, drove the blade through its armor and into its heart.

Cald looked around in time to see Flamarier fall to the axe of a mounted and heavily armored warrior. He dashed forward, leaping and swinging the blade, cutting away an armored shoulder as if the bone and heavy metal protection had been so much cheese.

His leap threw him against the rump of the horse, and he bounced off, stumbled on the ground, and fell back into the twisted branches of the fallen limb. As he put out his left hand to keep from crashing to the ground, he felt the smooth familiar guard that belonged to his own sword. He dropped the strange weapon, and the burden of evil fell away like a heavy load put down at the end of a journey. Yet the experience remained like a bruise on the mind.

The small part of his mind that had objected to his sudden power took on more force. He realized the evil he had felt was coming from the sword he had found under the fallen limb.

He stared down at it, feeling his mind shrink away from the malignancy. Even his flesh seemed burned by it. Next to his right foot was a rabbit hole, and he knelt, thrusting the blade into the ground. He kicked dirt onto it and stood, ready to fight again, but this time with a cleaner weapon.

He was just rising when Glisinda took a sharp blow to the shoulder, a gift from a ghoul's club. She drew back into the shelter of the forest.

Unable to fight, Glisinda suddenly raised her voice in the "Lirimira," the elven song of strong hearts and good purpose. Around the clearing, the other elves took up the song, and even some of the fighters gave voice to the tune that sustained them in times of darkness and evil.

Despite his furious battle with Klasmonde Volkir, the prince's voice was one of the strongest, and his armor and sword glowed the brighter. Even elven eyes turned away from the blinding glow.

Beside Cald, another elven warrior without a foe stood watching. He fingered the hilt of his sword, though it remained encased in his scabbard. Judging by his dress, he was no elf of Reilmirid, but his wholesome appearance denied any contact with the Shadow World.

Cald stared at him, wondering if the elf were friend or foe when he heard a rattling sound behind him. He turned to discover a humanoid horror—part skeleton, part rotten flesh—advancing on him. He leapt clear of the fallen limb. He could not afford to be tripped by it when his blade met the axe of his opponent. As quickly as his new foe advanced, it stopped, looked back over its shoulder, and withdrew. A hollow sound like a moan of terror escaped the fleshless mouth, and Cald glanced in the direction it looked, toward the portal.

Cald felt that same terror as a black shape approached the portal from the Shadow World. It seemed to have a discernible form, yet he sensed it was no being that he could name. When it passed a shambling ghoul, the undead creature disappeared, and the army from the Shadow World seemed as fearful of that striding darkness as the elves and halflings.

The monster was not to reach the portal. The strange wind that signaled the closing of the gate between the two planes whipped across the clearing. Limbs and branches of the trees from the Shadow World whipped in the gale. The dark leaves of the Muirien Grove remained undisturbed.

Individual fights broke off in midthrust as the invaders from the other plane were sucked toward the portal. The elves retreated to the eastern side of the clearing, untouched by the gale, yet they feared the possibility of being drawn into that other world.

The halflings threw themselves to the ground,

grasping the roots of the trees in the Muirien Grove to keep from being blown back to the plane they had fled. Most held tightly enough. A few did not.

Half the wood disappeared, the sky lightened, and the portal faded into nothingness. The only sign of battle was the trampled grass. No bodies remained.

Cald realized Flamarier's body had disappeared with those of Klasmonde's warriors.

Eyrmin sheathed his sword, and the glow emanating from blade and armor died. He looked around at the elves, his face registering relief and sadness as he seemed to tick off each face against a list in his mind.

"Flamarier?" He called when he missed the elven warrior from the eastern wood. "Kilrinis? Ursrien? Glisinda? Hialmair?"

Glisinda and Hialmair answered. Cald knew Flamarier would not. Neither did Kilrinis, the merry joker who, in times of peace, kept Reilmirid laughing. No answer came from Ursrien. Cald remembered the tale of the brave Ursrien refusing to come to the prince's aid and kill a child because his weapons were too large for the foe. Ursrien's weapons had at last met a foe for which they were undersized.

Cald wearily climbed out of the branches of the fallen limb and noticed his companion, the nobly dressed elf, had no need to step over the debris. He passed through as if it were not there. Cald felt the hair rising on the back of his neck.

"Well met, warrior," he said. The elf continued to pass through the debris as if he had not heard Cald, but the human had expected no answer.

The lie he had told eight years before had become truth. He *could* see the spirit warriors.

ANUIRE

sixteen

Lerien had been born to tales of the Crystal Palace, but his duties had kept him in Eisermerien, the elven village that guarded the southern eaves of the forest, near the swamps of Elinie. Like every elf in Sielwode, he had promised himself a journey to Siellaghriod, but elven lives, if not cut short by disease or a fatal blow in battle, lasted forever, and there always seemed to be plenty of time.

Months before, he had been one of the three warriors guarding the eaves of the wood near the swamps of Elinie when the black breath had surrounded him. As the darkness had enveloped his mind, he believed his death followed, and his deepest regret had been that he had never taken the time to visit Siellaghriod and the Crystal Palace of King

Tieslin Krienelsira.

He had regained consciousness to find himself caught in the gaze of the awnshegh Czrak, and for a full day, he had foolishly struggled against the will of his master. Now he deeply regretted putting the great Czrak to the trouble, and he was willing, even eager, to give his life for the great one who would one day rule Cerilia and possibly all of Aebrynis.

But the merciful Czrak had not asked his life, only that he be a messenger. First he would travel with Iswiel and Farmain, who had also been won to the master's cause, and then he would bring to the awnshegh all that they learned after they joined Prince Eyrmin in the western reaches of Sielwode.

Czrak had been intrigued by the tale of the spirit warriors in the grove, and enraged that his two servants had not been able to enter the clearing and retrieve the sword.

The awnshegh had received messages from his elf minions. Iswiel and Farmain had been accepted without suspicion into the forces in the western arm of the forest, but then had been sent to watch the borders. Twice they had feigned injuries so they could return to Reilmirid, but even then they had been kept out of the grove.

The elven prince's dedication to the protection of the spirits made him an unwitting enemy of the awnshegh, so the prince had to be destroyed. And how better to accomplish the deed than to feed the distrust of the king of Sielwode? If his people insisted on being the enemy of the master, then they must pay the penalty.

Lerien had the honor of serving his new master by feeding that distrust, and to that purpose he was in the Crystal Palace, on the way to an audience with King Tieslin.

A small voice kept telling Lerien Hierhielin that he

should be awed by what he saw. As he walked down the halls of the Crystal Palace in Siellaghriod, the faceted carvings reflected the light of the setting sun. Here and there a spark of green, blue, or yellow gleamed out, but red was the predominant color. Red glowed and sparkled, dancing from facet to reflecting facet as the spectrum of light from the dying day changed with the setting of the sun. Before he reached the end of the passage, the sun had dropped below the horizon, and the red spectrum died away.

As the light of day departed, the color of the walls changed. Far below the surface of the earth, the base of crystal from which the castle had been built held a single glowing candle. Its tiny light, magnified thousands of times by the facets of the cavern in which it was set, traveled through the glass, picking up power as the light danced from wall to wall.

No elf remained who had worked on the carving of the castle, and the secrets of their skills had died with them, but they had left a legacy of beauty and color behind them.

A little part of Lerien's mind was awed by the beauty around him, but the larger part roiled with anger, malice, and the will of the awnshegh, Czrak. He looked on the castle and wanted it for his master. Czrak could not live in it, and as a result, Lerien hated it.

But it would not long stand, he decided with a smile of complacency. When his master ruled Cerilia, he would order the destruction of all beauty he could not use.

Lerien turned a corner of the passage and found Brechian waiting for him. The sharp-faced elf's eyes danced with a malign excitement.

"You will tell the prince all you have learned," he said for the tenth time since Lerien had approached him with the tale Czrak had decided he should bring to court. Lerien had been in Siellaghriod only three days, but he had learned that Brechian and Prince Eyrmin were rivals for the love of the beautiful Vritienel. The king's advisor was avid to have his rival shown to be a traitor.

"It is my duty to my king to speak of what I have learned," Lerien replied. "Honor requires me to give my loyalty to the throne."

Brechian led the way into the audience chamber, where King Tieslin sat on his crystal throne, his hands gripping the glass arms. Lerien's first thought was one of disappointment. He had expected the king to be robed in finery or dressed in glittering armor, but Tieslin wore simple brown and dull green forest clothing. A spot of mud on the outside of his left boot indicated he had recently returned from the wood. Lerien paused as he read the forbidding expression, but the king motioned him forward.

"You are Lerien, in the service of Prince Eyrmin?" Tieslin asked.

"No, Sire," Lerien stopped before the throne and dropped to one knee as he bowed his head. "I am a *deserter* from the service of Prince Eyrmin." A sudden rush of murmurs circled the room, and Lerien waited until they ceased before he continued.

"I beg forgiveness of my liege for my crime, my only defense being that the love and loyalty I have for the throne would not allow me to serve one who plots against it."

King Tieslin leaned forward, glaring at Lerien. His knuckles were white against the crystal arms of the throne.

"You are saying Prince Eyrmin is a traitor?" His voice, hoarse and low with anger, was hardly more than a whisper, but it echoed around the chamber.

Lerien dropped his head and stared at the floor,

keeping his eyes averted to hide his pleasure in the king's anger.

"My sire will, I hope, understand that I can call no elf traitor, but I will not serve with humans, goblins, and halflings whose goals oppose those of our people. With the king's permission, I will tell my tale, and he can judge for himself."

Lerien's story, almost wholly a lie concocted by Czrak, was embellished by facts about Reilmirid and the activities of Eyrmin's forces, facts supplied by Iswiel and Farmain. Lerien claimed to have been restless one night when on watch near the southern border of the western arm and had overheard a conversation between Cald Dasheft and a spy in the service of the Mhor of Mhoried.

"The human boy was complaining. He wishes to return to Bevaldruor, which the humans call Shield-haven, but the messenger told him he must stay with the prince. He is a royal hostage and a pledge that the Mhor would supply an army to support Prince Eyrmin when the prince attacks Siellaghriod."

Lerien paused again as an uproar from the listeners threatened to drown the rest of his story. Like all elves, he loved tales and knew that any story twice told lost some of its drama.

"It's a lie! A false tale!" Romsien shouted, drowning out the others. He jumped to his feet, his hand on his sword hilt as he started toward Lerien. Then he seemed to remember where he was and realized his action was out of place. "I will not believe Eyrmin is disloyal to the king! It cannot be true about the human boy. He has been in Reilmirid since he was a small child."

"Since when have elves suffered the impatience of humans?" Brechian demanded. He, too, was on his feet, ready to move to the defense of the informer. "It is less than a score of years. Eyrmin would wish to be sure of his footing before he took the final step and attacked Siellaghriod."

"Cease this bickering," the king thundered. His voice echoed. Lerien noticed the other voices did not reverberate in the chamber. Tieslin, of royal blood, had power over the castle and the surrounding lands.

"If there is more to your tale, tell it," Tieslin ordered. His brow was furrowed and his face was dark as he glared down at Lerien. He seemed to understand the hesitancy in the messenger. "Speak the truth and do not fear the enmity of the court. The tale you bring is unwelcome, yet for the good of Siellaghriod and Sielwode, it is necessary that we hear it."

"There is little more, Sire, save that the messenger asked if the halflings and the goblins were still with the prince, pledging the help of their people. The human boy said they were. It is true that three halflings of amazing likeness have been in Sielwode along with two goblins for years."

"Goblins?" Jainnar rose, his eyes sparkling in rage. "Eyrmin would sink to allying himself with goblins?" In his youth, Jainnar had lived in a village at the northern eaves of Sielwode. It had been overrun and destroyed by goblins from the mountains of Mur-Kilad. In the two thousand years that had passed, he had never ceased to mourn his family. The hatred of all humanoids was a major force of his life.

Biestiel, carrier of the sword Verdos and one of the oldest living elves, rose. The murmur of outrage and dissension died away as the elves paused to hear his opinion.

"Sire, this tale is one that bears much thought," he said slowly. "If a messenger arrived at court and spoke of the prince using the magic of trans-leaping when in battle, we would never doubt it. It is a natural elven trait, and one we would all approve. If that same messenger spoke of the prince turning himself into a goblin, none would believe it because we know this is not possible."

The ancient warrior gazed about the room, his commanding gaze drawing nods from the assembly.

"I have long wondered if the descendants of Ealresid would one day wish to regain the throne, a possibility we all admit. But for Prince Eyrmin to align himself with our sworn enemies to take the throne would avail him nothing. No elf would serve a ruler who did so. Prince Eyrmin knows this. I would sooner believe he turned into a goblin than believe he is a fool. I find this tale beyond my ability to accept."

"I bow to the wisdom of General Biestiel," Romsien said. "Sire, I am another who cannot believe this tale. I point to the suggestion that the prince is supposedly allied with halflings. These small people are farmers and traders. Their chief concern is in filling their bellies. They are not warriors. I can believe many are escaping the Shadow World through a portal in the western arm. This would not in itself make them our enemies. We too would seek to escape a plane where evil has become so strong we could not fight it. Even Lerien admits the halflings do not stay in our forest. If the prince sees fit to keep three in Reilmirid to assist those who escape the horror of their world and see them on their way, I see no harm in that."

Lerien had remained kneeling before the king. The objections made to his story bothered him, but he had not thought of a way to counter them until Romsien brought up the halflings. He raised pleading eyes to the king.

"Sire," he spoke softly. "If I may speak of a new

thing being discussed in Reilmirid?"

"Speak." The king seemed relived to put an end to the bickering of his advisors.

"The halflings have the ability to open the portal to the Shadow World. Some wonder if the prince plans to use their ability to allow forces from the dark plain to invade and fight under his banner."

"Impossible!" Romsien said, still trying to defend Eyrmin, though his voice lacked conviction.

"Sire, we must urge you to take steps before the prince opens Sielwode to these fell forces," Brechian pleaded. Beside him, Cleomid, his face grim, nodded.

"My king, I would ask a question of the messenger."

"You may do so."

"Lerien, have you told us all you know of this plot?"

Lerien nodded. He dared not add more, since his master had told him only to lay the groundwork for suspicion and let the distrust of the court do the rest.

"This conversation you overheard," Cleomid asked. "Was Prince Eyrmin present?"

In the original tale, Lerien had not placed the prince on the scene, so he regretfully shook his head.

"We must learn more of this," Cleomid said slowly. "The previous tales speak of the prince's sheltering the goblins because they saved his life and that of the king's kinsman, Relcan. Honor demands he repay a debt."

"The child was said to be the sole survivor of a caravan of travelers attacked by gnolls," Romsien said. "It does not seem reasonable that the Mhor of Mhoried would risk his kinsman in such a way."

"There is much here we must doubt, yet the throne must be protected," General Biestiel said. "I disbelieve this tale of allies from the Shadow World and the assistance of humanoid armies, yet I would know more of the prince's activities. I caution vigilance and readiness."

Tieslin nodded. "You and I are of the same mind. I will say only that I have taken steps to learn what takes place in Reilmirid."

"Sire, if you delay . . ." Brechian was on his feet, but he was silenced by a wave of the king's hand.

"The time will come when we know the truth," Tieslin said, and he strode out of the chamber.

Lerien frowned, afraid he had failed in his mission and wondering what more he could have done. Czrak had set the limits on his tale, fearing that making it too dire might destroy credibility. Lerien could not place the blame for any failure on the awnshegh. His master was perfect and could not have been wrong. If the court did not accept his tale, the fault must be his.

Czrak had said the doubts would need time to work; perhaps Lerien was being impatient. He listened to the king's counselors, who had gathered together and were arguing about what should be done. Brechian, Cleomid, and Jainnar were insisting a force should be sent to Reilmirid to confront the prince before he could summon aid from his allies. Several others were listening.

Lerien decided his mission was a success.

ANUIRE

seventeen

The third night after the battle at the grove, Garienel slipped from his dwelling, moving slowly and painfully. He had fought in the grove and had taken a shallow cut on his left thigh from the blade of one of the Shadow World warriors. The wound was slight, and he would have made nothing of it, but some fell magic or poison—perhaps just the vileness of the land from which the weapon came— caused a throbbing pain and slowed the healing in what appeared to be a clean wound.

King Tieslin had sent him to discover the truth of the rumors that had caused so much distrust in Siellaghriod. He had expected to arrive and learn the truth in a matter of hours, but in that he had been disappointed. If Prince Eyrmin and his followers had heard the rumors circulating at court, they gave no indication of it.

They neither expressed dissatisfaction with the throne nor did they openly offer loyalty to the king. At first Garienel wondered at this, and then asked himself what he had expected. No elf in Siellaghriod went about spouting his loyalty; it was taken for granted. The warriors of the western arm were concerned with the invasions of the Gorgon. They spent their time guarding the wood, passing information, fighting, and in their idle hours they sang the old tales, drank wine, and laughed, as if pretending the danger did not exist.

Garienel had hoped he would be able to enter the Muirien Grove and see the spirit warriors for himself, if they really existed, but again he had been thwarted for more than a month. He had been kept on duty at the eaves of the wood and had only returned to Reilmirid two days before the battle in the grove.

Luck, not planning, had been his ally. Glisinda had taken a force into the grove, and he had been close by when she called for volunteers. When the portal opened, he had seen for himself the evils of the Shadow World.

Garienel was no longer concerned about the existence of spirit warriors. The prince protected Sielwode from a far greater danger than a few human hunters and woodcutters on the eastern fringes.

Garienel had already decided to leave Reilmirid and return to court. The king needed to know the full tale, but since he was wounded and could not travel, he would send the dove, Brissel.

He called it, giving a soft coo, and it obediently lit on his outstretched arm. The dove fluffed its feathers, more than doubling its size, and then settled them back in place. It stretched its neck to look up into the elf's face, head cocked, one bright black eye on him. With a thin thread, Garienel tied the golden ring with the white stone to the bird's leg. At least the king would know the prince was not his enemy. The reassurance would have to do until he could make the journey and give a full report.

"Alandas," he whispered to the bird, and raised his arm. The brown and buff feathers of the bird blended into the darkness as it silently took wing, flying east.

His mission accomplished, he remained standing on the highest of the limb paths, looking down at the lights of the others below him. No city or village on Aebrynis could compare with Siellaghriod and the Crystal Palace, but the tree village of Reilmirid had its own charms. The dark leaves of the sielwodes roofed and sheltered the limb paths until in places they appeared to be tunnels of greenery. The flickering lights of the torches gave life and movement to the village night, and the inhabitants, who lived in danger of the Gorgon and the lich-lord of the Shadow World, were quick to put aside their daily fears with song and congenial company.

While he stood watching for the dawn, a burst of laughter came from the bierieum, followed by the music of a flute and the strains of an old lay.

Garienel sighed. When his leg was healed, he would return to the king and tell his tale, but afterward he would come back to Reilmirid, he decided. Far from endangering the throne of Sielwode, the prince protected it. He would serve his king by helping to stand against the evils of the Shadow World.

He heard a light footstep on the walk and looked up to see Glisinda approaching. She frowned at him.

"It is too soon for you to be walking on that leg," she said.

"The wound should be healing," Garienel replied.

"I thought exercise might help."

The lorekeeper of Reilmirid shook her head. "Wounds from the weapons of the Shadow World do not mend quickly. It will be a month or more before you have strength back in that leg."

Garienel also sighed. The news he wanted to bring to the king would be delayed.

* * * * *

The dove, Brissel, was glad to stretch her wings and fly as nature had intended. She had spent more days than she could number fluttering from tree to tree, keeping the messenger in sight and waiting for his call.

Part of her small brain enjoyed the forest, foraging for food like the wild creatures. Part of it remembered the shining castle where food, water, and a protected perch awaited. Waiting too, was her master, whose mind touched hers, making her feel safe, secure, and loved.

The thing tied to her right foot belonged to her master, and she was taking it to him. She stretched her tiny mind, reached out for him, and felt his warmth from far away. The flight would be a long one, but the sun was rising, the air was clear, and the wind helped to speed her on her way.

As she flew into the sun, she was unaware of the hovering form high above her. Reaching for her master's warmth, she did not even notice the whistling of the eagle's feathers as he dived, straight and fast as an arrow.

She realized the danger as a clawed foot grabbed her, one sharp talon piercing her fluttering heart. She barely felt the fear and pain before she died.

* * * * *

King Tieslin jerked, feeling a short stab of fear, pain, and then only emptiness in that portion of his mind he shared with Brissel. The dove was dead, killed on its way to deliver Garienel's message.

For the first few minutes, his mind was caught up in the ache of losing a gentle, great-hearted companion, but then the political ramifications surfaced.

Brissel had been bringing him a message. Had the gallant little bird died as a result of her errand? Did someone kill her to keep him from receiving Garienel's message? Death had come so suddenly, she had not had time to dodge. Had she been brought down by an arrow? Was he allowing the intrigue of the court to lead him into unjustified suspicions?

Could he discount the possibility that Garienel's mission had been discovered? If Eyrmin had learned Garienel's purpose, and the prince did have designs on the throne, would he not kill the messenger rather than have his plans revealed?

Tieslin could not believe Eyrmin was a traitor, yet he could not afford to discount the possibility.

ANUIRE

eighteen

"They muchly worried, great Czrak, but they not able yet to get into grove," the gnoll said, giggling in his nervousness.

"They must get into the grove! I must have that sword!" Czrak lashed out with his left front insect leg and grabbed the hapless gnoll who had brought the news of the elves' failure. In his rage, the awnshegh bit into the neck of the humanoid and drained him of blood while his arms and legs still twitched.

Failure! Failure! Was that all he could expect of these puny humans, gnolls, and elves? He rolled in the mud, lashing out at the small trees, turning a burning glare on them and shriveling them to nothing.

An unwary otter splashed in a pool, and he grabbed it, throwing it a quarter of a mile across the swamp. Luckily, the playful little creature fell into a deeper pool and limped away, favoring a sprained joint in its right hind leg. It would never realize its good fortune.

Czrak slid through the mud, seeking any prey. His anger needed release. A small island in the mire became his target. He tore at the few saplings on the island, reducing them to splinters. He shriveled the grass. By the time his initial rage had cooled, a barren clump of charred ground was all that remained of the little island. Overhead, a pair of marsh warblers circled, unable to understand what had happened to their nest.

Czrak deliberately stayed away from the area where his new minions camped. His rage brought his bloodlust to an almost uncontrollable pitch, and he could not trust himself near them.

He had lost one force in Sielwode, and it had taken months to collect another. To destroy them in his anger would be to compound the failure. His mind rankled with the knowledge that he needed them.

As he calmed, he also considered the situation. When his gnolls captured the three elves, he had heard the story of the elven spirits in the Muirien Grove, and Prince Eyrmin's desire to protect them. The news had given him an understanding of why the grove was so closely guarded. The discovery of the court's distrust of Eyrmin had given him another weapon, and Lerien had successfully worked on that suspicion in the elven court.

Czrak slithered down into a pool of cool mud to ease the heat in his bloated body.

What had the gnoll said about the elf Relcan? A member of the royal kindred, and the prince's second-in-command? He had never seen the elven spirits, did not believe in them, and distrusted the non-Sidhelien that the prince had taken into service. Could Iswiel and Farmain make use of the elf's doubt?

Was the royal kinsman truly distrustful, or did he harbor ambitions for the prince's command? Czrak's centuries of experience had taught him there was nothing like a taste of power to build an appetite. Perhaps he could turn the dissatisfaction of this elf to his own purpose.

He'd send Iswiel and Farmain another message, if he had not terrified the stupid gnolls into fleeing the swamp. He rolled over, soaking his back in the mud, and gave a sigh. But intrigue grew slowly and took time to bear fruit. And when it did, would he get the benefit of his efforts, or would the Gorgon, with his more numerous forces, make better use of the trouble among the elves?

No, he must go for the sword himself. He would need some huge conveyance, a large wain, many horses or mules to pull it, and all his forces.

But one way or another, Deathirst would be his.

ANUIRE

nineteen

"Sire, the army is ready to march," Brechian prompted as he stood in the doorway of King Tieslin's chamber.

The first light of the morning sun turned the Crystal Palace rose and gold, a favorite time for the elves of Siellaghriod. The early morning light enhanced a beauty already breathtaking. But as Tieslin turned to face his councilor, he wondered if any light could mask or soften the malicious satisfaction on Brechian's face.

"They await you to review them as they leave, Sire," Brechian urged.

"And they cannot start soon enough for you, can they, Brechian?" Tieslin snapped as he pushed past his advisor and walked down the long passage that led to the main balcony.

Tieslin walked slowly, pacing his memories. He inspected each carving on the wall, remembering the time when, as children, he and Eyrmin had played in that wide passage. With toy swords they had battled the monsters in the carvings and fought mighty imaginary battles in crystal forests.

Tieslin and Eyrmin had grown up as friends. Now he was leading an army against his kinsman and childhood playmate.

Tieslin delayed as long as he could, but in the back of his mind he knew his loyal forces were standing in full armor with packs of rations on their backs and their weapons in their hands, waiting for him to start them on a long and tiring march. His delay would not prevent elf from fighting elf, though reasonable haste might keep Eyrmin from bringing terrible enemies into Sielwode.

He tore his gaze from the walls and stared at the floor of the wide passage as he strode forward, out into the morning air, and looked down into the courtyard.

Five hundred elves in full war panoply stood below, looking up at him. He gave a slow nod and raised his hand. On the morning air, he sketched a rune, giving them the sign of good fortune.

As General Biestiel led his forces out of Siellaghriod, Tieslin turned away in time to see the lovely elf maid, Vritienel, raise her eyes toward Brechian, who gazed at her with hopeful admiration. Brechian's face paled. The elven beauty stared at him with contempt. He might rid himself of his rival, but she would never forgive him.

When Brechian turned to his king, his eyes mutely pleading for royal intervention, his face went completely white. By Tieslin's expression, he could tell the king would never forget his part in bringing about the downfall of the prince of the western arm of Sielwode.

The king gave a slight nod of satisfaction, knowing his cousin's enemy would pay for his malice, but the feeling was fleeting. Armies might fight, and elves loyal to Tieslin and Eyrmin might die, but the true battle would be between the two contenders for the throne. He would have to face Eyrmin in battle.

He looked over the balcony to see two young elves, the proud bearers of his weapons and armor. They waited for him to give them a special sign. He waved them on, by gesture letting them know he would join them later.

Tieslin stood on the balcony and watched as his forces passed in review in the courtyard. After the last had passed through the main lemdair he turned back to the passage, heading for the exit from the Crystal Palace.

When he reached the forest, he set a fast pace, soon overtaking the bearers of his armor and the last of the line of warriors. His face was set in lines of determination, as was fitting for his people to see.

He hoped the sadness in his heart did not show in his eyes.

ANUIRE

twenty

Cald and Eyrmin walked in the forest west of the Star Mirror Stream. Since the last battle at the portal, Cald had spent all his time in the grove, eating at his post, sleeping rolled in a blanket on the ground, and bathing in one of the streams that formed the boundaries of the grove.

Eyrmin had been away from Reilmirid, walking the line of defenses, and had been present twice when the forces of the Gorgon made tentative forays into the forest. The decision to draw the perimeter back into the deep forest had provided the elves with unexpected allies.

Scenting the blood on the ground, the carrion crawlers, forest cats, and myriad other scavengers had moved in, and though they prevented few of the Gorgon's forces from attacking, they finished off Rae-sene's wounded when the invaders had withdrawn.

"They did us a service," Eyrmin said as he walked with Cald. "The second time the invaders attacked, they were so worried about what might be behind them, they exposed themselves until our archers were nearly out of arrows. We had less need for swords and spears."

"You once told me a disheartened enemy is one who fights your battle for you," Cald said as he paused and looked back across the Star Mirror Stream. He valued every moment he could spend with the prince, but he disliked leaving the clearing in the grove. When Eyrmin had discovered Cald had not returned to Reilmirid since the battle, he had insisted on dragging the youth away from the oppressive atmosphere of the strange trees.

They continued to walk up the banks of the Star Mirror Stream, trading gossip on the daily activities during the time Eyrmin had been away from the village.

"And Garienel's pet dove has disappeared," Cald said. "We expected him to be upset over it, but he pretends not to worry."

"He never admitted it was his pet," Eyrmin said. "Perhaps the little creature did not consider Garienel his particular friend. One stands with one's friends or loses them," the prince added.

Their stroll had taken them up the watercourse to the edge of Star Mirror Lake, and Cald paused, gazing at the reflection of the Star Stair on the smooth surface. He felt as if he were being held under a spell of peace and beauty. Eyrmin had continued to walk a few paces before he realized the human youth was no longer with him. He retraced a couple of steps and watched Cald.

"What bothers you?" he asked, and when Cald did not answer, he moved quickly to stand behind the young man.

The Star Stair was four miles away, but its size, height, and reflection in the water made it seem to stretch from their feet to the sky. The stone anomaly that rose out of the swamp at its base was not a single rock, but a series of huge granite columns of different heights. Glisinda had told him they stood completely alone. No small boulders or rock scree surrounded them.

The human had never been closer than the lower end of the lake. Eyrmin had always forbidden it.

"Come away," Eyrmin said, putting a hand on Cald's arm to urge him to move. "I know you've always been curious, but the tale is not for human ears, not even yours."

Cald resisted the pressure and remained where he was.

"I must know about them," he said quietly, though the voice hardly seemed to be his own. "Before it was only curiosity, but now it's something else. I don't know why, but now I must know."

"I'd need a better reason," Eyrmin said. His low tones did not quite mask his objections, but as always, he gave Cald the benefit of a doubt.

"The fortunes, whether for good or for evil, have made a lie into truth," Cald said. "During the last battle at the portal, I really did see the ghost warriors."

"You . . ."

Eyrmin's eyes had widened, and for a moment he was at a loss for words. When he fully understood the meaning of Cald's admission, his face hardened with his hatred of a lie. Then understanding and a hint of laughter lit his eyes.

"Years ago, you spoke falsely because you thought I needed your assistance," he said.

"Or because of my need to assist you," Cald replied. "Once caught in my lie, I could not find a way out of it."

"Such is the way of the false tongue," Eyrmin agreed. "It weaves a web stronger than steel and leads to mazes that have no escapes."

"But during the last battle, the lie became truth," Cald said. "I know they look to us to help them."

"I feel the same, but I don't know how," Eyrmin stared out over the water. His shoulders drooped, and he lowered his head. The change of stance was so slight no one except an elf or a human trained to see with elven attention to detail would have noticed. Still, there was a world of sadness in that movement.

"Yes, you do," Cald snapped.

Eyrmin's head jerked up, his eyes dark with angry denial.

The youth would not, could not keep silent. "They would not seek your help unless they knew you could give it. You have the answer—probably in some old tale you have forgotten—probably you have known it so long it no longer has meaning. It would have to be an old song from the most ancient of days, else the memory of their passing, the memory of a time when attire like theirs was worn by all your people . . .

"It has to do with the Star Stair and Star Mirror Lake. The sense of it is pounding in my head and through my veins. I don't ask from curiosity only. The spirits of the grove are forcing this on me."

"And why on you? Why not on me if they seek an answer?" The prince sounded uncharacteristically sharp, and with a shock, Cald saw a glint of jealousy.

"Perhaps they did," Cald said slowly, trying to think of a reason to sooth Eyrmin's ruffled feelings. This need was one he had never before been called upon to fill. Eyrmin's mind was too disciplined to give in to petty feelings. He realized no feigned excuse was necessary; in the strengths of the prince lay the true answer.

"Human minds and wills are not as strong as elven ones," he said. "It was easier for the spirits to reach me."

The prince seemed to accept the reason. His anger fled, and he turned away from Cald to stare out over the lake. His stillness seemed to affect the forest, and to any human eye but Cald's, trained in the tricks of elven sight, the prince would have blended with the wood to become nearly invisible.

Knowing Eyrmin was deep in meditation, the human waited patiently. Half an hour later, the elf moved, glanced around, and espied a fallen tree. He led the way, and they sat down on the moss-covered trunk, looking out over the lake. They sat for several minutes before the prince spoke.

"Every race knows that the forests, trees, sunlight, and dapplings of shade are loved by the elves, but it is the night we revere. It is in the night we see Tallamai."

Cald was well aware of what the prince was telling him, but the retelling seemed to satisfy the need pounding in his veins.

"When our firstborn walked the world, there were no lights in Tallamai. They saw the first glimmer you call starlight a sennight after the first immortal life of an elf was cut short in a fight with a roving dragon. There were many of the beasts then.

"More stars appeared in the sky, and we came to know that we were given two lives, the first here among the trees. When that is finished, we go to Tallamai. There we try to assist those we left behind."

"The fortunes," Cald said as Eyrmin stopped to take a breath.

"The fortunes," Eyrmin repeated the human term. "If the gods of humans really exist, they would be the fates, but in Tallamai they are the fortunes. An arrow that should have struck an enemy and is affected by the wind so it misses its target may have been deflected by the fortunes. Perhaps they can see into the future and know that the enemy may by some later deed aid us. Not all the stars are elves who have left this world. It is thought the dragons also become stars."

This thought was news to Cald, and he looked up quickly.

"They fought the elves in life, so . . ."

"The old enmity remains." Eyrmin nodded. "Many battles that begin on Aebrynis continue on other planes. We see that at the portal. So, too, they continue in the night sky.

"There was a time when the Star Mirror Lake was a primary focus of our lives. The mages of Siellaghriod would make a yearly journey to the Star Stair and climb it while the light was bright enough to see their way. During the night, they would watch the reflection of the stars in the still water, and from the patterns of the reflections, they could read omens of good and evil. Thus, many ills that would have injured our people were avoided.

"Then, as time went on, the ability of the readers of fortune dwindled. It is said some were chosen not for their ability but for their standing at court. There are many tales of that time, most muddled and full of half-truths. It could even be that the enemies of our good fortunes were distorting the patterns. The false readings of the omens led to deaths through battle and disease.

"After many deaths because of false readings, the elves of Sielwode no longer trusted the predictions and forbade the climbing of the Stair."

"But *someone* climbed it," Cald suddenly objected.

Eyrmin gave him a sharp look. "Who has been telling the forbidden tales?"

"No one . . . " Cald paused and shook his head. "It is not from an elf's telling that I speak, but something in my head." He rammed his two hands together, fingers interlinking, and made a double-handed fist to thump against his knees. Then he understood the revelation. It came partly from the strange sense of knowledge that had invaded his mind and partly from logic.

"*They* climbed the Star Stair," he said suddenly. He looked up to see the prince's face frozen in anger and knew he had to find a way to explain his conclusion.

"The Stair serves, or has served, another purpose besides platforms for the readers of fortune," he said. "Else your people would not be forbidden it. Those who are now the spirit warriors climbed the Stair, or were near it, and something terrible happened, something that drove them away. They took shelter in the thick wood just to the south."

"No old song tells of this," Eyrmin said. "You are making up a tale. We forbid imaginings about the Stair."

"It isn't mine," Cald said quietly, "Or if it is, it's not a tale, but conjecture. For elven spirits to be trapped on Cerilia, there had to be a terrible happening. . . ."

Eyrmin stared at the young human, searching his face. As always, the prince's trust in the boy won out, and he reluctantly joined in the conjecture.

"And one that had to involve forces outside the plane of Aebrynis," Eyrmin added, continuing the logical progression Cald had begun.

"It seems more reasonable to assume the happening involved the Star Stair than some other magical place, since it is so close," Cald said.

"You have divined the truth, I think," Eyrmin said softly. "I have taught you the elven skills of seeing detail, but the longsight ability is born in us. When you stand on the high platform of the Grove Father, you, as a human, are unable to see any details of the Star Stair." Eyrmin was stating another fact known to both of them.

"If I had longsight, what would I see?" Cald asked.

"The lights of our dead rising up from the swamp, climbing to Tallamai," Eyrmin said quietly. "That is why we are forbidden the area now that no one reads the omens. We must not impede their progress."

They sat in silence, staring up the length of the lake. Eyrmin's explanation had not satisfied the need in Cald. The elf seemed to understand the failure without being told. He waited with the patience of his people while Cald picked up a stick and jabbed it in the ground. He dislodged a small clump of earth. An ant, panicked at the sudden destruction of its part of the world, ran halfway up the stick before turning and racing down again.

Down . . . up and down. Cald looked up. "Stairs allow travel in both directions," he said. "What goes up might come down."

Eyrmin had also watched the ant and nodded as if Cald's remark had been a casual thought, unrelated to the subject, and accepted as such.

Suddenly the prince jerked. "Lightfall!" he announced, almost shouting his idea, it struck him with such force.

Cald felt the hair rise on the back of his neck, and goose bumps of awe rose on his arms as he felt the rightness of the prince's discovery.

If the old lay held the answer, he could understand why the spirits of the grove looked to the living elves and even to him so hopefully. Every elf knew the old lay; it was sung to every elven child to put him or her to sleep with its soothing melody and repeated phrases. It had long been considered a nonsense song about the sun:

Up goes the light.
Down comes the light.
Call illberin,
Call illberin.

Cald sang the first two lines and the refrain from the old tune. "I always thought the light in the song meant the sun, but the words are backward. You think of the sunlight coming up and going down, not going up and coming down. It would make more sense if it meant the lights on the stair."

When need and deed
Have not agreed,
Call illberin, •
Call illberin.

Eyrmin sang the second part of the song and lifted an empty hand, palm up, as if offering Cald the gift of the last verse.

"Together—you taught it to me," Cald said wanting to share the secret, and they both sang:

Then they who stay
Will find their way.
Call illberin,
Call illberin.

"It's so simple. Why have we not thought of it before?" Cald asked.

"Perhaps the spirits laid the burden of finding it on you because you learned the song in Reilmirid," Eyrmin said.

"You, and the rest, learned it in Siellaghriod, or in other parts of the Sielwode," Cald added. "No elf child has ever been born here in the western arm?" He knew the answer. Reilmirid was considered a village for warriors. There were no settlements in the western arm of Sielwode. The elven infants were cared for deep in the forest, either in the capital or in one of the villages close by.

Eyrmin leapt to his feet, his eyes ordering Cald to waste no time.

"Now that we know the secret, we must free the spirits," he said. "If they can leave this place, perhaps the danger of the portal would be destroyed."

Two hundred yards to the east, they waded across the shallow stream that flowed from the lake and entered the Muirien Grove. After nearly an hour's wandering through the grove, they found two spirit warriors sitting beneath a tree, as if resting. When they saw the prince and the human gazing at them, they stood, nodding and smiling.

They spoke between themselves, but neither Cald nor Eyrmin could hear them.

"I'll try just the word," Eyrmin said. "Illberin."

Nothing happened. The ghost warriors continued to nod.

"You try it," Eyrmin said, his eyes dark with his sense of failure. "They looked to you for the answer."

Cald spoke the word, again without result. He tried singing the song. Eyrmin joined him in the song, but the spirits could not hear them.

"I thought it was the answer," Cald said as they walked away to leave the ghost warriors in peace. "It felt so right.

"You were not alone," Eyrmin said. "I still believe we *are* right. We have the weapon to cut their bounds; there must be a secret to using it."

ANUIRE

twenty-one

In the clear night, the stars of Tallamai twinkled
down on Sielwode. The air was cooling after a warm
day, and many of the elves of Reilmirid had left the
village. They gathered in a clearing half a mile to the
south of the sielwode grove.

Tall, slender poles with torch heads of tightly
woven range grass gave light and movement to the
shadows as the gentle breeze caused the flames to
flicker. The elves could have done without the
torches, but the moving shadows added mystery to
the evening.

The elves had ranged themselves in eight groups,
each numbering between eight and a score. The size
of each group shrank and grew as the elves moved
about, listening to and joining in different songs and

conversations.

In most of the groups, laughter was frequent, but in one, the listeners were silent, their brows furrowed. Iswiel and Malala were engaged in an argument. The elf from the southern village of Eisermerien, near the swamp of Elinie, was complaining about not being allowed into the Muirien Grove. He was hinting the prince wanted to keep the elves from learning the elven ghost warriors did not exist.

"Prince Eyrmin has seen them; that's proof enough," Malala said, her eyes flashing.

"So we hear," Farmain said. "You've spent months on duty near the clearing where the portal opens, and you've never seen the spirits?"

Iswiel firmed his lips to hide his smile as the female warrior shifted, uncomfortable because she had to admit she had not. Iswiel had deliberately chosen Malala because she was a dedicated follower of Prince Eyrmin, with unshakable faith in her leader, but she lacked verbal skills. In her determination to convince him, she would argue for hours on end, scoring few points. He in his turn would be able to say everything necessary to sow doubt and distrust among the prince's followers. The argument continued for a few minutes, and when Iswiel lost his train of thought, his comrade Farmain, who had been listening, joined the conversation.

"The only other person to claim the distinction is the human, Cald Dasheft," he observed. "I do not trust any human."

"Cald Dasheft has the honor of an elf." Hialmair, who had just joined the group, took immediate issue with the remark. On the day the human child had been found in the forest, Hialmair had risked the anger of the prince in refusing to kill the child. Since that time, he had considered it his responsibility to assist in the youth's education and training. Farmain leaned back to gaze up at the warrior.

"Is this human of the blood also?"

The suggestion startled Hialmair, and he frowned, staring down at Farmain for a moment before shaking his head.

"It's not possible," he said. "He was a survivor from a settler's caravan. I saw the dead."

"If he had been a member of the Mhor's royal kindred, he would have been sought with diligence," Malala added.

"Unless he was meant to be where he was," Iswiel suggested. "In Siellaghriod, they are saying he is a hostage to a promise. Mhor of Bevaldruor is to aid Eyrmin when he marches on the capital to take the throne.

Malala was on her feet in an instant, her blade in her hand. "You lie!" She advanced on Iswiel, who hastily scampered backward. He refused to stand to meet her challenge. The female warrior was too adept with her blade for him to face and live. Instead, Farmain rose, laying a gentle hand on her shoulder.

"Of course it is a lie," he said soothingly. "But it has been suggested in the Crystal Palace. They are saying why else would Prince Eyrmin give such care to a human child?"

"What else are they saying?"

The others turned to see Glisinda, the lorekeeper-warrior who was a trusted councilor to the prince. Her voice had been quiet but commanding. "What other doubts fill the minds of the inhabitants of the Crystal Palace?"

"Some say quite a lot," said the elf Garienel, who was known to have joined them after living at court for many years. The reason he had given for journeying from the comfort of the Crystal Palace to the rigors and dangers of the western arm was the need to use his arm in defense of his land. "But those who misunderstood and doubted the prince will soon learn of their error. . . ."

"Enough of this!" Iswiel cried out. "My questions have taken the joy from the celebration, and I regret it. Let us sing together so the fortunes of Tallamai will know we are a united group. Let them hear we revere those who have gone before us and seek to keep their land pure."

He raised his voice in the "Lay of Sielwode," a song that described the virtues of the forest. Once the others joined in, however, he drew back with Farmain.

"You were doing well; why did you stop?" Farmain asked, speaking too quietly for the singers to hear.

"We could not allow this Garienel to finish his say," Iswiel said. "He has a quick wit and faster tongue. He might have undone all we set out to do."

"We made a good beginning," Farmain said, his eyes on a group of elves who were listening to Mimilde, one of the newer arrivals. He stood on the fringe of the singers. Judging by his gestures, he was telling the tale of the argument to others, and the faces of the listeners showed they were taking in the doubts with the story.

None of the elves who heard the tale of the argument were surprised when Prince Eyrmin called Garienel to his dwelling the next morning. Their talk lasted for more than an hour. No one knew what passed between them; none of Eyrmin's counselors had been present, not even the human youth who shared the prince's dwelling. Iswiel and Farmain exchanged dissatisfied glances when the prince and the elf from the Crystal Palace reappeared. They both walked with light steps, their brows uncreased by anger or worry.

Still, the two elven minions of the awnshegh Czrak soon learned the seeds they planted were bearing fruit. Relcan, the royal kinsman who stood second in leadership to the prince, had been away from the village when the rumors started. On his return, he listened avidly to every word spoken against Eyrmin. His eyes flashed when he heard the suspicion that Cald Dasheft was secretly a hostage to the promise of Benjin Mhoried, ruler of lands not far west of Sielwode. He chewed on the information for days, walking about the village during the day, his face twisted with dark thoughts. At night he refilled his wine cup with unusual frequency.

Three days later, the portal opened again, this time to forty-one halflings fleeing the Shadow World. They were not pursued, and the portal closed behind them.

When the door to the Shadow World had first opened, the elves had looked on the escaping half-lings with suspicion, but they soon learned the little people bore them no ill will and had no designs on the forest. Most of the inhabitants of Reilmirid saw the residue of terror on the faces of the halfling refugees. As time passed, they rejoiced over every escape from a world turned evil through no fault of the refugees.

That evening, a gentle breeze blew beneath a star-lit sky, and most of the inhabitants of the elven tree village had gathered in the southern clearing. Any opportunity to celebrate was a welcome break from the tensions of guarding against and fighting their enemies, and the arrival of the refugees made a good excuse.

The halflings were resting in the shallow caves on the eastern bank of the Moon Stream. At full dark, the elves gathered in the southern meadow. Some were still lighting the torches when Bigtoe, Littletoe, and Fleetfoot Rootfinder arrived. The halfling triplets, who were so alike in their elven clothing they could have been a division of one being, marched up to Eyrmin. They gave a formal, perfectly synchronized bow that caused the elves to smile.

"The new arrivals are resting," Bigtoe said.

"Getting a well-deserved rest," added Littletoe.

"All with wet feet," Fleetfoot said, putting in his customary jarring note.

The elves had brought food and wine to the meadow. In a burst of goodwill, they had even invited Bersmog and Stognad to bring their cooked meat, though the goblins had been told to cook it earlier in the evening.

The celebrants took turns singing and dancing for the entertainment of the diners, and the evening was well advanced when the three halflings, merry on elven wine, decided to take part in the leaping and cavorting.

Cald, who had been ordered to relinquish command of the Muirien Grove guard for the evening, was sitting by the prince. He doubled over with laughter at the antics of the halflings, whose short legs and heavy bodies made them awkward. They tumbled in a heap and rolled on the ground in a tangle of arms and legs.

Relcan, who had been giving his attention to the wineskin and ignoring the food, suddenly threw his cup across the clearing, narrowly missing Bigtoe Rootfinder.

"Are we now to have even our songs and dances tainted by the short-lived, short-bodied vermin who invade our land?" the royal kinsman demanded in a wine-slurred voice.

The singing and dancing stopped in midnote and midstep, as if the merriment had been slashed with a sword.

The only movement was Eyrmin's as he carefully set his flagon on the ground and rose. His face was a mask of implacable anger.

"Those who are guests at my feast are not insulted," he said quietly, his voice echoing in the sudden silence.

"And who next will be guest at the feasts of Reilmirid?" Relcan asked as he also rose to his feet. His voice was clearer, and despite the wine, he stood rock solid in his contempt, though his hands jerked from the handle of his knife to the hilt of his sword.

"Will we next find Klasmonde Volkir feasting on our land and our people? Is that not why these three halflings are here, to open the portal for him? Are these . . ."

"Untrue!" Bigtoe objected

"Surely untrue," added Littletoe.

"Must be sour wine," Fleetfoot observed.

Around the circle, voices muttered their objections, but Eyrmin raised his hand for silence.

"Let him finish," the prince said, his voice cold. "Let him ask his questions and spew his poison in the sight of the fortunes of Tallamai, who know all. They will judge him. We will have these suspicions discussed in the open and over with, but know, Relcan, that speak or not, by moonset you will be gone from Reilmirid. I am done with you and your dark thoughts."

Even in the torchlight, the paling of Relcan's face was evident, as was the flush of rage that darkened it afterward.

"Then I will say and will say all! You are harboring these non-Sidhelien not for any honorable purpose, but as liaisons between your fell plans and your evil allies! The human hostage from Mhoried . . ."

"That tale is false and even you know it," Hialmair shouted.

"Silence! Let him finish," Eyrmin ordered, but the sturdy elf warrior jumped to his feet.

"Forgive me, my prince, but I will not be silent in the face of his lies against you! And there are many here who know the truth of that human massacre."

"Which proves nothing," shouted Iswiel, also gaining his feet. "It is possible that the massacre of the humans in the caravan was a ploy of the Mhor in order to get the child into the wood. Humans are not even capable of honor and loyalty to their own. They could have killed many of their own to achieve their aims."

"And I myself have seen this *human* meet with messengers traveling from Markazor to Mhoried," Relcan shouted. "And since the prince was present at the meeting, he cannot deny it."

Cald and Eyrmin exchanged puzzled looks, since at that moment neither could remember a circumstance that could have been the foundation for the remark.

"Does he speak of the time I taught that family to braid the grass for fire logs?" Cald asked the prince.

"Have you spoken with any other travelers?" Eyrmin asked, and Cald shook his head.

"See, they must confer to cover their evil acts with a tale!" Relcan shouted.

Looking around the circle at the elven faces, some full of doubt, others closed, having decided on the truth or falsity of the accusations, Cald realized that his and Eyrmin's frowns and their sudden conference had worked against them.

"You came here to aid in the defense of the elven spirits in the grove, but have you seen any?" Relcan demanded of the warriors sitting in the circle. "You were drawn by a ruse, and if you stay, it will be to betray your king and Sielwode to the very races that are your enemies."

Relcan looked as if he would say more, but Eyrmin pointed a finger that seemed to freeze the other elf in midbreath.

"Enough!" the prince shouted. Then he lowered his voice. "You have had your say. The king knows I am loyal to his aims, but if you doubt it, begone from here now, and all those who choose may go with you. I will have none in Reilmirid who have not the heart for defending the helpless, assisting those who flee evil, or standing against the vile forces that try to invade this land. If you seek the safety of the court and Siellaghriod, then go. And take your tales, for the truth is known there and your lies will fall on deaf ears."

With a face still set in anger, Eyrmin strode across the clearing, back toward the village. He looked neither right nor left. Cald followed, and knew that several others fell in behind them, but he decided it would be unseemly to turn and count those who were leaving the clearing. Out of the corner of his eye, he saw the halfling triplets moving east, toward the caves by the Moon Stream, and he heard the heavy shuffling of the goblins as they followed Cald.

Still, there were too many elves still sitting on the ground, their faces thoughtful or angry.

By the time they reached Eyrmin's dwelling, Cald had made a decision. Speaking of it was the hardest thing he had ever done.

"I will leave," he said. "I will take Bersmog and Stognad with me. We can go south into Elinie, where they will be safe from the wrath of the goblin chief. We'll travel with the halflings. . . ."

"No!" Eyrmin shouted at him. "You . . . you and the goblins and the halflings have proven *your* loyalty. I will not allow you to be driven out of your home.

You—you, Bersmog, Stognad, Bigtoe, Littletoe, and Fleetfoot—are valued inhabitants of Reilmirid." The prince paced the room twice before he continued. "Each of you, in your way, contributes as much to the welfare of Sielwode as Relcan, and does less to destroy the unity of our people."

"But we are the reason for the distrust," Cald argued.

"No, only the channel. Distrust and dissension are malevolent springs that seek any available course to flood and pollute. If you were not here, Relcan would find something else, nurture it into full growth, and the result would be the same. I have often believed he had an ambition for my place, and once he got it, he would eye the throne itself."

"But if he takes his tale to the king, he could cause trouble," Cald argued, desperately hoping to be talked out of leaving the forest, but still believing he should go.

"The damage has already been done, and the repairs made; there is trust between my cousin and myself," Eyrmin said. "It was Tieslin himself who chose to seek the truth, and by now he has his answer. He will not be swayed by Relcan."

"But Relcan can still cause trouble," Cald said.

Still, he allowed himself to be ordered to his bed, to spend the night in the village.

At sunrise, he learned his last words to Eyrmin had been prophetic. Two thirds of the warriors who had come to defend the Muirien Grove and the western arm of Sielwode had left in the night.

A scant hundred warriors were left to hold back the Gorgon's forces and the attacks at the portal.

ANUIRE

TWENTY-TWO

Czrak squirmed within the large wain, silently
cursing his minions, blaming them because he felt
cramped. The skin on his sluglike body was dry, and
relieving his misery drew on the power he had been
hoarding. He would need all his resources when he
reached the western arm of Sielwode.

Rage boiled inside his bloated body, rage at having to leave the swamp. He was sure he was endangering himself by coming out of hiding. He might be
found by other awnsheghlien more powerful than
he. In addition, he was suffering the discomfort of
the dry air and having to stay inside the wagon.

Still, he controlled himself. Taking his bad mood
out on his army of a hundred fifty humans, four
hundred goblins and orogs, and twice as many

gnolls would reduce his forces, all of which might be needed when he reached the wood.

The cart came to a halt. Czrak sighed with relief. The jolting irritated his eight exoskeletal legs, which were cramped from being trapped within the bed of the wagon. Still, his frustration rose. Each stop delayed the journey, lengthening the time he must stay confined and hidden. He was restless, and raised a pair of glowing red eyes as Demloke Winsin lifted the rear flap and looked in.

"Master, the end of the journey is at hand. The lead wagon is even now at the bank of the stream."

"We have not yet been discovered?" Czrak cursed himself for the needless question. If the elves of Siel-wode had learned the secret of the caravan, he would have heard their whistled alarm as it traveled through the forest.

The awnshegh had laid his plans carefully before starting his own assault for the possession of Deathirst. He had sent his forces more than a hundred miles to the south with orders to bring back large trading cara-vans. This time, obeying his orders to the letter, Dem-loke Winsin had completed the mission, though it had taken many months. He had returned with sixty large freight wagons, canvas coverings, and enough sturdy horses, oxen, and mules to pull heavy loads.

Czrak and the gnolls, goblins, and orogs rode inside, hidden by the canvas coverings. The humans, wearing homespun over their armor, walked in plain sight, leading the animals. The sharp eyes of the elves, and any other travelers they encountered, saw only a caravan of settlers on the plains of Markazor.

The spring rains had left the ground soft, and Czrak had fumed as the large, heavily laden wains mired down in the mud. Twice they had waited for darkness so the humanoids could leave the wagons and help push the vehicles onto firm ground, but they had completed the first part of the journey without being discovered.

The elves in the western arm of Sielwode kept an eye on the plain near the eaves of the wood, but seldom bothered travelers who stayed out of the forest. The elves even expected the caravans to angle close to the outlying trees, since the only place the Star Mirror Stream could be forded by wagons was less than half a mile from the wood.

"How long before nightfall?" he asked.

"The sun is even now on the horizon, Great One," Demloke replied. "An hour. Two at most. We are even favored by the weather. The sky is clouding over and will hide the moon this night."

Impatience pulsed in his veins, and the discomfort of his long journey seemed to double as Czrak waited for full darkness. His first failures had made him cautious. He ordered Demloke to bring his wagon up close to the stream, turning it so he could slide out into the water. With luck, any elf watching would think they were planning to fill water kegs. Before they crossed the stream? He decided not to worry about that one little lapse in logic.

At full dark, he gratefully slid out of the wagon and into the water, discovering the one complication he had not considered. The recent rains had swelled the stream. He could move easily on the water, but after many years in the swamps, he had not given a thought to the current. His progress up the Star Mirror Stream would be difficult. Before they could travel a mile into the forest, the elves would be alerted.

* * * * *

Cald, back on guard duty in the Muirien Grove, had learned not to spend all his time standing. He was sitting at the base of the tree that for months had been his station. He was fighting to keep his eyes open when he heard the whistled alarm.

"Intruders following the Star Mirror Stream . . . humans, goblins, gnolls, orogs . . ." They were accompanied by some creature the watchers could not identify.

Cald jumped to his feet but stayed at his station. Around him he could hear the slight movements of the elves who also stood guard. They strung their bows and loosened their swords in their scabbards.

"Are we needed?" Cald whistled back. He waited while questions and answers passed through the forest.

"Hundreds of invaders . . . Come."

Hialmair stepped out of the shadows, a dark object separating himself from the black column of a tree. Cald, with his human eyes, would not have recognized the elf if he had not known his position.

"Will you take the lead?" the human youth asked. Elven eyes were better at finding a path in the darkness, and speed was necessary if they were to hold the invaders at the edge of the forest.

But could they hold them? Cald wondered. Since the defection of two thirds of their forces, the defenders of the western arm numbered just over a hundred, and a third of them were patrolling different sections of the wood.

Cald followed Hialmair as the elf led at a run. They leapt across the stepping-stones in the Moon Stream and paralleled its course, racing along the eastern bank.

From the west came the calls of a great cat of Sielwode, and from closer, the deep rumble of a carrion crawler. The beasts of the wood were anticipating a feast when the battle was over.

For five miles, Cald followed the leading elf until they came to a bend in the stream and another set of stepping-stones, hidden by the high water.

Hialmair leapt from stone to stone, relying on his

memory. Cald, traveling partially by memory and his ability to see the faint splashing, followed. Directly to the south, they heard the sounds of fighting. They traveled less than a mile when they came upon Eyrmin and the thirty elves who had been in Reilmirid when the alarm sounded through the forest.

The prince was sheltered behind a large tree, listening to the report of two elves. One was being bandaged by Glisinda.

"I don't know what it is," Saelvam said as Cald arrived. "Huge, bloated, but with a face that is a parody of humanoid . . ."

"It has some terrible power," the other said.

"And stink like the Gorgon," Stognad, the goblin, said as he trotted up. He saw Cald. "Told you about that stink, but you didn't listen."

"How could it be the Gorgon?" Eyrmin asked, ready to listen to the goblins at last. "The tales say he cannot leave his mountains, and if he did he would come from the north, not the west."

"Like Gorgon but not him," Stognad said. "Me plenty good remember stink of power from awnshegh."

"Another awnshegh?" Eyrmin's eyes sparkled in the light of his sword, Starfire, which had been lightly glowing. The blade detected the presence of evil.

"It's traveling up the stream," Saelvam said as Glisinda finished his bandage. "From what we could see of it, a huge human"— his eyes flickered as he noticed Cald—"humanoid face, a sluglike body. I think I saw two humanoid arms and eight large, hairy legs like those of a water spider. A creature out of nightmares."

A dozen elves came in sight, sprinting from tree to tree as they retreated. Behind them, a party of goblins appeared, and the prince waved the wounded elf back deeper into the woods. The rest took up positions and waited. The goblins were in bow range, but they, too, ducked from tree to tree.

Eyrmin forsook the shelter of the tree to crouch behind a thick bush, and Cald joined him.

"They're very cautious," Cald said as he waited by the prince for a target.

"Saelvam and Cloasien have accounted for nearly a score." Eyrmin said. "I'm short six arrows, but they all found targets."

"Are they protected by any sort of magic?" Cald asked, thinking of the deflected arrows in the wood when they had first faced this new awnshegh's forces. He and the elves had thought that first fifty to be the minions of the Gorgon. Looking back, he remembered the warnings of Bersmog and Stognad. Neither Cald nor Eyrmin had listened to the goblins, but if they had understood, what could they have done about it?

Cald spotted a creature sticking its head out from behind a tree, but before he could be sure of his aim, the creature ducked back. It peered out twice more, and by then, Cald had recognized the pattern of its movement. The fifth time it stuck its head out, Cald's arrow caught the humanoid in the eye.

Eyrmin struck down two, but part of his attention was on the wood around them and farther to the south. He lowered his bow, giving a whistling call for retreat.

"They're flanking us," he told Cald, who lacked the sharp hearing of the elves.

By Eyrmin's orders, they moved back, spreading out through the wood on both sides of the stream. Every arrow brought down a goblin, gnoll, or human, but even if every shaft found a target, scores of invaders would remain in the woods after the defenders' quivers were empty.

The elves harried the front ranks, slipping from

tree to tree, planting their arrows deep in the thick bodies of the goblins, who were in the vanguard. Every time they killed one, two others took its place.

Eyrmin whistled to Cald, ordering him to drop out of the line and move north to discover how far the advancing forces were spread. Cald reluctantly obeyed, knowing the elven prince was trying to keep him out of danger. Still, they did need to know, so he backed away from the retreating line and hurried off. He had traveled only a few steps when he was joined by Bersmog. Over the goblin's shoulder was draped a ragged fur, badly tanned and smelly. The fresh blood that stained one side indicated its wearer no longer needed it.

"Maybe Gapemouth Clan think me one of them and not shoot," Bersmog explained.

"And maybe the elves will think so, too," Cald warned. "Their arrows are surer than any others."

Bersmog acknowledged the flaw in his thinking and pulled off the cloak. Using a leather thong from his belt pouch, he tied it to his belt and pushed it behind him, out of his way. It bumped along behind him as he trotted at the human youth's side.

A quarter of a mile to the north, they discovered an elf who had heard the alarm and had been on the way to join Eyrmin when he was ambushed by goblins. The elf was on the ground with a wound from a thrown spear, desperately trying to hold off the enemy soldiers.

Cald joined him, but Bersmog faded into the night.

"I knew those goblins would turn traitor," Wiermar said as he clamped his hand to his bleeding leg and stared into the night.

"And do you believe the same about me?" Cald snapped, his tension built to the point where he could no longer keep quiet. Part of his irritation was caused by the fear that Wiermar might be right. He was watching the wood when a shout from behind the goblins startled the defenders as well as the attackers.

"Hoi—you scum in plenty trouble!" They heard the voice of a goblin, though only Cald recognized it as Bersmog. He appeared briefly between two trees, now wearing the captured fur. "The master, he think you desert, you so far from stream."

"You scum, yourself," a gruff voice called back in the goblin tongue. "We told to scout out to side."

"Scout where you please, but I go back plenty quick. He not think me a deserter," Bersmog said, and turned as if he were heading for the stream.

"Aagh—could have killed them elveses, too," the second voice growled as he trotted off after Bersmog. His companions followed him. Cald saw the invaders run past Bersmog in their hurry to join the rest of their forces.

"We should get out of here while we can," Cald said, helping Wiermar to his feet. They had only gone a few feet when Bersmog appeared out of the shadows.

"Me help elf, you be ready to use bow," he said, taking the weight of the wounded elf from Cald.

"You owe Bersmog an apology," Cald told Wiermar, who limped along with the help of the goblin.

Bersmog needed no explanation for the remark. He gave a low chuckle that sounded, to those unfamiliar with goblins, like a rumbling growl.

"You think me go with them and join Gapemouth Clan? Your brains leaking out your leg?" he asked with a grin.

Cald led the way, angling toward Reilmirid rather than toward the stream. Eyrmin was harrying the invaders in a delaying action, hoping to pick off as many of them as possible. Cald knew the prince would not be able to stop the awnshegh from reaching the grove.

ANUIRE

twenty-three

When they neared Reilmirid, Cald left Bersmog to
make sure Wiermar reached the village. He hurried
through the wood, listening to the receding sounds
of the wounded elf furiously objecting to his loss of
dignity. The goblin, tired of the elf's slow, limping
progress, had hefted him bodily and draped him
across his shoulders.

Wiermar will carry his resentment for a long time,
but he will at least live to complain, Cald thought as
he saw a large forest cat stalking through a clump of
undergrowth. The animals had heard battle and
were gathering, waiting their chance. He froze until
the cat was out of sight, then hurried to where he
heard the loudest noises.

Prince Eyrmin would be in the thick of the battle.

Cald was not quite right. The battle was taking place between the forward ranks of goblins and the retreating elves. Eyrmin was nowhere to be seen. When Cald met Glisinda, she wore a worried frown.

Cald took time to shoot three arrows in rapid succession, catching one humanoid in the knee and another in the upper arm. His third arrow missed its target. With a silent gesture, he directed Glisinda to move farther upstream. He noticed the gleam from the lorekeeper's scabbard. Her own sword was tucked, sheathless, in her belt.

"You're carrying Starfire," he said, stating the obvious. "The prince?"

"He left it with me," she said, frowning. "I've no knowledge of his intentions." By her look, he knew she suspected more than she was willing to tell, and so did Cald. Eyrmin had stayed behind, likely near the stream.

They needed to know what sort of creature they faced and whether or not the awnshegh was vulnerable to their weapons. Dread caused the hair on the back of Cald's neck to rise. If Eyrmin faced the monster alone, he could be facing his death. That would not deter the prince, and Cald knew it.

Cald turned away, as if taking a position in the line. As soon as he slipped from Glisinda's sight, however, he worked his way west, crouching in a clump of bushes when the first of the goblins passed.

Slipping from tree to bush and staying in the shadows, he used the Embrace of Sielwode to blend in with the trees when no other shelter offered itself. He had worked his way more than half a mile downstream when the call of a startled night bird chirped above him. The faintest up-scaling of the call alerted him to the elven presence.

Cald scaled the tree as silently as an elf, though with less skill. When he reached the first large limb, he found the prince glaring at him.

"Humans are not known for wisdom," Eyrmin hissed at him.

"Where is the wisdom in a prince who risks his leadership on a foolhardy mission?" Cald asked, incensed at Eyrmin for endangering himself. The prince was the heart of his warriors, and as such, his life was the most precious of all.

He knew Eyrmin had been relying on the darkness to help protect him, but the clouds were breaking up. Below them, the moonlight flooded down on the stream for a few seconds before the clouds hid the light again.

Neither Eyrmin nor Cald was concerned about being overheard. The goblins had passed. The gnolls and humans treading below on broken limbs and twigs muttered to themselves as they pushed through the heavy undergrowth near the banks of the Star Mirror Stream.

Sounds of splashing and occasional roars of frustration approached slowly. The awnshegh was working its way upstream. It barked orders with every splash, and as it drew nearer, the humans and gnolls accompanying it ran back and forth like ants.

Minutes later, the monster came into view, and Cald felt his gorge rise as he looked on the bloated creature. Awnshegh were usually human, though a few were members of the humanoid or demihuman races. This creature was none of these.

As the thing crept upstream, it passed through a patch of moonlight. The bloated humanlike face seemed three times its original size, and the mouth was wider in proportion than was natural. The neck disappeared into the body of a giant slug that was at least twelve feet long. Two human arms extended out of the bloated shape, not far below the head. Behind them, eight hairy exoskeletal legs worked to move the monstrous body upstream.

"Can it be killed?" Eyrmin murmured. "If we can destroy it here, its minions won't continue. Remember the spells thrown by its first mages. Keep to this spot." He jumped, grabbed a second, higher limb and ran along it until he reached another tree. Cald stayed where he was. While he waited, he pulled a thin, strong, elven rope from his belt pouch and tied one end to the limb, preparing for a hurried escape. Eyrmin did the same in another tree.

When the prince gave a birdcall, they both shot three arrows in rapid succession. All six hit their target, and for several seconds, the awnshegh screamed and thrashed in the pain. Cald thought he might be able to lodge another arrow in the bloated body, and it was nearly his undoing.

The awnshegh was still thrashing, but he recognized the direction of the last arrow and turned a glare on the tree. The great trunk withered, and Cald caught the rope, swinging down just in time to avoid the spell. He had not, however, been fast enough to reach the ground before the rope above him gave way. He fell the last fifteen feet. Luckily, his fall was broken by a pair of gnolls, whose attention had been on the awnshegh.

"Yi-i-i!" Eyrmin gave a call, drawing attention to himself as Cald picked himself up and raced for the nearest cover. Eyrmin shot another arrow, but it went wide as Czrak turned his withering attention toward the prince's perch. Eyrmin swung away on the rope, arcing up as the spell destroyed the anchor. He went sailing out into the darkness beyond Cald's sight.

From the area where he disappeared came the roars of a forest cat—two cats—and Cald, fearing for the life of his prince, dashed in that direction. A gnoll popped out from behind a tree, ready to do battle, but the human knocked aside the spear with a swing of his bow and ran the short, squat humanoid through with his sword. He stumbled as the blade caught in the body, and he nearly fell before the momentum of his stride pulled the weapon free.

He raced around two more trees and nearly ran into Eyrmin. The prince grabbed his arm and whirled him around, retracing Cald's path. When a party of gnolls rose up out of the undergrowth to stop them, Eyrmin suddenly changed direction, sprinting around the bole of a tree.

His sudden and surprising turn came just in time. Cald felt the hot breath of a cat just behind him. The forest hunters had lost their elven prey, but they found five times as much gnoll flesh in front of them. With a roar, they leapt in the midst of the gnolls, tearing with claws and teeth. In their frenzy, they caught two other humanoids that had taken shelter within another bush.

Eyrmin and Cald slipped away, their progress covered by the snarls of the cats and the screams of their victims.

Less than fifty feet from where the cats attacked, Eyrmin gave Cald a sign, and they both found trees, accepting the Embrace of Sielwode. Not knowing what the prince had planned, Cald stayed within the tree until Eyrmin came for him. The waiting was hard, and time dragged with torturous slowness, but when Cald left the tree, he could see, by the course of the moon, that only a few minutes had passed.

The awnshegh had also passed, and with it the main body of the invading force. The unlucky warriors in the rear were having their own problems with the big cats and the carrion crawlers. The blood of the first dead had drawn the forest predators, who were attacking savagely.

"We'll work our way north and flank them," Eyrmin said, moving through the forest like a shadow.

No sooner had they passed the northernmost group than they turned west, harrying the fringe of the marchers. The humans had concentrated closer to the stream and had left it to the humanoids to brave the deeper forest. Eyrmin and Cald used their arrows until their quivers were empty. Where they could, they picked up the spears of the fallen gnolls and hurled them, but Eyrmin had no sword, and he insisted they did not have time to engage in hand-to-hand combat.

When their arrows were gone, Eyrmin led the way at a fast trot. Not many minutes passed before they reached Reilmirid. The long stairs, or lemdair, had been raised so the only access to the tree village was by rope or climbing the giant sielwodes. Platforms had been attached to several ropes, and two wounded elves were being hoisted up to the first path. Another platform was being lowered. On it were baskets of arrows.

Hialmair stood waiting with two companions, looking up anxiously as the baskets descended. His face glowed with pleasure as he recognized Eyrmin, approaching through the first of the dawn light.

"My heart sings at the sight of you," he said. "Glisinda has been pushed back to the fork in the streams. The monster has taken the Moon Stream, as we supposed he would."

"It will bring the creature closer to the clearing and the portal," Eyrmin said. "There can be no doubt of its destination."

"Perhaps it means to pass through the portal to the Shadow World," Hialmair suggested. "Should we not let it go?"

"If I could believe that was its intention, I would gladly do so," Eyrmin agreed. "But I cannot count on so much good fortune. From what we hear, even the rulers of the dark plane seek to leave it. He's here for the elven spirits, or to meet the lich-lord who keeps trying to enter our world."

"And we must prevent either or both from happening." Hialmair nodded. "Though how we can is a mystery to me. More than a score of us have serious wounds, and six will be journeying to Tallamai."

"We will stand," Eyrmin said, his face full of sadness for his people. "In honor we can do nothing else. . . ."

The air rang with whistled alarms: warnings of a sudden enemy, a description of the awnshegh, and a call to rally to the king.

Cald was not sure he had understood.

"The king?" he asked Eyrmin.

"The king!" the prince cried, grabbing a handful of arrows from the basket that had just reached the ground. He sprinted away before Cald could fill his own quiver.

ANUIRE

TWENTY-FOUR

Cald followed Eyrmin, who raced along the Star
Mirror Stream. They met Glisinda and her fighters,
who were attempting to hold back the gnolls and
goblins that pressed toward Reilmirid. She was urging her people across the Star Mirror Stream into the
Muirien Grove. Their fording had been slowed by
the danger of being in the open as they crossed the
wide, normally shallow stream. The elves were
retreating. Though cutting into the numbers of
invaders, Glisinda and her band were too outnumbered to risk making a stand.

The sounds in the forest indicated that the awnshegh had split his forces at the fork of the water
courses, sending some up the Star Mirror Stream
while the rest took the Moon Stream.

While five elves took shelter and watched, their shafts ready to bring down the advancing humanoids, Glisinda hurried to Eyrmin, her eyes wide with puzzlement.

"You're here? I thought the call was to rally on the other side of the Moon Stream."

"That call was to rally to the king," Eyrmin said, listening to the sounds of battle in the distance.

"I just thought some young warrior, excited by the battle, had slurred his message," Glisinda said as she raised her bow and sent a missile in the direction of a gnoll that had moved too close. She barely missed it, and sent it scurrying back for better shelter.

"No, the noise of battle from the east is too loud," Eyrmin said as he cocked his head, birdlike, to listen. "We have too few people in that area for so much activity. Tallamai has seen to it we have reinforcements, but I doubt they know what they face. We will abandon Reilmirid and join the king." He whistled a message that was repeated and echoed through the village. He had ordered the elves who cared for the wounded to take them deeper into the forest. If the goblins and gnolls set the sielwode grove afire, anyone left up in the tree houses would be burned alive.

At Eyrmin's orders, Cald crossed the stream with six elves who carried the baskets of extra arrows. The halfling triplets went with them, clinging to the sides of the baskets, their short legs pumping as they attempted to find the bottom and propel themselves along. Fleetfoot lost his grip and went spinning off in the current. Luckily, Cald was close enough to grasp his shirt sleeve and pull him to safety.

From the shelter of the trees in the grove, the human and the elves rained arrows on the goblins while the others forded the stream behind them.

Cald's feet felt weighted with fatigue as he raced

behind Eyrmin. They sprinted toward the sounds of battle. They entered the clearing where the portal often opened. At the moment, it seemed the quietest place in the western arm of Sielwode. They crossed it at a run. Two hundred yards farther on, Eyrmin came to a stop, faced by elves unknown to Cald. They numbered about fifty and were all in full battle dress, yet they milled about in confusion.

When they caught sight of the new arrivals, they raised their bows, threatening both the human and the prince. Eyrmin's name echoed through the group.

From out of their midst stepped an elven warrior in shining armor trimmed in gold and heavily decorated with magic runes. From the scabbard at his side rose a knotted form reminiscent of the twigs of the sielwode trees. Cald had often listened to Eyrmin tell the tale of the making of the famous sword Emieline, and knew the magically armored elven warrior who stood before them was the king.

The spells on the shining helmet had not protected the king from a small wound on the cheek. The cut was only a scratch, but the blood still seeped out and ran down his chin.

Behind the king, Cald saw Relcan and several of the elves who had deserted Reilmirid. The royal kinsman's face was white, and he stayed well back from the meeting of the rulers of Sielwode.

The king stared at Eyrmin with eyes wide with shock. He raised his sword, hesitated, and lowered it as Eyrmin gave a deep bow to his king.

"I rejoice at the reinforcements, Sire, but regret you put yourself in danger. I did not know Garienel asked for help when he sent you the message."

"Message? Garienel? Eyrmin, what happens here, and why have I heard nothing about this creature that approaches?" King Tieslin spoke with the breathlessness that accompanies shock.

"The dawn has just broken on the first day of this tale," Eyrmin replied, his eyes searching the wood for danger. "Until this past night, we thought all our troubles stemmed from the Gorgon and the evil beyond the portal."

"We were crossing the stream when the monster rounded the bend," King Tieslin said. He paused as a goblin spear hurtled through the forest and fell just outside the ring of listeners.

With hand gestures, Eyrmin ordered his people to take up defensive positions in the trees. Many of the warriors who had traveled from Siellaghriod with the king followed Eyrmin's orders, relieved to be given direction.

King Tieslin's worried followers had moved well back from the stream, and while they paused in a relatively safe area, the two royal commanders exchanged information. Neither had good news for the other.

King Tieslin had marched with five hundred warriors. He had met the deserters on the way and added them to his forces. He had crossed the Moon Stream with the fifty who were with him. Another group of seventy or so had been caught in the open when the awnshegh had rounded the bend in the stream. The monster had slain them all. The rest of his warriors were still on the other side of the creek.

He had been stunned by the power of Czrak, and almost as shocked by the defection of three elves who had scurried toward the awnshegh, calling him master. They had died with the rest.

"We must mourn their departure from the true paths, but not their deaths—if they served the awnshegh," Eyrmin said.

The king nodded, took a deep breath, and seemed to be trying to marshal his mental forces.

Stognad, together with the halfling triplets, came

trotting up. King Tieslin's attention fixed upon the four, who carried elven-made weapons. The halflings carried small bows and Sidhelien swords and wore elven helmets. Stognad's long-handled, double-bladed axe had been made in the fashion of goblin weapons, but its craftsmanship was elven perfection, and it glittered with magic runes.

"Where is Bersmog?" Cald demanded of Stognad. His concern for the second goblin caused him to forget he was in the presence of the king.

"Him find subchief helmet and give orders," Stognad grumbled. "Sending goblins back downstream. One day he talk too much and somebody shut his mouth good."

"What is he saying?" the king demanded.

Cald explained Bersmog's tactics. Cald saw the doubt in the king's eyes but could think of no way to convince him the goblins were loyal.

While they waited for the advance of the awnshegh, Eyrmin warned the king about the portal in the grove.

"A horrible creature is Klasmonde Volkir," Bigtoe Rootfinder announced with no more awe of the elven king than of one of his own brothers.

"As horrible as the awnshegh is," Littletoe agreed, nodding wisely though the halflings had not seen Czrak.

"And neither respects mealtimes," Fleetfoot grumbled as he hitched up his trousers and peered into the woods.

Cald, who had been standing behind Eyrmin, had also been watching the forest. From between two trees, an elf appeared. By the movements of his legs, he seemed to be walking slowly, but his speed was faster than that of a sprinter. He passed through the side of a thick tree trunk as if it didn't exist. The apparition looked straight at Cald and pointed to his back trail; he wiggled the fingers of his left hand, mimicking the multilegged walk of a spider. Eyrmin had also seen the ghost warrior.

"The awnshegh has left the stream; it's coming this way," he told the king.

"You know your area better than I," Tieslin said, and then paused, giving Eyrmin the opportunity to chose the most easily defended area.

"We should move back fifty yards," the prince said with the ready authority of a leader familiar with his terrain. He pointed to a place in the path of the awnshegh, where the trees were the thickest. "If we cannot hold him there, we won't stop him."

Cald had not counted the numbers, hoping against hope that more warriors were hiding in the grove, harrying the enemy. Only twenty elves had accompanied Eyrmin. Even the fifty who had arrived with the king seemed a pitiful number to pit against the awnshegh and his army.

The defenders retreated to shelter behind the thick growth of trees only fifty yards from the clearing. Near Cald, Stognad and the halflings waited. The small bows and short arrows of the demihumans looked like toys, and the human youth noticed the elves of Siellaghriod shaking their heads when they saw them. Cald wondered what they would think when the halflings tried to shoot.

The halflings often bragged about the warriors among their people in the Shadow World. According to them, the brave little fighters were the scourge of the evil rulers and their foul servants. Even so, the survivors of the Rootfinder's village had been farmers and woodworkers who knew little of fighting. The halfling triplets were courageous, but their small arrows were as much a danger to the elves as to the enemy.

The noise of the approaching awnshegh preceded

it through the forest. Added to the sounds of crashing and breaking limbs were the roars of frustration and the repeated orders for the goblins and gnolls to advance. By the number of shouted orders, it seemed the humanoids feared the elves as much as the creature they served.

Lightning flared through the grove. The screams of gnolls and the odor of burning flesh preceded a rush of humanoids as they rapidly advanced into a shower of elven arrows.

A few fled to the right and left, out of the reach of Czrak's rage. Others tried again, throwing their spears ahead of them. Enough were moving out in a determined flanking movement to worry Eyrmin, who kept motioning the elves to lengthen their line of defense, thinning their already inadequate numbers.

As the gnolls and a few goblins moved off to the sides, their places were taken by human invaders. The center core wore the magical protection Eyrmin and Cald had seen in the forest. The wide leaves simmered indistinctly and the shafts of the elven arrows veered away.

"What is this power?" an elf from Siellaghriod asked Cald.

"Some foul magic of the awnshegh, but we learned the protection is limited to the leaves," he told the warrior as he waited for a clear target. The humans also moved away to the side. Behind them came the sound of a huge body being dragged over the ground, and the clatter of exoskeletal legs as they cracked against the trees of the grove.

Directly in front of Cald, the bole of an ancient tree withered away. Beyond it, out of the gloom, appeared the bloated face of Czrak. It was distorted by rage, his fangs dripped venom, and the power of his eyes filled his enemies with terror.

"Don't look in his eyes!" Eyrmin shouted, and he

gave the call for retreat.

Cald fell back with the others, wondering how they could stop so vile a creature. The magic of the elves could not stand against it, he knew.

What power . . . no power he knew . . . only another evil could stand against the awnshegh.

"An evil power . . ." he murmured, suddenly knowing what he must do.

The elves moved back, an orderly retreat, but Cald shouldered his bow and sprinted for the clearing. Behind him, he heard the elves' contemptuous remarks about his lack of courage as he fled the defensive line, but he had no time to explain.

Eyrmin, with his brave and great heart, must not know what Cald intended. If he understood, he would take the task to himself. Cald trembled with the thought of the evil in that terrible sword he had found and used during the last battle with the forces of the Shadow World. Afraid the evil that had coursed through him might become a permanent part of his being or twist anyone that used it, he had buried it and forced it out of his mind. The thought of using the weapon a second time, and what it might do to him, filled him with horror. Still, he could not allow the prince to know of it. That great goodness that was the prince might be tainted. Better that the evil of the sword destroy a short-lived human than an immortal elf, he decided.

The clearing was deserted. He rushed into the center. There, the huge, old tree limb still lay where it had fallen during the battle in which Eyrmin had destroyed Mmaadag Cemfrid. Cald scrambled beneath the thick leaves and brittle branches as he searched, trying to find the rabbit hole where he had buried the sword. He had hidden it too well. He dug around in the moist earth, unable to find it.

Roars of the awnshegh's frustration echoed

through the grove, followed by the crash of another fallen tree. In the quiet that followed, Cald heard the rapid patter of halfling footsteps and the heavier tread of Stognad. The defenders were retreating into the grove.

Cald looked about in desperation, and as he moved, he fell over a thick branch broken from the fallen tree limb. That branch had been one that supported the debris, he realized. When it broke, the limb had shifted and rolled.

But how far?

Only a few feet, he decided, no more than three. He turned and searched again as he heard the *thirrp-thirrp* of elven bow strings and knew the battle had reached the clearing.

Suddenly, his fingers were digging in softer soil, and as he tore at the dirt, he felt the curved guard on the handle of the evil weapon.

He stood, bringing up the blade with him. His flesh shrank from the pulsing evil in the blade, but he kept his grip on it as he looked around. At the eastern edge of the clearing, the elves were taking what shelter they could. Judging by their stances, they were determined to hold.

Czrak's human vanguard pressed forward, too close for the bows. The fighting was hand to hand. The elves, far outnumbered by the invaders, were forced out into the clearing. Their blades flashed in the morning sunlight.

Eyrmin was trading blows with a tall, black-clothed human protected by the shimmering leaves. The elf was clearly the better swordsman, but the magical protection provided by the awnshegh was deflecting Starfire every time the prince found an opening for a potentially fatal blow. A second magically protected fighter stepped into view and came up behind Eyrmin. Cald shouted a warning and scrambled over the fallen tree limbs, but he knew he would not be in time.

The halflings, who had been crouching low to stay out of the reach of the larger fighters, had also seen the prince's danger. They dashed out, striking at the human. Bigtoe and Littletoe jabbed him in the back of his thighs, where the dweomered atwer leaves were loosely joined. Fleetfoot held his blade until the man fell, and then rammed his short sword though the human's throat.

Stognad, axe in hand, gave a howl and rushed across the clearing, his weapon raised as he charged a goblin who had just entered from the south. He belatedly recognized his intended opponent as Bersmog, still wearing the bloody fur cloak and sub-chief's helmet. Stognad tried to halt, but his momentum carried him into his companion. They both tumbled to the ground in a tangle of arms and legs.

"You plenty stupid!" Bersmog roared as they scrambled to their feet.

"Always you have plenty too much to say," Stognad growled as he groped for a firmer grip on his weapon. He faltered in his search, his small eyes wide with fear.

All across the clearing, the invaders paused uncertainly, and so did the elves from the city far to the east. The sun had suddenly disappeared, and the dread brooding that preceded the opening of the portal leached the color from the morning. The heavily rune-trimmed armor of the elves glowed in the growing darkness. The prince's sword seemed to take on a power of its own as he cut down his opponent.

With a heave of his heavy body, the awnshegh forced himself between two trees, but even Czrak paused as if testing the strange atmosphere.

The trees of the Shadow World appeared like smoke, and then solidified. Six halflings raced out of the shadows. Behind them came the black-armored warriors of Klasmonde Volkir . . . and the lich himself.

Beneath that column of darkness thrown by the crown, the lich-lord's eyes glowed with hatred, sweeping the clearing until he found the adversary he had faced twice before. He forced his terrified mount forward, galloping directly toward Eyrmin. His mount had moved less than twice its length when Bersmog's spear caught the beast in the chest and brought it down. The lich-lord jumped away as the horse fell.

His decision made for him, Eyrmin forsook the battle with the forces of the awnshegh and dashed to meet his archenemy. In the presence of the evil from the other plane, his armor glowed, and his sword was lit with an inner fire. When their blades clashed, the sound dampened the other noises of battle.

The awnshegh recognized the newcomers as rivals at least, even enemies. His eyes glowed red as he glared at them, but the withering spell had no effect on the denizens of the Shadow World. He roared and raised one of his muscular arms, though they looked puny beside his bloated body. Fire flew from his fingers. Two elves, who had turned to face the warriors from the Shadow World, screamed as they writhed in the flames.

Cald believed that only the evil blade he held could destroy the awnshegh, so he avoided other, easier opponents. He slowly backed to the edge of the clearing, knowing his best chance was to approach the awnshegh from behind, using any surprise he could manage. His plan faltered; the clearing filled with undead. The stink of their rotten bodies polluted the air, making it hard to breathe.

Still more elves were arriving, he noticed. But why weren't they assisting with the fight? Then he realized they were not the warriors who had marched with the king, but the ghost elves who lived in the grove.

They stood in fighting stances, their weapons in their hands, but instead of attacking the invaders, they all seemed to be looking straight at Cald.

Malala, her feet flying in her battle dance, had just injured a gnoll. As he backed away, his left shoulder bleeding, she followed for the kill, passing through one of the warriors. The female elf did not falter. She had not seen the ghost fighter, nor did he seem to see her. The apparitions were all watching Cald.

Then he understood his ability to see them. It came from the blade he held in his hand. He also remembered that he had heard a ghost warrior's voice the last time he held the evil sword.

"Why don't you help your people?" he shouted at the closest ghost warrior. The spirit had been turning away, but when Cald shouted at him he looked back, gazing at the human. He made no move to join the battle nor to answer Cald, but he had heard.

He *had* heard!

"Free us," the ghost warrior said, as if making a decision to try again for help. "Free us and we will join you."

Cald repeated the words in his mind. Free them. Only a short time before, he and Eyrmin thought they had discovered the way to call on the trapped spirits, but they had been wrong.

They had tried the old song that had been a lullaby for so long.

Up goes the light.
Down comes the light.
Call illberin,
Call illberin.

It sounded as if it might have referred to the Star Stair and elves who had lost their lives on Aebrynis. So had the next line:

When need and deed
Have not agreed,
Call illberin,
Call illberin.

If there was ever a time when they faced a need, it was at that moment. At that moment! When Cald and Eyrmin had tried to call the spirit warriors there had been no *need!*

"Illberin!" Cald shouted, and was startled by his own voice. It rang through the grove as if it had sprung from a thousand throats.

The eyes of the spirit warrior lit with joy and purpose. His body took on solidity. As he took a step, the grass crushed beneath his feet. He drew himself up straight and raised his blade as one of the awnshegh's humans charged toward Cald. The human, with the lust of battle on him, shied, and his eyes focused on the elf who had not been visible a moment before. The human's blade had been raised for a strike at Cald, and he was not fast enough to prevent the suddenly visible ghost elf from skewering him through the magical protection.

Malala faltered as a strange elf appeared beside her and hacked at one of the two opponents she faced.

Glisinda, backing away from three humans, found two strange warriors at her side. The three elves quickly dispatched the confused foes, who had been startled to see two opponents appear out of thin air. Around the clearing, elves and enemy alike faltered in their attacks as in their midst appeared more than fifty warriors whose existence came as a surprise.

Several appeared directly in front of the awnshegh, who raised his hand and tried to flame them, but his fire proved ineffective against the ghost warriors.

Realizing the ghost warriors were occupying the attention of the awnshegh, Cald raced forward with the blade he had drawn from the rabbit hole. He plunged it into the side of the monster.

Czrak screamed in agony and twisted, nearly jerking the blade from Cald's hand. The human stumbled and was knocked sideways by one of the exoskeletal legs. Czrak turned on him. Using another leg, the monster pinned him to the ground. As the giant head turned toward him, Cald felt the pull of the awnshegh's gaze, invading his mind, robbing him of his will.

The master wanted the sword . . . the master must have the sword. Cald would be rewarded if he gave the master the sword. The puny elves, evil because they stood in the master's way, would be destroyed, and the master would rule all Cerilia. Cald would rule with him. . . .

A wail of terror erupted from the fighters, but Cald, caught in Czrak's spell, only dimly heard it and gave it no heed.

Suddenly he was free of Czrak's gaze. The bloated face twisted in pain, and the awnshegh gave a tortured scream. He rolled on the ground, nearly crushing Cald with his weight as he passed over the human.

Breathless and feeling as if his ribs had been crushed, Cald staggered to his feet.

He found himself facing the foreleg and shoulder of a gigantic black deer. As he looked up, the Stag of Sielwode lowered his head. His silver antlers, glowing like fire in the darkness cast by the portal, gored Czrak in his bloated side. The sluglike body was torn by ten antler points, sharp as rapiers.

Czrak roared in pain and outrage and slashed at the Stag of Sielwode with two of his long, claw-tipped spider legs. One missed as the Stag leapt away; the other slashed down the shoulder of the gigantic black deer. The deer backed away, limping on his right foreleg. The deer's hind legs became entangled in the branches of the huge fallen limb.

Czrak whipped his swollen, torn body around, two long insectlike legs reaching for the encumbered and wounded Stag.

When the Stag attacked, Cald had pulled his mind free of Czrak's influence. Eyrmin had said the elves had never been truly sure whether the Stag of Sielwode was good or evil, but now Cald knew. The creature was graceful, beautiful with its gleaming black coat and silver antlers. He fought the evil, bloated Czrak that had killed so many elves.

"No!" Cald dashed forward. The wicked claw on the long, exoskeletal leg was reaching for the Stag's throat. The human jumped and raised his arm, hacking at the leg as he reached the top of his leap. He had barely touched the ground when the claw and first joint of the insect-leg fell beside him. He stood between the Stag and Czrak.

With a heave, the giant black deer freed himself of the thick, confining branches of the fallen limb. The Stag lowered his head. At first, Cald thought the creature meant to gore him, but with an abrupt move, the Stag used the side of his head to push the human out of the way. Cald went staggering back as the Stag charged into Czrak again.

The force of the shove sent Cald stumbling toward the eastern side of the clearing, where the portal had opened.

The fight between the two awnsheghlien would be theirs alone, that much was clear. The battle would be to the death, and the survivor would absorb the strength of the dying.

Inside the shadowy wood, the light that blazed from Eyrmin's sword and armor set the human youth's goal. He worked his way toward it, through a knot of fighting skeletons and ghouls. He leapt and dodged, putting the evil blade to use in behalf of the elves, whether living or dead. The spirit warriors little needed his aid; so long denied battle, they were attacking with a vengeance.

A moan of fear from the rotting mouth of a ghoul warned Cald of a new arrival, a monster he had seen before. He turned to see a black, formless shape winding between the trees. This time it ignored the fighters as it approached, and he sensed its attention on him.

He shut out the individual battles around him, and their noise hushed to silence as the darkness approached. Again he looked on a blackness so deep it seemed to be a hole in the existence of both worlds. Still, it had movement and purpose. If it had a mind, its thoughts were centered on Cald.

Fear caused him to back away a few steps, but as the horror approached, it neared Eyrmin and Klasmonde Volkir. The elven prince was too caught up in his fight to see it, and the lich-lord was attempting to force the elf back into the path of that approaching menace.

Cald started forward, though his feet felt as if they had grown roots. Fear slowed him; still, he knew he held the most powerful weapon in the battle, and if this new danger was to be stopped, he would have to stop it.

Then behind him, he heard the clear, sweet voice of Glisinda as she began the "Lirimira," the elven battle song of courage. Howls from the undead tried to drown her out, but other elven voices took up the song, swelling the noise of battle and giving heart to their allies. Cald felt his own courage grow, and he ran forward, his blade cutting into the unsubstantial darkness when he reached it.

Remembering the creatures that had disappeared into that void at the last battle, he ducked quickly aside. At his feet, a black feather shape, almost weightless, drifted to the ground, and the apparition drew back. Cald dodged the smaller portion of blackness, not sure if it contained any power. He quickly learned it did. The severed head of an undead warrior rolled from a nearby skirmish, and the grisly skull, with its rotting flesh, disappeared into that scrap of blackness.

Stepping carefully to avoid the remnant, Cald advanced toward the main shape of the void again. It waited, spreading huge wings like those of a bird. Above his head, Cald saw the shape of an avian neck and head.

The huge wings whipped together to surround him, and suddenly he was cut away from the clearing on Cerilia, the Shadow World, the battle. The light of his elven armor showed the ground at his feet, but around him was only black void. Above him, the shape of the birdlike head had disappeared into the formless blackness, but he remembered where it had been.

With a leap he had not thought himself capable of making, he launched himself upward. The sword hacked into the darkness, part of the blade disappearing only to reappear again as he pulled it out and stabbed again. With each thrust, he felt the drain on his strength, as if his life force were being pulled away. But from deep within that void, he felt rather than heard a scream of pain.

He knew he did not have the strength to make another leap, so he jabbed with the blade, each time hearing the scream, and each time feeling a drain on himself. Would he last long enough to destroy the monster?

He hacked at it twice more. The third time, he fell

to the ground, the tip of the blade still wedged in the darkness. He did not have the strength to pull it out. He could not even draw a full breath. The light of his dweomered armor dimmed and almost died. . . .

But then it brightened again. He jerked, energized. He suddenly felt overfilled with strength, his own strength and more.

The blackness shuddered and fled into the treetops. Cald could hear the elves still singing and smell the stench of rotting flesh from the ghouls and the other undead.

He looked across the clearing in time to see the Stag of Sielwode, for the last time plunging his antlers into the torn body of Czrak. The huge deer's head shook as he tore at the bloated body of the awnshegh.

Cald looked around, trying to find Eyrmin. The prince was nowhere in sight. Nearby, Saelvam was holding off two grotesque orogs, minions of Czrak. Cald ran forward and, with a mighty thrust, dispatched one with a sword through the heart.

Behind him, the fatally wounded Czrak gave a death gurgle and was still. The second orog blinked and suddenly lost heart. It turned to run. Saelvam, wearied from the long fight that had begun before dawn, let it go.

All around the clearing, the minions of Czrak were pulling back. The death of the awnshegh had released them from their need to fight. Some looked confused, as if they had no idea where they were. Many who yet fought undead in the three-way battle lost their lives in the confusion. Some turned and fled the clearing.

Adding to the confusion was the sudden wind that heralded the closing of the portal. The battle ended with a cry of rage from the undead as they were swept away by the wind, a wind that did not touch Cald or the elves.

Cald looked around. He glimpsed a light within the portal, and recognized it as the armor and sword of the prince.

"Eyrmin!" he shouted, but he was too late.

As the portal closed, again shutting Klasmonde Volkir out of Aebrynis, the prince disappeared with him.

ANUIRE

twenty-five

The closing of the portal disoriented the elves of
Siellaghriod and the invaders. The elves of
Reilmirid, most of whom were not aware of the loss
of their prince, took full advantage of the confusion,
using arrows, swords, and spears to their best
advantage.

Glisinda, struck out at one of the human warriors
and drove him back. It was pure accident that his
swinging sword, in a backward thrust, struck the
king on the helmet. The impact of the blow knocked
the king unconscious, and he fell beside the human,
who had been pierced in the heart by Glisinda's
blade.

The field of battle, a moment before crowded with
three armies, was quickly emptying of all but the

dying and dead. A few of the forces of Czrak fought a retreating action. More turned their backs and ran into the forest with the elves in victorious pursuit. The undead were already gone. The ghost warriors had disappeared into the Shadow World, going willingly and hacking at ghouls and skeletons as they went. Only the elves remained, and their numbers had dwindled by nearly three score.

The Stag of Sielwode backed warily away from the closing portal. He bumped into the huge fallen limb, accidentally rolling it over and concealing the body of the king. With one gigantic leap, the huge deer was across the clearing, and with a second leap was out of sight.

Cald saw it all happen: the defeat and death of evil, the victory and escape of the Stag. But with the loss of Eyrmin, what should have been cause for rejoicing had become a misery.

Still staring at the place where the prince had disappeared, Cald was only vaguely aware that Bersmog was using his axe to cut away the fallen limb and expose the king beneath it. Stognad stood over Tieslin, his axe in his hands.

"Hey, you king elf! You dead or not? I waste plenty too much time looking after you. Could be having some *fun,* you know," Bersmog complained.

The three halflings approached and critically eyed the royal body. Bigtoe reached down and laid a finger against the king's throat, which caused Tieslin, who had been feigning death beneath that raised axe, to jerk.

"He's not dead if he can move," Bigtoe announced.

"Surely not," Littletoe agreed.

"I'd play dead too, if two goblins with axes were standing over me," Fleetfoot said, finally making a comment that fitted the occasion.

Their conversation had brought Cald out of his grieving apathy. He walked over and laid a hand on Bersmog's arm.

"Move back. You, too, Stognad. He probably thinks you mean to cut his head off." He reached down, offering a hand to the king, who rose, chagrined at being caught in his pretense.

Stognad unintentionally drew attention from the king's embarrassment as he eyed Cald.

"You find plenty strange thing to fight. What you call that black thing?"

"I don't know," Cald admitted.

"No elven song tells of it," the king said.

"A regog," Bigtoe volunteered, speaking the name in a whisper. He shuddered at the thought. "An elemental from the void, it is said."

"And said only in whispers," Littletoe added.

"It interrupts mealtimes, too," the irrepressible Fleetfoot said.

Cald noticed the king was still eyeing the goblins' axes.

"Sire, did we tell you Stognad and Bersmog were loyal defenders of Sielwode?" Cald realized after he spoke that, as a non-Sidhelien, his loyalty might also be in doubt.

"It is time for a new song when the elven king is defended by only those races he thought were enemies," he said, looking around for his own people. Cald explained about the fleeing armies of the awnshegh.

"You were hidden beneath that branch. They probably thought you were leading the advance," Cald suggested, not sure he was right, but his explanation sounded probable. No elf would have left his king helpless and undefended.

"I agree with the gob—Bersmog. We should not be missing the fight altogether," King Tieslin said, and he reached down to pick up his sword. He led the way out of the clearing, heading an unlikely group of two goblins, one human, and three halflings. After a few steps into the shadows of the grove, he lost one member of his band.

In his grief, Cald had dropped the evil sword when the portal closed, but he knew he could not leave it lying exposed on the ground. He slipped behind a tree, and when the others were out of sight, he returned to the clearing.

He picked it up and felt the burning power coursing up his right arm and through his veins again. He studied it. A new thought crossed his mind.

Everyone had believed the spirit warriors were the reason for the attacks on the grove, but they had been wrong. Once the warriors had been freed, they went willingly into the Shadow World, their eyes gleaming with honor and purpose. Klasmonde Volkir would not have wanted them and their integrity in his world.

That meant the lich-lord had a different reason for wanting the portal to open. It had to be the sword. If Klasmonde wanted it, its evil was useful to the lich-lord, and that was reason enough to keep it from him.

Czrak had wanted the sword as well. He had demanded it when he held Cald in a trancelike state. Was the mysterious weapon also the reason the Gorgon's forces attacked? Evil attracts evil, Glisinda had said. War and death had come upon Sielwode because of the weapon. He could take it away. If it were out of the forest, the elves would be safe.

No. His skin prickled as he imagined the prince's dislike of that idea. His senses reached out, searching, and knew the thought had come from his own mind. It came because he had known his foster father's heart, and the prince would not have inflicted that cursed blade on anyone of any race.

But where could Cald hide the weapon? He took the blade in both hands as he stared at it, and felt the same evil power in his left hand. The cut on his palm suddenly began bleeding profusely. He raised his arm to stem the flow, allowing the blade to slide down onto his gauntlet. His left arm was abruptly shielded from the evil emanations. The power of the weapon did not penetrate the magically runed armor. And if the armor could protect him from the sword's evil power, it might also mask the sword from the senses of those who sought it. . . .

"No!" He gave an anguished cry as the realization struck him like a blow. His hunch had to be wrong—that he should give up the armor Eyrmin had given him in order to hide the sword. That was asking too much. It was Cald's last and most precious gift from the prince.

But no one was asking him to give it up, he reasoned. There was only the possibility that elven magic might trap the malevolent forces of the blade. Not even he knew it for certain.

Hoping he was wrong, he stripped off his right greave and, with a silent apology to Eyrmin, placed the sword on the ground and the greave over it. Then he set his hand on the armor and sighed, thinking he had been wrong. He was both relieved and disappointed. He could still feel the evil power. The awnshegh of Aebrynis and the rulers of the Shadow World could still find it easily.

He removed the other greave, and this time he covered the weapon with the two pieces of armor. When he placed his hand on the soil he felt nothing.

His heart felt heavy. He realized he had discovered how to imprison the power of the blade. The method would cost him, but he knew he had to pay the price. He could feel nothing, but what about the powerful forces that wanted the blade? To be safe from them, he would need to use his entire suit to shield it.

He stripped away all his war gear and started to dig a hole in the ground, thinking he would bury it. Bad idea, he decided. Occasionally hard rain storms swept across Sielwode, and the runoff dug gullies in the soil. Once he disturbed the soil, he would leave the hiding pace vulnerable to a washout.

Then where? He wanted to keep the location secret, unknown to the elves. With their sense of honor, they would never understand the evil of the blade, and they might try to use it. To taint the immortal courage of Malala, the knowledge of Glisinda, or the dedication of Hialmair was unthinkable.

He leaned against one of the great trees of the grove, and felt the warmth, the welcome of the giant trunk.

He would leave it in the Embrace of Sielwode!

But not in the Muirien Grove, he decided. The ancient trees had suffered enough. Leaving it there might be dangerous to the elves. They would be watching the portal. They might enter the Embrace during a time of danger and find it.

Where would it be safe? Where were they least likely to go? They were forbidden to go near the eastern shore of the Star Mirror Lake, where it bordered the Star Stair.

Cald retrieved the leaf-covered pieces of his armor along with the sword, and he started north.

The sun had set, and the last of twilight was passing when he rounded the eastern knuckle of the lake and found a huge, ancient tree. It stood at the edge of the swamp that surrounded the Star Stair. He had found a perfect place, he decided.

Mournfully, because he had always valued the

armor the prince had given him, he stripped it off. He placed the sword in the smaller pieces, wrapped his mail shirt around them and used the leather straps of his breastplate and backplate to make a tight bundle.

With an apology to the tree, he began the incantation that opened the tree's Embrace. He stepped into it, holding the bundle in front of him, and released his hold as he backed out again.

"Keep it safe, so your forest will remain free of trouble," he murmured to the tree. He felt a slight breeze, and a branch, moved by the wind, touched his shoulder as if in agreement.

Out in the swamp, the sounds of the night creatures seemed to hush. Cald's head filled with a trilling music, so far away his mind could not conceive of the distance. The darkness of the night faded, and lights began rising from the swamp, traveling up the Star Stair.

Knowing no mortal was to watch the ascension of the departing elves, he turned, but the light stayed with him. He looked up and realized he and the ancient tree were being targeted by beams of light. Above his head, the leaves of the old tree seemed transparent in the starry glow. The bark of the tree glistened with a silvery sheen. In his head, the music swelled until he thought he would burst, and then the sound and the beams faded, withdrawing to twinkle in the night sky.

Tallamai itself would guard the secret of the sword.

Only one faint beam remained, shining on his sword belt where his own blade hung in its scabbard. Beside it was his helmet, which he had removed and had forgotten to use in shielding the terrible sword.

The guilt he would have felt if he had deliberately

kept the helmet back was washed away by the gentle light that faded when he picked up his remaining belongings and started his long walk back to Reilmirid.

* * * * *

Two hundred miles north, the Gorgon roared in frustration. From the mountain encampment of his marching army, he had felt the use of the blade Deathirst and had focused all his senses upon it. Some strong magic prevented him from discovering the mind of the creature who wielded it, but he had felt the force when the weapon had been used.

Then it was gone!

He could feel no emanations. He decided it had been taken back into the Shadow World, where not even his power could easily overcome the wielder.

He roared again and shook his giant bull head. His horns gored three orogs unlucky enough not to flee in time. His diamond-hard hooves raked the rocky ground, sending out sparks and setting the mountainside alight with small fires. When his rage calmed, he sought the minds of his generals and ordered his armies to return to the mountains.

He was too intelligent to waste his forces attacking the elves when they had nothing he wanted.

* * * * *

Cald walked slowly through the wood toward Reilmirid and arrived before daylight. He joined several others who were also returning. By the talk, the elves had spent their time driving out the remnants of Czrak's army. They had scoured the forest for any lingering foes, and had found some of their own people, too badly hurt to reach the village.

The tree village had escaped injury. Wounded elves were being assisted up the lemdair—those who could walk. Others were being lifted on platforms hastily fastened to the long ropes that dangled from the high limb-paths.

Hundreds of uninjured but battle-weary warriors were gathered at the base of the Grove Father, where King Tieslin stood on the boulder used by Eyrmin when he wanted to speak to all the inhabitants of the village.

Strange elven faces looked at Cald, most with contempt, but the elves of Reilmirid eyed his lack of armor with unspoken questions. Cald moved close enough to hear the king and stopped.

". . . and they're fleeing faster than we could drive them out," the king was saying. "I will risk no more Sidhelien lives on them today. Tomorrow we will search the forest again, and we will take no mercy on those who linger."

The elves nodded. The lives of most invaders were forfeit for entering the forest. These forces, however, had been impelled into Sielwode by the power of the awnshegh, and they seemed willing enough to leave once their master was dead.

The king stood for a moment, staring out at nothing, and many of the tired elves shifted their feet restlessly. The king looked back at them and spoke again.

"Many immortal lives have been lost this day, and Sielwode will never recover from the loss of Prince Eyrmin."

In a public show of emotion, the king wiped one hand across his face. When he lowered it, his grief was still plain.

"My cousin, a true descendant of the line of kings, was lost, not to the creature he fought, but to distrust and deceit among his own people."

More of the elves shifted; discomfort, not restlessness, was the cause.

"I am also to blame for this, since I listened to tales and let the love of power convince me my loyal and brave kinsman was plotting against me. Many of us will walk in shame for the rest of our lives."

He paused and stared down at someone in the crowd. Several elves moved away; Relcan stood alone and white-faced.

"You, Relcan, my kinsman, have always coveted the command of the western reaches, and it was your enmity that drew away the forces so badly needed here. To you I give what you thought you wanted, the command of Reilmirid and its warriors."

Cald could not believe what he was hearing.

"Your punishment," the king continued, "is to fill the shoes of one of the greatest warriors in our long history."

It was a punishment, and it was fitting, Cald realized. Every step Relcan took, every word he spoke, would be compared with those of Eyrmin. The prince, no longer present to make the occasional error, would gain perfection in the memories of the elves. Soon, tales of him would grow far beyond reality, far beyond what any other elf could attain. Ashen faced, Relcan stumbled away.

Punishment was not the only subject on the king's mind. He commended many elves on their courage, and then moved on to the subject of the non-Sidhelien. He told the assembled warriors how he had regained consciousness with none but a pair of goblins, three halflings, and a human standing guard over him.

He had to pause. A roar of elven outrage at their lack of care for their ruler drowned him out for a few moments. When he could speak, he absolved them of blame and told the tale of the circumstances.

"I name these six to be citizens of Sielwode."

Cald heard no more of the king's speech. He was glad Bersmog and Stognad would have a home and the halflings would not be driven out.

Sielwode itself would not mean so much to him in the future. He moved behind a tree and, using it as a shield, turned back to the grove and the clearing. For him, it was not a time for celebration.

One day that portal would open again, and when it did, he would either rescue Eyrmin, or join him on the other side.

ANUIRE

εpilogue

Three and a half years later, every detail of that last battle in the grove was still fresh in Cald's mind. It could have happened only an hour before. The image of the prince disappearing into the Shadow World had returned in a thousand dreams. If Eyrmin had been killed, Cald could have mourned, and the grief would have lost its razor edge with time. But the prince had crossed to that evil plane as a living being, and might still be alive.

Cald had lived in the Muirien Grove for half a year after the last closing of the portal, waiting for it to open again. In less than a month after Eyrmin had disappeared, his hope dwindled. The power that had kept the grove out of pace with the rest of Siel-wode had disappeared.

The ancient trees began dropping their old leaves, pushed away by new growth. Grass sprouted in the clearing, and wildflowers sprang up in such profusion that the elves, in spite of their grief over the loss of the prince, took great pleasure in the grove. The huge limb that had been broken from a tree in the battle between Eyrmin and Mmaadag Cemfrid, the limb where Cald had first hidden the sword, had remained nearly intact for more than ten years. It suddenly crumbled away, rotting into the ground. Within two months, new trees had sprouted from seeds and the birds had returned to the grove.

Still, Cald remained for an additional four months before he decided the portal would not open again. Then he left the grove and the forest of Sielwode, seeking another entry into the Shadow World.

He had traveled through Mhoried, Alamie, Avanil, and crossed the Seamist Mountains into Taeghas. At first, his elven clothing had brought him enemies on sight. Changing his clothing helped a little, but because he spoke the human languages with an elven lilt, few humans trusted him.

He found his answer in the Aelvinnwode, where, because they had heard tales of him, the elves allowed him to enter their domain. There he spoke with the loremaster, an ancient elf crippled by many battles.

"Free yourself of this grief, Aerienis," he said. In the elven language, he had called the human Greatheart.

"The halflings have the power to open the portal, though many do not seem to know it. I doubt you will find one in Cerilia who will attempt to open it from this side.

"Prince Eyrmin showed you another way to enter the Shadow World. It is entered by embracing some great evil. In his just desire to destroy the lich-lord, Klasmonde Volkir, he held to his purpose, and so was taken to the other plane with his enemy. You would need a malevolent force at least as strong in order to reach him."

Cald had left the Aelvinnwode in a mood of hopelessness that lasted for three days before he realized the loremaster had unintentionally given him his answer.

The sword, that terrible weapon that he had twice held, might be used to open the portal. Why had he never considered it? The answer was simple enough; he had hidden it and used every elven discipline he knew to rid his mind of its evil residue.

He had turned his face toward the Sielwode and traveled each day until hunger forced him to hunt or buy food. He walked until he staggered, but, sure he had the answer, he had been determined to reach the grove again.

Lienwiel, the elf who escorted him now, stayed well back, sensitive to Cald's need to be alone as he entered the clearing south of Reilmirid. That was where Iswiel, Farmain, and Relcan had challenged the prince and deserted his cause.

Half a mile farther, they passed through the sielwode grove and the village. One of the lemdair had lost several steps and had not been repaired. Many of the torches were gone from their holders on the high tree paths, and the structures were in need of new shingles. Even the houses in the village seemed to have lost their heart along with their prince.

Cald continued on, crossing the Star Mirror Stream above the fork. He walked into the Muirien Grove and jerked to a halt as a goblin stepped out from behind a tree. It took him a moment to recognize Bersmog, mainly because of the goblin's clothing. He wore traditional goblin attire—short trousers and a vest made of poorly cured animal hide—though for years he and Stognad had worn elven clothing.

"You gone plenty long," Bersmog said. "Now you come back."

"And you're still here." Cald, like the goblin, was stating the obvious, not quite knowing how to express his pleasure in seeing an old friend. Along with the pleasure was also a hesitation. He could not afford to renew the friendship only to suffer the pain of separation again.

"Is Stognad here too?"

Bersmog grunted his assent while industriously scratching his chest beneath the vest. During Eyrmin's time, the goblins had been ordered to bathe regularly. As Cald continued through the grove, Bersmog strolled along at his side.

"Stognad, he hunt. We need food for camp. Rootdiggers still here, watching for portal to open, but things plenty quiet for a long time."

"Rootdiggers—Rootfinders? The halfling triplets?" Cald was surprised. Halflings preferred towns and tame, well-tended lands. The three brothers were certainly dedicated to helping the refugees if they had remained in Sielwode.

"Finders become diggers. They plant food in clearing north of here," the goblin said. "They build little house and one for us. We wait." Bersmog shrugged. "Splitear dead now, but clan bossed by Gorgon. Stognad and me, we not go back. Boss elf king say we can stay here if no cut trees. You go to place where shadow trees come?"

"Yes, and you stay far away from it," Cald said, impatient to continue his journey. "If possible, I'm going through the portal to find the prince."

To his surprise, Bersmog nodded and took a firmer grip on his spear. He eyed the human hopefully.

"Maybe plenty fighting over there? Nothing happen here for long time. Me and Stognad have no fun for plenty long time."

"You want to go?" Cald could not believe the goblin.

"We go along, see this place," he said. "See Be-gelf again." The goblin had used his name for Eyrmin. "Where is Be-gelf is always plenty fun."

They had been walking toward the clearing, and Cald could see the sunlight through the deep shade of the grove. He nodded, hoping Bersmog could not read the lie in his face.

"Go find Stognad and meet me here at sunset tomorrow," he said, leaning against a handy tree. His body enjoyed the rest, but his intention was merely to give Bersmog the impression he was in no hurry.

Lienwiel had hung back, tactfully giving Cald and the goblin privacy. When the goblin trotted away out of sight, Cald moved around the tree and spoke the incantation to enter the Embrace.

After a few minutes, Cald's elven escort realized he had been left behind and began searching for him. The human remained in the tree until Lienwiel was well out of sight.

Slipping out of the tree and skirting the rest of the grove, he turned north, walking through the afternoon. By sunset, he reached the last forest monarch on the edge of the swamp.

Knowing the elves would not find him there, he slept on the ground. His mind and his body needed rest. If he was able to open the portal with the sword, he had no idea what he would be facing. He awoke at dawn, still fatigued from his long journey, but he refused to wait any longer to try for the sword.

Will I be able to retrieve the weapon? he wondered as he spoke the incantation. Within the Embrace, he raised his hands, and his left gripped the edge of his breastplate. He stepped out with his armor, still bundled as he had left it.

The breeze sighed in the limbs of the old tree as if it was glad to be rid of its burden.

He untied the bundle and donned his armor, marveling again that the magic of the elves made it seem almost weightless. His fatigue fell away as if the armor had absorbed his exhaustion and filled him with new energy. He buckled his sword belt around his waist, his scabbard and his own sword at his side. He slipped his bow and quiver of arrows over his shoulder and carried the dreaded blade as he returned to the clearing in the Muirien Grove.

The sunlight glinted on his armor and threw sparkles of reflected light onto the flowers, but the human saw none of the beauty. He stood, staring at the western eaves, willing the portal to open.

He had no words, no magic incantation, only his desire, but he reasoned the halflings had opened it with need and desperation. His heart thudded with hope. His blood ran hot in his veins, like rivulets of fire running down his arms and legs, the curse of the malevolent power of the sword. It would help him do what he could not manage alone.

He waited, willing the portal to open. Time dragged by, but he refused to give up hope. Then he felt the change in the mood of the grove. The sun disappeared, color drained from the flowers in the clearing, and slowly the shadows of the trees seemed to become vertical and take on mass and solidity.

Behind him, Lienwiel, who had finally found him again, called his name, and then gasped at the change taking place in the grove. Cald heard him stumble, probably backing away, though the human did not turn to look.

Someone was moving in the shadows, and when he stepped into full sight, Cald's heart leapt.

Eyrmin!

"My prince!" Cald cried, and he started forward.

Eyrmin raised his hand, palm out, ordering Cald to remain where he was. The elf stepped out into the clearing, and the human's hope died.

Eyrmin walked through the flowers, but they remained unbroken behind him. He passed through a small bush as if it were not there.

The prince had not survived his journey into the Shadow World.

"I-I wanted to help you," Cald said, blurting out the words like a child. "It took me three years to understand how to open the portal. . . ."

"I know," Eyrmin said softly. "I know how you have grieved. Your pain kept me close to the portal. Through it, I knew you had found the answer, and I have been waiting for you."

"I'm sorry it took so long," Cald said. "And I don't know how long the portal will remain open. Come away now, so when it closes you'll be on this side."

"I cannot." Eyrmin shook his head sadly. "I am of that world now and must remain."

"Then I'm going back with you," Cald said, but the prince shook his head again.

"No. You are needed in Aebrynis."

"I'm going with you," Cald insisted. "I won't leave you to fight alone in the Shadow World."

"I'm not alone," Eyrmin said. "You freed the spirit warriors, but there was no place for them on Aebrynis, so they came with me. We are a strong force here." He saw the questions in the human's face and sighed.

"The old song, 'Lightfall,' gave us the answer to their entrapment. Not all the lights of Tallamai are departed elves. Dragons also exist in Tallamai. When they are killed, they become lights, as do others from other worlds who were meant to be immortal.

"There have been great battles fought in the

sky. . . ." His face twisted with painful images, but Cald was not to learn what caused that terrible memory. "I have heard of terrible battles. We have seen the lights fall, streaking across the sky. We have seen others brighten suddenly and then disappear. It is all we see of epic battles in the sky.

"The ghost warriors of the grove were newly dead, having lost their lives in a great battle between the elves of Sielwode and four elementals that had been swept into this world though a portal from another plane—not the plane of the Shadow World. While a battle raged between the elves of Cerilia and the elementals, so too a war had erupted in Tallamai. The ghost warriors, just climbing the stair to reach the sky, were faced with terrible forces they did not understand or know how to fight. They fled back down the stair and were trapped here."

"And your people were off fighting the elementals and never knew what happened to them?" Cald asked, feeling like a child again, asking obvious questions as he learned his lore from Eyrmin. The prince shook his head.

"We never knew, though we were somehow given the knowledge in the old lay. As you said, they found it easier to plant the quest for the answer in your mind. There are those of our people who are not so open to new ideas." He sighed again.

"That, my human son, is the last lesson I can give you. Be content that I am not alone, and we will be a powerful force against the evils of the Shadow World."

"But I can fight at your side. . . ."

The elf's face turned dark with anger. "Free me! Cease this grief that entraps me. Rejoice that I can still fight. Use the lessons I taught you to help the land I leave behind." He took a step forward and held out his hand.

"That blade belongs in the Shadow World. With it I can close the portal and protect Sielwode. With it I, and the spirits who crossed with me, can make a difference in the dark plane."

Cald's hope died as he took the blade in both hands, ceremoniously presenting the hilt to the prince. Eyrmin, in turn, held his weapon by the blade, presenting the hilt to Cald.

"We will exchange weapons, and you will have Starfire, a sign that I am always with you."

As they traded swords, the prince suddenly seemed to take on more solidity; the shadowy gray of his armor glowed in the silver and gold of the world of Aebrynis.

"Prince Eyrmin!" Lienwiel cried out and bowed.

"We fight for the day when the passage between the two planes can be opened in peace," Eyrmin said, his eyes on Cald. He raised the blade, and the wind that signaled the closing of the portal rose, roaring through the clearing.

The prince stood, the short cloak that covered one shoulder whipping in the breeze that had no effect on Cald, Lienwiel, or the trees of Aebrynis. Eyrmin was still gazing at the elf and the human when he disappeared with the trees of the Shadow World. Just before he disappeared, he raised the blade in salute.

The portal closed, and the sunlight returned. The first rays had just lit the clearing when the goblins trotted into sight, carrying their weapons. Behind them raced the halfling triplets, with all their weapons. One look at the sword Starfire, gleaming in Cald's hand, told them they were too late.

"Aw, it's closed," Bersmog growled. He glared at Stognad. "You plenty dumb, plenty slow, and now we have no more fun."

"There's no fun beyond that portal," Bigtoe said

with a sigh.

"No fun at all," Littletoe agreed.

"And everything tastes like straw and makes you belch," Fleetfoot added.

"Then why have you come, bringing all your weapons?" Cald asked the halflings.

Addressed directly, the halflings traded looks as if not sure how to answer.

"They think they go back to help more shorties find the portal," Stognad said. "Bersmog say is good idea."

"But if Eyrmin is right, this portal will not open again," Cald said and saw the distress in the faces of the triplets. He smiled and softened his tone.

"If the prince can permanently close a portal, he might be able to open another, so your people can still reach Cerilia. He likes them, you know." He ruffled Bigtoe's curly hair. "You can join your people in that land called the Burrows, and live in the open again," he suggested.

"Maybe they've found something fit to smoke in a pipe," Fleetfoot said hopefully.

"Maybe they have," Bigtoe agreed.

"And turnips," Littletoe added.

Cald noted the change in precedence.

Lienwiel had been gazing at Cald in wonder, completely ignoring the conversation.

"You will forever live in a new song among my people," he said.

Cald swallowed, his muscles struggling around the emotional boulder in his throat. Rejoice, Eyrmin had said. Rejoice that the prince still had purpose, hope. The grief slowly faded, and in its place, Cald felt the stirring of desire, the need to justify the prince's teachings.

"Don't start my tune yet," he said, raising the sword, contemplating the magical weapon. "There are deeds yet to be done before all the verses can be written."

"How come you not go with Be-gelf?" Stognad demanded.

"Because he said there were still battles to be fought on this world," Cald said quietly, careful to hide his disappointment. Eyrmin had said the human's grief tied him to the portal, so Cald must not allow himself to grieve.

Rejoice, Eyrmin had said, and if a merry, joyful heart would aid the prince in his dark duties, Cald would attempt to give it to him. He smiled, knowing the curve of his lips was belied by a heavy heart, but he would win the battle over grief for the prince's sake.

"You want fun?" he demanded of the goblins. "Pack your belongings and sharpen your axes. We'll escort the Rootfinders on a journey to find their people and then have some fun."

He led the way out of the clearing.

ANUIRE

appendix:

Deathirst and Starfire

The farmers of Reichmaar, near the southeastern coast of Aduria, looked up from their seedlings with worried frowns. The weather during planting season was usually mild, with a few gentle rains. The clouds that were forming in the sky were black and roiling. They promised a deluge that could wash away the tender shoots that had not yet had time to anchor their roots in the soil.

The farmers weren't to know the storm would not hit Aebrynis in the form of weather, and when it struck it would not fall on Aduria.

High above the heads of the worried mortals, the

dark clouds hid a meeting of gods. The roiling black-
ness shrouded Azrai, the god of strife and evil.
Nearly as dark was the angry camouflage of Reynir,
Masela, and Vorynn.

The beast-men of Azrai, the Shadow, had invaded a
woodland under Reynir's protection. With the assistance of their evil god, they had found a vein of iron
ore in the nearby hills. In the process of mining and
refining the ore and forging weapons, they had deci-
mated the small forest, fouled the waters of the stream,
and slaughtered the woodland creatures for food.

Since the small, new forest was Reynir's pet pro-
ject, he had been incensed. The streams, carrying the
filth of the beast-men, had fed into the ocean and
angered Masela, mistress of the seas. Vorynn, god of
the moon and magic and an ally of Reynir and
Masela, had joined them. He contributed his efforts
to blast the beast-men out of the remainder of the
forest.

Their actions had brought on a confrontation with
Azrai, whose cloud boiled in the heat of his rage.

"You will pay for your interference," he threatened the others. His voice reached the other gods,
but the mortals below heard only the rumble of
thunder.

"It is you who will suffer the penalty for the
destruction you brought to the forest," thundered
back Reynir, usually a placid, thoughtful god.
"Attempt to destroy another of my forests, and I will
wipe your abominable beast-men off the face of this
world."

Far below, the farmers looked up from their planting as the blackest of the clouds seemed to move
contrary to the wind, closing in on the other clouds
with roiling menace.

Lightning streamed across the sky from the blackest cloud to the other three. The brilliant shafts then

streaked back again, all aiming at the darkest, though none of the bolts seemed to find their target. The mortals crouched on the ground, hoping against hope the terrible storm overhead would not kill them.

Then, as suddenly as the storm had appeared, the clouds swept across the sky and out over the sea. The darkest was in the lead, and the others followed as if they chased it.

Even when the danger had passed, the farmers watched. The darkest cloud continued north over the sea, while the others slowed their progress and stopped. None of the humans understood the strange weather pattern.

"Where is he going?" Vorynn asked the others as they slowed, unwilling to chase Azrai farther.

"He seems to be turning north, toward Cerilia, the land of the demihumans and humanoids," Masela said. She drew in the wisps of her cloud, rearranging the wayward tendrils as if she were combing her hair.

"There are deep forests and bubbling streams on Cerilia." Reynir sounded worried and then thoughtful. "I have never considered them a part of my domain. . . ."

"Those bubbling streams feed into huge rivers that run to the sea," Masela said. "He will seek revenge on us—and all that falls within our spheres of responsibility. We should keep an eye on him."

* * * * *

Lord Drien Veyamain walked in the deep forest, far from the crystal palace of Siellaghriod. As the elf ruler of Sielwode and loyal vassal of King Bliemien Oriaden of Aelvinnwode, king of the elves of Cerilia, Drien spent much of his time with the business of his land. Occasionally, he hungered for the shadows of the wood and the opportunity to enjoy the forest like any elf of lesser or no rank.

He seldom found the chance to leave the concerns of office behind, but for several weeks his duties had been light. He decided to give himself leave to enjoy the land he ruled. He was strolling though the forest when he paused, backed up slowly, and murmured the incantation that took him into the Embrace of Sielwode.

Elf magic allowed his race to take temporary shelter within the huge trees of the forest. They most often used this ability to prevent frightening the forest creatures, and to observe the animals as they went about their daily lives.

From within his camouflage, Drien watched a family of rabbits that had hopped into sight around a bend in the forest trail. The large female appeared first, and following her were three youngsters, getting their first experience of the world outside the burrow. Their eyes stretched wide as they gazed at the trees and the thick undergrowth that walled in both sides of the path.

Two paces from the tree where Drien hid, a small brook crossed the trail. The mother rabbit led her family to the edge and lowered her head to drink. The first youngling watched and put out a tentative paw to investigate this moving strangeness. It drew back, shaking the paw, but was cuffed back to the stream by its mama. The second, after watching the experience of the first, edged closer, touched its tongue to the water, and obediently drank.

The third, who had stopped to bat at a leaf that had been wafted along the trail by the breeze, watched the other two and decided this newness was something to be enjoyed to the fullest. He gave a leap and landed in the brook in three inches of water.

With a shriek of terror, he leapt out and scuttled behind his mother.

Like any good parent, the mother rabbit knew when her child had learned a lesson. She turned and licked his face, removing the water from his eyes as she reassured him. She pressed her soft dry fur against his wet side until he stopped trembling. He needed no instruction to rid himself of the excess water. He shook himself, and she turned her head to keep from being struck in the face by the flying drops.

When the kits had finished their drink, she led the way a few feet upstream to where the cowslips were thick on the ground. She was just passing over the first plant when she gave a squeal and was whipped into the air in a cunningly laid snare.

Drien's keen elf hearing had heard the snapping of her neck, and before he could step from the Embrace, she had stopped kicking. He stood for a moment and stared, disbelieving, at the snare. Shock, disbelief, and anger chased each other through his mind. For a moment, he thought of trying to revive the mother rabbit, but she was dead, and no elf magic could bring back life. Nor would Drien want to, since it would be against the will of nature.

On the ground, the three kits were in tharn; fear had frozen their minds and bodies, a state nature gave them to keep away the torture of terror and impending death.

Drien opened the pouch at his waist, dumped out the berries he had picked on his walk, and scooped up the young rabbits. They were old enough to eat and drink, else the mother would not have brought them out of the burrow. They could be saved.

When the kits were safely stored in the bag and Drien had trotted a quarter of a mile from the stream, he whistled a soft birdcall. Five minutes later, he saw movement ahead. Trialien, a young warrior in training, was also enjoying the forest on a day away from her training. She had raced to the whistled call for assistance and stopped, dipping her head respectfully to the lord of Sielwode.

Drien handed her the pouch as he told her what he had seen. Inside the silken bag, the kits had come out of tharn and were struggling against their confinement.

"Goblins, orogs, or gnolls this far into Sielwode, my lord?" Trialien gazed at Drien with wide eyes.

"I've never known the humanoids to set such cunning traps," Drien replied with a frown. "I passed it by without seeing it."

Both elves paused to consider the implications. Elves were naturally sharp eyed and knew their forest with an intimacy unimagined by other races. The trail was one of Lord Drien's favorite walks. His memories held the height of every tree, the exact width of the streams in wet weather and dry. As he passed through the wood, he even noted the movement of the fallen leaves as the wind stirred them about.

Yet he had not seen the trap.

"When you cross Laughing Brook, give a call for warriors," he instructed her. "I return to see who comes for the dead rabbit."

Trialien's eyes darkened with worry for her lord, but she nodded and turned away, racing through the forest.

Drien retraced his steps, far more cautiously than on his usual strolls. Back at the stream, he waited for the elves who would be joining him within the hour. They would not arrive in time, he realized as he heard a low voice and the breaking of twigs.

He entered the Embrace of Sielwode and watched as two creatures came into sight. They were part humanoid, part animal, as if some twisted imagination had brought its nightmares to life. Their legs and feet, arms and hands were thick and sturdy—humanoid. They stumped up toward the snare. The tallest was slender in body, with a long, tapering face and a blunt nose, reminiscent of a deer's. A rack of antlers stood up from its skull. Its expression was malignant, bearing no kinship with the timid forest creatures.

The other was shorter and stouter, with a large head and tiny eyes. It had the snout and tusks of a boar. Their bodies were covered with fur, and they wore no clothing, but both carried spears. Around their waists were belts hung with pouches and knives in sheaths.

They spoke a strange language, one unknown to Drien. Judging by their tones, they were disgusted that they had caught only a rabbit. The tallest reached up and pulled the snare down, removed the rabbit, and tossed it away. The other snarled and picked up the carcass. It stood watching while its companion reset the snare. They turned back in the direction they had come.

When they were out of sight, Drien left the protection of the Embrace. He took time to spring the snare before following the intruders through the forest.

The lord and principal protector of Sielwode had found it hard not to kill the creatures when they first appeared, but he thought it more important to discover if there were more of them and where they made their camp. From the rabbit's snare, the beastmen pushed their way through the undergrowth, avoiding the easier travel on the forest trails as they traversed a set course, moving from one trap to another. In one they had caught a fox, and in two others they had snared deer, both caught by the necks, which hung broken and limp when taken from the traps.

As Drien followed, one, two, and in time a score of warrior elves came up behind him. They obeyed his gestured orders to remain out of sight and silent as they trailed the beast-men. They tripped the snares as they passed. The invaders would kill no more creatures of the forest if the elves could prevent it.

More than forty warriors had joined their lord by the time the misshapen trespassers reached a ramshackle village that had been built between two low hills in the forest.

As he stood sheltered by the trees, Drien saw the destruction of part of his forest, and rage nearly blinded him. Dozens of ancient trees had been cut, the white of their stumps weeping sap. Any one of the forest monarchs would have provided enough timber for the entire village, but the beast-men had cut dozens just to use the smaller limbs.

The buildings were ramshackle affairs. Logs had been driven into the ground and stood more or less upright. The walls were horizontal logs, placed one atop the other and tied in place with vines. The roofs were logs laid across and covered with leafy branches.

To his left, twenty beast-men were hacking limbs from a tree and carrying the timber into a hole in the side of the hill, a mine of some sort.

Drien forced himself to be still until his mind cleared of his rage and he could think clearly. He watched the activity of the village, moving from tree to tree until he could accurately estimate the number of invaders. A hundred, possibly more. How had so many of the creatures invaded Sielwode, and how had they avoided discovery?

But it would not be difficult to hide in Sielwode for short stretches of time, even from the sharp eyes of the elves. Sielwode had a far smaller population for its size than most of the elven territories. The Aelvinnwode covered much of the southwestern quarter of the continent, reaching into the mountains and the area called Tuarhievel. To the east, the great forest Coulladaraight blanketed the land, covering the mountains and the level lands to the south. The huge forests were divided into elven territories, each ruled by an elven lord who reported to the king.

Only Sielwode stood alone, a small forest in comparison to the others, bounded by plains, mountains, and a swamp to the south. To many, it was not a friendly forest; its bogs and traps were as dangerous to the elves as its invaders were.

These trespassers had managed to avoid the traps, but Drien determined they would not remain. He rejoined his people and gave the order.

"Death to the destroyers of our forest," he decreed, and led the attack himself.

He ordered his warriors to surround the village, and at his call, their arrows flew. With his first arrow, Drien caught a huge creature, as much forest cat as humanoid, in the chest.

Thirty beast-men died in the first second of the battle, but the survivors were canny and intelligent. They took cover and produced bows of their own, though the elves, dressed to blend with the forest, did not make easy targets. After the invaders dived for cover, more than three minutes of stillness prevailed. Then, not far from Drien, one of the younger warriors, too impatient to wait, left his shelter to dash to another tree, closer to the eaves of the new clearing. When a boar-man stood to aim a spear at the elf, Drien found his second target. His arrow pierced the beast-man's left eye and penetrated deep into the brain.

The moans of the wounded creatures and their harsh, guttural muttering were the only sounds in the forest as the elves watched for targets. But the next attack was against them, and not from the trespassers in the village.

To Drien's right, an elf screamed as a bolt of lightning struck the tree that sheltered him. The tree and the elf burned fiercely. More lightning fell from the sky. A second and a third elf died, along with the trees where they sheltered.

The rest of the Sidhelien retreated rapidly, their eyes wide, their faces pinched with the fear of a foe they could not fight. Bolts of lighting followed them as they fled. A mile from the camp of the intruders, they paused, but the lightning had not pursued them more than a quarter mile beyond the ramshackle village.

When they stopped, Eiresmone, a small slender elf, was close to Drien. He gazed at his leader with fear-filled eyes and tried to smile to hide his recent terror.

"What power can direct lightning?" he asked. "No song I remember speaks of it."

"No lore I know can answer you," Drien said, looking back toward the settlement. He stepped out into a small clearing and looked up at the cloudless sky. "I cannot believe it was an act of nature."

The elves huddled together in groups, asking questions of each other. For the first time in their long lives, they were afraid of the trees.

Drien, shocked, angry, and thoroughly confused by what they had faced, paced between two large trees. He was reluctant to return to the Crystal Palace while the intruders remained in the forest, but how did he fight lighting?

He was still considering when he realized the soft sound of elven voices had changed from questioning to wonder and then fear. He turned to see a misty wall moving through the forest, traveling faster than an elf could run.

"Away! Scatter!" he shouted to his people, and took his own advice, but the mist swirled around him, and he felt himself held by a great power. Reluctant and fearing what he might see, he turned.

Within the mist, he saw three deeper concentrations that could have been clouds that descended from the sky. They roiled, and then cleared slightly, and within them, he saw three beings, human shaped, though they stood twice as tall as an elf.

The first shrouding mist to clear sufficiently for him to see within it held a female whose skin was the color of the sun on the sea, her hair as black as a raven's wing, and her robes made of wide leaves of seaweed. The second was a male whose skin and hair were as white as the snowy robes he wore. His garments were trimmed with runes that radiated power.

The third could almost have been an elf. His clothing was wood-hued, and he was slender as a Sidhelien.

Drien had no knowledge of their kind, but he sensed them to be immortals, with powers the elves had never imagined. He knew he was helpless in the grip of their power, but not even the fear of death could hold back his anger.

"Why did you bring your monsters to our forest?" he demanded. "Why did you kill my people?"

The pure white figure grew brighter with anger.

"It is not for you to question powers you do not understand!" Vorynn boomed at Drien, nearly knocking the elf off his feet with the tremendous sound. "Be grateful that we stopped the bolts before they set the entire forest ablaze."

"How should he not question?" Reynir, dressed in woodland clothing, countered in a softer voice. "He is not one of our followers, and I cannot fault him for wishing to protect his land."

"And while we are not guilty of his accusations,

we did drive the Shadow here," said the female, Masela. "So in a sense we are at fault."

The volume of sound roared around Drien's head. Those words he could make out were strange to his ears, but the meaning entered his mind and somehow soothed him. He was forming new questions when a crack of thunder directly overhead startled him. He jumped, but before he could retreat to the protection of the nearby trees, Vorynn flicked his fingers. By the change in the air, Drien knew himself to be enclosed by some magic he did not understand.

The three immortals who had addressed him rose rapidly into the sky. Thunder rumbled and lightning crackled, but as far as Drien could tell, no bolts had been aimed at the forest. Many fell among the trees, but they struck the ground without causing harm.

Drien tried to escape the force that held him, but on every side he met a resistance he could not overcome. He could see nothing holding him, but he was unable to move more than four feet in any direction.

An hour later, he was pacing the area of his imprisonment when one of the gray clouds descended, and as it thinned he saw the tall white figure inside. By this time, Drien was too angry to care that the being within the cloud could probably kill him with the blink of an eye.

"By what right do you hold me?" he demanded. "What have you done with my people? They would have returned for me if they could."

"Your people follow an image of you, and will continue to do so until you return to them," Vorynn said. "I hold you by my power and your desire."

"*My* desire? What do you know about what I want? Who are you?" Drien had learned the boundaries of his prison, and he walked forward, prepared to push against the invisible wall, but it had disappeared. Free, he perversely decided to stay and confront the tall white figure within the shroud of mist.

"To you I will remain nameless, since this is not my dominion," Vorynn said. "Neither is it the realm of my adversary." The god sighed. "By a miscalculation on our part, we drove him here, and we will attempt to rid your land of him and his beast-men, but this can be done only if you assist."

"I want them gone from Sielwode," Drien said slowly.

"That is what I meant by your desire. If we each succeed in our respective chores, you will have your forest in peace again."

"What must be done?" the elf lord asked.

"I am the chosen for our cause. You will champion us and your land," Vorynn said. "If you lose, my adversary and his minions will keep this forest. If you win, you and your people will be free of the beast-men. This is the bargain we have made."

"You need a champion?"

"It is our way. We menace and threaten, and throw bolts of lighting, but we do not battle each other." Something in the voice of the strange being seemed to be saying, "Not yet." A feeling of foreboding came over Drien. The last thing he wanted to see was a battle between those titans of power.

From the south came a distant rumble of thunder, and Vorynn raised his head to listen. When the sound died away, his fierce gaze turned back to Drien.

"Speak, Sidhelien. Say if you champion your land. There is no time to lose. Our adversary is about the task of making a powerful weapon. If it is completed and put in the hands of your enemy, you will surely die and your land be destroyed for your enemy's pleasure. If we can possess it, you will as surely win."

"I stand for Sielwode," Drien said, realizing he

could do nothing less and keep faith with his people.

He had hardly finished speaking when a tendril of the cloud reached out and gathered him up. He rose above the forest with the white entity. They sped through the air faster than a bird could fly.

Far below, he saw his woodland as no elf had ever seen it. The deep green of the ancient forest was seamed with silvery streams, dotted with lakes and the pale green of swamp grass in the bogs. Many areas appeared brown, but the color was deceptive, caused by the height and speed of his passage. He was seeing the blurred colors of the forest leas, meadows with green grass mixed with a profusion of red and yellow flowers.

Their direction was southeast, and Drien had only just caught his breath after the first wonders of the journey when they began their descent into northern Baruk-Azhik. The mountainous country was a land of dwarves, which seemed fitting since the short, stocky cavern dwellers were famed for their weapons.

Dwarves, though seldom overfriendly with outsiders, were known to be a gregarious people who liked the company of their own. But a few, so dedicated to their skills that they had no time for others, lived as hermits. It was to the caverns of a solitary dwarf that Vorynn took Drien.

They whisked through mountain valleys and into an underground passage that wound through the inside of the mountain in a tortured path. Vorynn traveled at breathtaking speed until they reached a large cavern.

Set on his feet and with the freedom to look about him, Drien shivered. Across the chamber, the roiling blackness that hid Azrai was not the only cause. The cavern was stifling, the air foul, and the heat oppressive. The darkness was only partially dispelled by the torches on the wall and the forge of glowing coals.

Standing by the forge was what must have been a dwarf, but he was more than eight feet tall. His arms and legs bulged with muscles that were out of proportion to his size.

As Drien and Vorynn entered, the dwarf picked up a pair of tongs that seemed like a toy in his large hand and drew a glowing red-hot sword from the fire. The blade was more than six feet long. The giant dwarf picked up his hammer and began beating out the shape as if he were unaware of the intruders. His eyes were glazed, as though he were in a trance.

Drien looked back at the huge sword again and up at his strange ally.

"The blade is overlarge for an elf," he said quietly. He did not want to admit he would hardly be able to raise such a weapon, much less use it effectively.

"There is magic and magic," Vorynn replied, dismissing Drien's doubts.

Across the chamber, a rumble came from the dark column of cloud. An insubstantial tendril, like wayward smoke from a torch, stretched out from the column. Fire flew from it directly toward the sword, which was even then on the anvil. As the fire moved across the blade, a dark rune appeared on the side of the blade. Drien had no knowledge of this strange magic, but his mind recoiled from the evil of that mark.

Before the dark rune had been completed, Vorynn thundered at his enemy. He sent out a slim tendril of white smoke and a thin shaft of blue fire. It, too, wrote on the blade, leaving a glowing, silvery white rune.

Azrai thundered back, and the chamber reverberated with noise and power. Drien was forced back against the wall, and across from him, only dimly seen behind the shadow of the evil god, a beast-man—part cat, part humanoid—pressed back against the far wall. Drien lost all hope as he saw the size of the creature. It stood more than twelve feet tall, more than twice the height of the elf.

With the dimness and the roiling mist that shrouded both the gods, Drien could discern little of his opponent save its size and its yellow eyes, which reddened and glowed as it glared at the elf.

But the elf had little opportunity to worry about the enemy he would face later. The two gods stood on opposite sides of the forge, each more than ten feet from the fire and the anvil. Their thunder caused the stone of the mountain to tremble. The power that sprang from them seemed to eat up the breathable air as rune after rune, dark overlaid with silvery white, appeared on the blade.

The thunder increased; the atmosphere of the underground chamber closed in on the elf lord, as if the mountain itself pressed its weight against his chest. The air was thick with sparkles of fire that bounced off the blade and danced around the cavern like living creatures.

Black flames and white chased each other around the walls and through the air. The light produced by the white was consumed by the black, though an eerie glow escaped. Where the two touched they died, but the air was full of tiny potential battles.

The dwarf kept hammering the sword, his mighty arm and hand that held the child-toy hammer rose and fell. His chest heaved in rhythm as if he, too, found it hard to breathe. He continued to work in his trance, seemingly unaware of the contest that was being recorded on the weapon he fashioned.

The making of the sword was as much a part of the contest between these two gods as the battle would be. And they would need other champions if they kept up their part of the contest, Drien thought.

He wondered if he could live through the pressure in the chamber much longer. Then he saw the giant beast-man stagger and slump against the opposite wall. The lights in the cavern began to swim in and out of the elf's focus. No living being could withstand the force of that entrapped power for long.

Both gods thundered out at the same moment:

"I name you Deathirst!" Azrai shouted, but his words mingled with Vorynn's.

"I name you Starfire!"

The power that filled the chamber was greater than anything that had come before. The breath was forced from the elf lord's lungs. He felt as if his bones had been crushed to powder and was astonished that he was still alive.

Not even the stone of the mountain could bear the force of power in the chamber. With a crack so loud it deafened him to even the thundering of the gods, the mountain split apart. Light fell into the cavern, suddenly open to the air and sun. With it came a shower of small stones, but by the power of the gods, the debris disappeared before it reached the floor of the chamber.

Pale gray smoke rose from the forge, where the fire had died under the force of the exerted power. The dwarf lay on the floor, reduced to his original size—fewer than four feet in height. He was not dead; his fingers weakly clutching the handle of his hammer. Against the far wall, the beast-man had also lost size. Still, it would overlook the elf by at least a foot and had to be twice Drien's weight.

On the anvil lay not one, but two swords. They too had been reduced to their natural size. One gleamed with dark runes, and the other seemed blank.

Vorynn reached out with a more substantial tendril and whisked up the blank blade, thrusting it into the hand of Drien in a movement too quick to see. He reached for the second as well, but Azrai was before him.

The blade that had been put in the elf lord's hand was feather light, and Drien thought it just as well. He would not have had the strength to hold a heavy blade. The tendril that put the sword in his hand ran up his arm. He felt the chill of the void and wondered if he were frozen, but when the tendril withdrew, it took with it the physical and mental wounds he had suffered in the battle of the gods.

Before he had time to think of it, he was enveloped in the cloud again and they rose through the crack in the mountain. Below him, the world of Aebrynis receded until he was above the clouds. A few hundred feet away, a dark column of mist rose with them, and just visible within it, Drien could see the beast-man holding the other sword.

Even through the dark, roiling cloud that held Azrai, he could make out the features of his opponent, though not the color of the fur that covered most of its body.

A cat-man, less humanoid that most of the creatures Drien had seen at the shack town, it could still stand upright with elongated toes that gave it the foundation for balance. Its body was long in comparison with its arms and legs, and its shoulders were rounded like those of an animal used to walking on all fours. Instead of paws, it had large hands with long claws at the ends of the fingers.

The head was more feline than human, with ears laid back as it snarled across the empty air between the two rising gods. Long fangs extended from its upper jaw, and its eyes glowed a flaming orange as it glared at Drien.

The beast-man would have the strength of an animal, and probably the cunning. Added to that would be the intelligence of a humanoid. The elf lord would face a formidable foe.

"The time has come for you to do your part," Vorynn said as they reached their destination. He released Drien onto the soft, yielding surface of a cloud. "The gathering will see that there is no interference in your battle."

Drien spared a glance around and saw five misty columns forming part of a circle more than a hundred yards in diameter. Vorynn moved to take his place, and once Azrai had placed his warrior on the cloud, he too drifted back, closing the gap. Drien raised one hand to shade his eyes from the glare of the sunlight on the billowing white surface. The six tall, white columns added to the brightness. Azrai's darkness, the tawny brownish-yellow of the beastman's fur, and Drien's forest-hued clothing stood out in bold relief.

Drien's mind was a turmoil of objections. He was angry at these strange gods and their intrusion into his life and his forest. He was terrified at being set on a cloud to do battle with a monster that was part humanoid and mostly beast.

But he had been given a choice, he reminded himself. He had agreed to fight for Sielwode and had not asked to choose the battleground.

He drove the anger out of his mind and took a tighter grip on the sword. As he turned it slightly, he became aware of a sparkle and looked down at the blade, marveling at the silvery-white runes that decorated one side. Then he understood why there had been two swords when the dwarf had forged only one. The power of the gods had split the sword as well as the mountain.

Vorynn had named the white sword Starfire, and that was the blade Drien held. Azrai had named the black one Deathirst, and the runes on one side of the beast-man's blade stood out blackly, as if they ate the light of the clear air.

Drien stepped to the side of his position and back again, making no move toward the beast-man, who stood more than fifty yards away. Not in any immediate danger from his opponent, who also blinked against the glare, the elf took a moment to study the surface on which he would fight. A mist, rising nearly to his knees, hid his feet and the relative solidity beneath him. As he took a step, his foot seemed to sink, and then the resiliency of the surface sprang back, as if he were walking along a strong but supple tree limb. Drien ignored his opponent and continued to move about, trying to adjust to the spring the cloud gave to his step.

The beast-man did not give a thought to the surface, its advantages, or its dangers. It charged forward, overbalancing, just catching itself in time to keep from falling. It gave no real attention to his movements. It was too intent on killing its adversary.

Still cautious, Drien danced away from the creature's first charge. He leapt sideways, brought both his feet down at once, and rebounded off the pliable surface.

Around him, the low thunder of the six gods seemed to hold disappointment, but the elf was more concerned with the overall victory than meeting the first charge. The huge cat-man had finally lost its footing. It fell flat on its face, disappearing into the mist that hid the surface.

Drien did not even try to take advantage of his enemy's fall. He was too far away; the mist hid the creature, and he had troubles of his own. He had moved onto a section of the cloud where the mist at his feet was thinner. He could see his ankles clearly, but the surface seemed thin and unstable; it sank ominously as he stood on it. He hurriedly climbed out of the depression and back onto a more solid surface.

By the time the elf was on his feet again, the cat-man was up and racing toward him. Drien had learned all he had time to, and he stepped forward, meeting steel with steel.

Lightning flashed from the clash of the two swords, half blinding both the elf and the cat-man. Drien blinked away the spots that danced in front of him. He saw the irises of his enemy's flame-colored eyes close to slits before they opened wide again. The rumble from the circle of gods held a satisfaction. The elf had felt the power of the huge beast-man's swing and knew he could not meet many blows that were wielded with that much force.

The swords seemed an even match, but Drien could never equal the strength of his adversary. He would need to depend on skill. His hope that the cat-man would not balance as well on the springing surface was fast fading. At first, the beast-man had been working from the part of its mind that was human-oid, but even as the elf watched, the features became even more bestial; the animalistic side of its nature was controlling its balance.

Drien backed away, closing his eyes and opening them again as he used Starfire to parry Deathirst, blocking out the blinding fire each time the two blades came together.

The glare of their fight hung in the air like brilliant balls of swamp gas that rose from the bogs. Before one fire died, the blades struck again, adding more fireballs until the combatants were walled in with them.

Drien's hope that his skill could overcome that of his wildly swinging foe came to nothing. Using sheer strength and an animalistic speed, the cat-man forced Drien's retreat. All the elf could do was parry the blows. Just meeting them and fending them off was wearing him down.

From the circle of gods, the tall black column thundered victoriously, and the others rumbled more softly, as if voicing doubts.

Even if Drien had misread the tone of the gods' thunder, the suggestion that the dark god could be doubted drove the elf to stronger action. He parried the next blow and slipped his own blade past the guard of the cat man, slashing at its left arm.

The beast-man howled and charged again, as if driven to madness by the pain. The flurry of blows drove Drien back until he stepped onto the thinner area. The surface sagged, and he fell backward. The mist swirled around his face, but he could still see the bestial grin of the cat-man and hear the triumphant rumble of Azrai.

Above him, the cat-man sprang into the air, intending to fall on the elf with the point of its sword aimed at Drien's heart.

With only one desperate hope of saving himself, Drien clutched at the barely substantial surface with his left hand while he slashed at the yielding surface with his sword. He rolled to the side just as the beast-man descended, blade first, widening the tear. The cat-man howled in terror as it fell though the slit in the thin fabric of the cloud.

Drien desperately gripped the sloping, yielding surface. Instinctively knowing he should not loose his hold on the sword, he gripped the blade with his teeth while he pulled himself onto the firmer surface with both hands.

The thunder of the gods was deafening—triumphant rumbles of six gods and outraged roars of Azrai—but not even they blotted out the scream of the cat-man as it fell. Its voice, growing thinner with distance, seemed interminable as it fell toward Aebrynis far below. Then the creature was too far away to hear, but it would still be a long time falling through the empty air.

The black cloud that was Azrai disappeared.

As Drien rose to stand on trembling legs, one of the shrouded gods drifted toward him. The small column of cloud that covered him seemed to drift, yet remained a part of the surface. Within it, Drien could barely see the white figure of Vorynn.

"You were a worthy champion, elf lord."

Knowing the power of the immortals he faced, Drien held out the sword, offering it to the god, but Vorynn made no move to take it.

"Such a blade is made for the use of those who are condemned to walk the lands below. It is not for those of us. You have used the blade with courage, and it is yours if you choose to keep it."

"It is a wondrous blade, and more reward than the winning of one battle deserves," Drien said, turning Starfire in his hands.

"Reward?" Vorynn thundered softly. "A curse as well, I think. Our enemy has dropped below the clouds. He cannot prevent the death of his champion, but he can retrieve Deathirst. He will give that sword to another he chooses as his champion, and the two blades will be drawn together in the future. Think well, elf lord. Do you accept the challenges you and your descendants may face in the years to come?"

Drien considered the words of Vorynn. By will rather than strength he gathered himself to stand his straightest and tallest.

"If Deathirst is to enter our world again, it is as well that Starfire is there to meet it. By such power as I possess and by the honor of my name, neither I nor my descendants will fail in fighting the evil of our joint enemy."

Drien was not aware of having moved, but he opened his eyes to see dawn breaking over the Sielwode. He lay wrapped in his cloak. Beneath him was a pile of fallen leaves, hastily pulled together to make a bed.

Around him, the warriors who had survived the battle at the encampment of the beast-men were also rising. They watched him covertly, some with confusion, some with a judgmental look, quickly hidden.

He understood their feelings. Though they had been willing enough to escape the lightning that fell on them, they expected him to lead them in another attack and could not understand why he had not.

Drien neither understood nor questioned it. His night had been filled with strange dreams. Powerful beings had shrouded themselves in clouds. They had split swords and mountains. He had fought a battle on a white surface. A strange dream, caused by his need to drive away the intruders in the forest, he decided. He had slept with a mind full of the fight to come.

As he rose, he adjusted Starfire within its sheath. To him, it had always been his weapon. His mind never questioned its history, nor did he connect it with his dream. He pulled the blade from its sheath and held it aloft. The elves around him looked on it and smiled, as if they had long experience of seeing that blade leading them into battle.

"Forward!" he shouted to his warriors. "The battle will be swift and sure, and no longer will we suffer intruders in the sacred forest of Sielwode!"